Pleasures Unkown

maria isabel pita

an erotic romance

First Magic Carpet Inc. edition October 2003

Published in 2003

Manufactured in th United States of America
Published by Magic Carpet Books

Magic Carpet Books
PO Box 473
New Milford, CT 06776

Library of Congress Cataloging in Publication Date

Pleasures Unknown Maria Isabel Pita
ISBN 0-9726339-6-0

cover design: stella by design contact: stellabydesign@aol.com

*For my family, who loves me no matter what,
but especially, inevitably, for Stinger*

AUTHOR'S NOTE

One etymology of the word Druid derives it from "dru-wid" meaning "knower of oak trees" but "deru" also means truth and can be interpreted as "knower of the truth". It is believed Druid priests fashioned wands from the wood of oak trees that had been struck by lightning, and everyone knows they met in the dark hearts of forests, but for the most part Druids remain a class of men and women shrouded in romance and mystery...

PROLOGUE

A cigarette burning between his fingers, a man wearing a black leather jacket lightly caressed the moist rim of his scotch glass and exhaled a stream of smoke as he smiled sadly. Then he raised the glass to his lips and took a sip of the dark-gold spirit, his eyes never leaving the face of a young woman seated only a few feet away from him in the intimate restaurant. Votive-like candles trembled in the center of each round table covered with a pure white cloth and he was using his as an ashtray.

Maia frowned. 'We need a new candle,' she observed, 'this one's nearly dead.' For some reason this seemingly insignificant detail made her somewhat cross. She was a grown woman of twenty-three, yet whenever she went out to dinner with her parents part of her felt like a little girl again, pouting and frustrated that none of her dreams of love and adventure had come true, at least not yet.

'My dear, you have innocently stumbled upon a serious philosophical issue here,' her father replied gravely. 'Would it be right to end its struggling life prematurely or should we let it burn out to its natural end?'

The man in black leather sitting by himself smiled as though he could hear this conversation, and raised a free hand to caress shoulder-length dark-brown hair away from his strong jawed, fine-featured face set with intensely blue eyes. Then with the ball of his thumb, he idly traced a faint white scar just below his thin lower lip as he took a final drag off his cigarette, and casually tossed its remains into the flame.

The resulting sparks captured Maia's attention. Suddenly, she couldn't understand how she had failed to notice this man before, a man who made her intensely aware of her own mysterious melancholy as he got up to go. This strikingly handsome man dressed entirely in black seemed to embody all her deepest, darkest feelings, and his leaving did not make her feel better, on the contrary...

CHAPTER ONE

Stoneshire Hospital's Emergency Room was never crowded. State-of-the-art medical facilities were housed inside a Victorian factory that had been gutted, its rotting wooden beams replaced with a less vulnerable metal skeleton. Nevertheless, the centuries-old town refused to outgrow its narrow winding streets and quaint historic buildings.

The hospital's elegant waiting room boasted large chairs upholstered in burgundy leather, softened by years of comforting the stressed bodies of people waiting for news of their loved ones, a far cry from the cold plastic slap to your backside suffered in most modern hospitals. Large potted plants helped soothe eyes strained by the inevitable fluorescent light, and encouragingly hot fragrant tea was brought around by quietly sympathetic nurses wearing traditional white knee-length outfits.

Stoneshire's Chief Resident, Eric Christianson, was personally responsible for the waiting room's aesthetic charm; the furniture had come from his family estate, which he was aching to get rid of. Lately, the endless, lifeless rooms surrounding him at night felt disturbingly like cancer cells threatening his altruistic health, yet for some reason he couldn't bring himself to sell the place.

The thunder-filled night they brought in the old woman and her niece – a strikingly lovely creature in her early twenties – he had just slipped off his lab coat and was reluctantly preparing to drive to his palatial home through the storm. He was almost relieved to be spared another lonely night in his study as the paramedics quickly informed him that a tree had fallen across the victims' car. One of the elderly female's knees was crushed beyond repair. The young woman appeared unharmed yet she was unconscious, and Eric immediately suspected she might be suffering from serious internal bleeding. After only a few minutes with her, he was able to staunch the flow of her life's blood, thereby saving her life, but a heavy tree branch had struck her womb with such force no life would ever be able to take root inside her.

* * *

Eric had done everything he could for her, but Maia Wilson's vital signs were still fluctuating dangerously. It was a desperate, unorthodox impulse that caused him to dismiss his nurses and to bend over the young woman's unresponsive body. He whispered passionately in her ear like a lover, begging her to hold on to life, pleading with her to let him save her, fervently urging her to stay alive.

Even though he definitely should have been, he was not surprised when her pulse suddenly grew stronger and a warm hint of color returned to her snowy cheeks. Not yet daring to hope, he gently raised one of her marble-white eyelids and shone a light into her deep brown iris, but it was as though a tiny round sun moved instead of the dark cloud obscuring it, because she remained unconscious.

* * *

Dr. Christianson was exhausted and frustrated, but at least he had not lost his lovely patient, who uncannily evoked the legend of Sleeping Beauty as she smiled peacefully in her unnatural sleep. Her parents were still out in the waiting room (they had been there for over twenty-four hours) and his smile as he approached them was reassuring if also somewhat abashed. He was feeling just a little guilty about the unorthodox way he was going about the desired end of saving their daughter's life.

'How is she?' Peter Wilson demanded, anxiety making his voice sound uncharacteristically harsh.

'She's still unconscious,' Eric informed Maia's father reluctantly, 'but as I said, she's stopped bleeding internally and all her vital signs have stabilized. She's very weak, naturally, and she's still not responding to stimulus, but her strength seems to be returning gradually. I've done every possible test and there's no evidence at all that she was injured anywhere except…' He glanced at the dark leaf of a plant brushing against his white sleeve. 'She won't be able to have children,' he concluded bluntly, 'but other than that, she should be perfectly healthy.' If she ever decides to wake up, he thought despondently. As a scientist, he both respected and resented mysteries he could not solve if they were ones that thwarted him in some way.

'But then why is she still unconscious?' Stella Wilson pleaded to know, clinging to her husband's arm. They were a strikingly attractive couple; it was easy to see where their daughter had gotten her looks.

'I don't know,' Eric admitted softly, studying the plant intently. 'It could be shock, some sort of psychological defense mechanism against the trauma she suffered… she slipped into the safety of unconsciousness to escape the pain and she's not ready to come out yet.' He was taken aback by his intuitive diagnosis and somewhat concerned by how casually he expressed it, with absolutely no scientific evidence to back him up.

'I see.' Surprisingly, Maia's father apparently found the explanation reasonable and convincing. 'What about my sister, Carol? Is she still in stable condition?'

'Oh yes, no need to worry about Carol. She's heavily sedated, of course, and I'm afraid she'll need a cane to walk from now on, but she will be able to walk, she won't require a wheelchair. Don't worry, please, I fully intend to stay by Maia's side until she comes around. She's not in a coma, not in the traditional sense… you see, I believe she can hear me. When I spoke to her…' He thrust his hands in his pockets and cleared his throat decisively. 'When I spoke to her, her vital signs responded.'

'You spoke to her and she heard you?' Stella's hand resembled a bird's claw clinging to the solid branch of her husband's arm. 'What did you say to her, doctor?' She sounded fascinated.

'Nothing, really.' He cleared his throat again self-consciously wishing there was something in his pockets he could hold onto. 'I simply urged her not to give up.'

'Please,' Peter slipped a supportive arm around his wife's shoulders, 'tell us what you said to her.'

Eric glanced over at the plant again knowing it wouldn't judge him no matter what he thought or did. 'Well, I said, "I want you to live for me".' Looking back at Maia's parents, he tried very hard to sound as though he was only reciting his grocery list as he went on. 'I said, "don't fight me, you know you want to live, you're so beautiful, you have to hold on", and so on.' Attempting to look innocently relaxed, he ran the fingers of his right hand through his silver-blonde hair even while his other hand clenched into a fist inside his lab coat.

Stella gazed fervently up at her husband. 'Then what Drew said is true, Maia is-'

'Thank you, doctor,' Peter cut her off abruptly. 'We know she's in good hands.'

* * *

After two final introspective drags, Drew Landson killed his cigarette and then gazed down at its broken body for a moment before at last meeting the eyes of the man and woman seated before him. 'You both know,' he began quietly, 'that there's no such thing as an accident or a coincidence.'

'This is too much!' Peter struck the table with his fist, but made no impression on the snowy plain of the cloth. Even the candle kept burning steadily in its glass sphere as though mocking the uncontrolled heat of his anger. There was so much pain written on the lines of his face as he focused on the small flame that he might have been watching the distant tower of his castle burn beneath an enemy's torch.

'Please, dear.' Stella spread the soft, pale roots of her fingers over her husband's rock-hard fist. 'You heard what the doctor said, there's no rational explanation for Maia's condition, it's as though she's being held-'

'There's always a rational explanation!' Her husband's chin dug into his chest as he closed his eyes and struggled to gain control of himself.

Drew sat back in his chair holding Stella's eyes, their thoughts in such perfect harmony they might as well have been caressing each other beneath the table. They were meeting in the restaurant where only last Sunday evening he had seen Maia for the first time having dinner with her parents. Their eyes had met, and he had felt the sparks literally fly between them as he tossed his cigarette into the flame. And because of this, because of the desire and longing he had felt her touch him with, he was in the position to reach out to her now, because her beauty had evoked the same intense response in him...

'I am extremely upset,' Peter muttered tightly in an oblique apology for his emotional outburst.

'Your emotions have their roots in the limits of your perceptions,' Drew stated mildly. 'Why don't you try actually thinking about what Maia is experiencing for a change instead of selfishly dwelling on what you're going through? For all we know, she's enjoying herself. In the dream she's living now, she has absolutely no awareness of her body lying in a hospital bed, and you need to stop thinking about her that way, too. Her soul is very much alive and well in another dimension, or another frequency of being, or however you want to think about it, and in whatever adventure she's living out, I suspect it's you, her parents, who are dead. In her psyche, she has to accept the fact of a car crash, but instead of the victims being herself and her aunt, Carol, I imagine she thinks you both were in the crash, and since she can't communicate with you, in her mind it's her parents who were killed in a fatal accident. I'm just speculating here because I haven't gone in yet, but I'm assuming since Carol was involved in the trauma with her that Maia imagines herself living with her aunt now, instead of with you. Her personal history will be slightly different in her subconscious fantasy, but other than that, she'll be completely herself, and I mean completely, much more herself than she is normally in so-called real life.'

'What do you mean?' Stella breathed in wonder.

'I mean her deepest self, all her most intense longings and desires, will have full reign in her dream. You say she's an artist?'

'Yes, she's a painter,' her mother said proudly. 'Her work is haunting, full of standing stones and blood-red sunsets and women lying across altars…'

'Jesus!' Peter heaved a deep sigh. 'All right, man, what do we do?' The rational and Christian portions of his brain surrendered abruptly. 'Just tell us what we have to do to help Maia.'

'It's the soul's delicate organs of fear and desire, hope and despair that we're dealing with here,' Drew responded matter-of-factly. 'We have to read the events and come up with a diagnosis. I'm relatively certain Maia has entered the haunting sensual world of her paintings.'

'We trust you, Drew.' Stella handed him the intangible yet infinitely heavy gift of their hope. 'Just tell us what to do.'

'I will try my absolute hardest to help you.' His charismatic smile was broad enough to contain several meanings, but it dimmed almost at once as his face resumed a respectful lack of expression. 'First things first,' he stated briskly, and draining his glass of scotch rose abruptly. 'I have to sleep in her bedroom tonight, in her bed.'

* * *

Peter locked himself in the library, to Stella's mingled relief and dismay. She longed for the solace of his presence, but his negative attitude in the face of the unknown was no comfort at all to her. She was grateful Drew had given her the nearly impossible task of digging up an ashtray in a house where no one had smoked cigarettes for years. At least the search kept her from stalking around the telephone, very much like a panther walking on two legs in her form-fitting black dress; she was desperately fighting the hunger she felt for constant news of her daughter. Doctor Christianson would call her as soon as there was any change in Maia's condition.

Stella finally found what she was looking for in the bottom drawer of a wooden cupboard hidden away in a back hallway. She held the round clay object reverently in both hands, treating it like an archaeologist unearthing an ancient relic. Maia had made this ashtray for her father in kindergarten when he still smoked. A crude, heavy little sphere the dark-gray of stone, its entire surface was covered with the mysterious spirals of her childish finger-prints, which had grown as she aged yet never changed. Inevitably, Stella found herself comparing the rough childish art project with a Celtic artifact, and she smiled for the first time in over forty-eight hours as she pressed it against her heart. The object's earthy appearance, combined with the pure love that had shaped it, reas-sured her that she was doing the right thing with Drew, whom she knew would be very pleased with her discovery.

He was perched at the foot of Maia's single bed looking slowly around him when Stella entered her daughter's bedroom. The sight of his black jacket spread across the blue-and-white quilt made her heart skip for an instant it looked so much like a big black bird with its wings spread wide, and she paused anxiously in the doorway, at once questioning and understanding why she had put her daughter's life in this man's hands. He was wearing a sleeveless black T-shirt that fully exposed his powerful arms, and as she watched him, he abruptly leaned forward as though listen-ing intently to something beyond the range of her own hearing.

'What is it?' she whispered, her heart racing.

He sat up again. 'Nothing.'

The casual smile he tossed her felt like a boomerang momentarily carrying her fears away, but then the desire it hit her with made her feel even worse. 'I found what you wanted,' she told him, thrusting the ashtray towards him as though it was suddenly burning her hand.

He got up and quickly took it from her. 'This is perfect,' he murmured, caressing the rough surface imprinted with Maia's sensual identity in the form of her unique fingerprints. 'She made this for me.'

'She made it for her father,' Stella retorted weakly, for she was already half drugged by his heady aura of leather and male flesh irresistibly blended with his spiritual and physical self-assurance.

'Your daughter is testing your faith, my lady.' He set the ashtray gently down on the nightstand.

'You mean she deliberately chose to almost get herself killed,' she snapped, her husband's attitude inevitably rubbing off on her, 'and to never be able to have children of her own?'

'Stella,' he gently grasped one of her arms and urged her down onto the edge of the bed beside him. 'Without your blessing, it will be impossible for me to reach your daughter,' he trapped both her hands firmly between his while looking earnestly into her eyes, 'and your doubting rational mind is an utterly unacceptable chaperone on this blind date Fate has chosen to set up between Maia and me. So please do your best to relax and trust me. That's the most important thing you can do right now, because if you don't trust me and believe in me, neither will Maia.'

Red hair licked around the waxy pallor of her face as she lowered her head submissively. 'I trust you,' she sighed.

CHAPTER TWO

The evening of May Day, the anniversary of her parents' death in an automobile accident, Maia Wilson drove to the cemetery where they were buried, their bodies lying eternally side-by-side in a single coffin. Another year had passed; the earth had made yet another full turn around the sun like a girl in a country dance, her vulnerable green eyes meeting her partner's penetrating regard as she raised such a lovely skirt of flowers in the Spring you could almost forget her skeletal legs.

Tears streaming down her face, Maia drove slowly along the path between the graves while stars appeared overhead as if in sympathy with her glistening cheeks. The last thing she expected to happen was for her engine to suddenly give a loud metallic cough, shudder ominously, and die.

A deafening silence settled around her as in her rearview mirror a pair of headlights shone indifferently on their way outside the cemetery gates. She was miles outside of Stoneshire surrounded by a crescent of woodland, all that remained of a once vast ancient forest. She had no way of getting home; it was much too far for her to walk, especially in the dark. She would be forced to take the dangerous option of flagging down a pair of anonymous headlights hoping they would stop for her and that there wouldn't be a rapist or a killer behind the wheel who would have her completely at his mercy...

She switched on her emergency lights. They flashed an urgent rhythm with her pulse, giving the deepening darkness a small, hopeful heart. She doubted, however, that anyone would notice her luminous plea for help, and she knew absolutely nothing about the inner workings of the metal shell that carried her around everywhere.

It seemed an absolute miracle when after only a few minutes a pair of headlights turned off the main road outside the gate and shone her way, effortlessly penetrating the night with sword-like shafts as the modern armor of another car pulled up just behind hers.

Maia gratefully opened her door and leaned out to watch a tall man's silhouette rimmed in gold approaching her, his blond hair catching the glow of his headlights so that his dark face seemed surrounded by a halo.

'What seems to be the trouble, miss?' he asked in a kind, quiet voice that instantly made her feel better.

'I don't know,' she replied, 'the engine just died.'

'I'll take a look at it for you.'

'Oh would you, please?' She stepped out of the car gratefully. 'Thank you so much!'

He walked back to his own vehicle to fetch something from the trunk, and it struck her that his small red sports car looked exactly like the one she had seen parked between the standing stones yesterday evening, its polished body shining beneath the setting sun making her think of a yoke inside the egg-shaped circle. She heard the trunk slam shut, then carefully stepped out of his way so he could walk past her. He lifted her hood, and holding it up with one hand he shone a flashlight into her vehicle's dark bowels. Above the small light his pale features rose out of the darkness like a cresting wave flooding her with feelings. Not only had someone come to her rescue out in the middle of nowhere, that someone was amazingly handsome. 'I think I saw your car parked at the standing stones last night,' she said impulsively, even though she really had no way of knowing if it had actually been his car. 'You know which stones I'm talking about, the small group just outside Stoneshire?'

'Yes, I know them,' he responded absently, neither denying or confirming her assumption as he concentrated on diagnosing her mechanical problem, lightly touching something here, then something there. In the dim halo of illumination cast by his flashlight, her car's organs were serpentine, evil looking things to her.

'Are you an archaeologist?' she asked him curiously.

He laughed briefly. 'No, I'm just interested in standing stones, that's all.'

'So am I,' she confessed.

'Isn't everyone? Well, I don't see a problem here. Why don't you try starting it again and see what happens.'

She slipped obediently back into the driver's seat, and was paradoxically disappointed when the engine rolled over just like normal, as though there had never been anything wrong with it at all, effectively killing her hopes of getting to know him better. She stepped back out of the car as he slammed the hood closed. 'I can't understand it,' she murmured, somewhat embarrassed and intensely distressed that he was going to drive out of her life again forever. 'I'm sorry to have troubled you.'

'It was no trouble at all,' he assured her, switching off the flashlight and plunging them into a darkness alleviated only by the distant stars. 'Nevertheless, you now owe me a favor.' The mating music of crickets punctuated his statement in a strangely sinister way.

'I do?' she asked both hopefully and anxiously.

'Yes, you do. My name is Christopher Thorn and you are now obliged to grant me whatever I request.'

'With pleasure... I mean...' But it was too late to slip a proper corset on her naked eagerness. 'My name is Maia Wilson.'

'It's a pleasure to meet you, Maia, and I would be honored if you would join me for dinner.'

It felt very strange being asked out to dinner by a featureless silhouette, yet what she had seen of his face was branded into her brain and there was no way she could pass up the opportunity to get to know him better. 'I would like that,' she replied, and felt wonderfully daring. Stoneshire wasn't exactly full of attractive eligible men and she had already dated (as well as almost immediately discarded) those who were.

'My place isn't far,' he said. 'You can follow me in your car. I'll keep you in sight just in case it stalls again.'

'But... but we just met...' She had believed they were to dine together in public. It was another thing entirely to enter the home of a man she didn't know at all.

'I understand, Maia, please don't be afraid. You can trust me. I won't do anything you don't want me to, and I mean that.'

She knew perfectly well she should be afraid, but there was something about him she was finding it absolutely impossible to resist. How instantly she had been attracted to him killed all her natural misgivings. She heard herself say, 'Okay, lead the way' even as part of her cringed in dread of what she was daring to do in defiance of everything she had ever been taught by everyone.

* * *

Back behind the wheel of her mysteriously moody car, Maia followed Christopher Thorn out of the graveyard. They took the main street for a few miles, then he turned onto a much narrower road flanked on both sides by ancient oak trees. Their headlights washing over the massive trunks turned them a ghostly gray color, illuminating lower branches so the darkness seemed to open its arms for her in a menacing illusion of welcome. She had never felt comfortable around large old trees, not since the accident years ago when an oak tree struck by lightning collapsed across the car she was in with her aunt, permanently crippling Carol in one knee and making it impossible for her niece to ever have children. Fortunately, Maia had never wanted to be a mother; paintings were all she desired to create.

Christopher's turn signal flashed a bright green and she followed him off onto several increasingly narrow roads, until she found herself in a pitch-black tunnel formed by tree branches embracing high above her. By now her nerves were sharp as restless kittens squirming in the basket of her belly. She was regretting having agreed to follow a strange man to his home in the middle of nowhere, but there was literally no going back now; they had made too many turns in a pitch-black darkness unrelieved by a single streetlight for her to be able to find her way home without his direction.

She was nearly breathless with panic when they at last pulled up in front of such a narrow two-story house it might have been made from a hollowed-out tree trunk. It was the only house in sight, the crescent of grass cleared out in front of it surrounded by an impenetrably dark forest.

Still refusing to really think about the dangerous thing she was doing, Maia got out of her car, then calmly preceded Christopher's silent silhouette onto a miniature porch framed by hanging vines. She stiffened when his hand suddenly reached past her, but it was only to open the unlocked black door.

She entered a room of highly polished wooden walls illuminated by a chandelier and the ceiling was so high the black wrought iron chain from which it hung vanished into darkness. She caught her breath gazing up at the light fixture, for it was beautifully carved to resemble a winter-bare bush glimmering with dozens of warm golden lights. 'What a beautiful chandelier!' she exclaimed, for a moment forgetting all her fears. 'It looks like a bush covered with dew drops shining beneath the light of the rising sun. It's exquisite. Where on earth did you get it?'

He closed the door behind them. 'I made it,' he replied. Brushing past her, he walked over to a small wooden cabinet with doors carved in an intricate bas-relief of intertwined grapevines. He sank to one knee before it. 'Perhaps it's a little too obvious that I'm a carpenter.'

Above his kneeling form, elegant in a long-sleeved button-down burgundy shirt and black slacks, Maia spotted a steep, narrow stairway carved straight into the wall and suffered the impression that it led up into the darkly powerful branches of a tree. She could not shake the impression of being inside a hollowed out trunk as she walked over to a loveseat made from the slender barks of a silver birch tree, and covered with thick, sky-blue cushions impossible to resist. She hadn't meant to sink all the way back in the loveseat, but the way it was constructed made it impossible to merely perch tensely on its edge. She hadn't realized before how short her sleeve-less white dress was, and she quickly covered her half bare thighs now with her red purse. Too small for all the things she was carry-ing, it sat in an awkward heart-shaped lump on her lap as her host approached her holding a bottle of red wine in one hand and two sparkling crystal glasses in the other. 'Does that mean you made everything in here yourself?' she asked in anxious wonder.

'Yes, it does.' He set the bottle down on a coffee table carved from a thick slab of wood that seemed to be floating just above the floor; she had to look to catch sight of the delicate black wrought iron legs actually holding it up. He seated himself beside her and handed her one of the empty glasses. 'What do you do for a living, Maia?' He reached for the bottle and poured wine for them both, politely beginning with her.

'I paint,' she said at once. 'But unfortunately that's not what I do to make ends meet. I work as a receptionist for a solicitor to pay the bills. What I love to do is paint though.'

'That's wonderful,' he stated earnestly. 'Money is inconsequen-tial.' He held her eyes as he took a sip of wine. 'May I see your work sometime? I have a feeling I'd like it.'

'I think you would, especially if you're interested in standing stones. They're in most of my paintings.'

'Is that so? Would you care to describe one to me?'

'I don't know…' She bought herself some time by taking a long sip of wine, then gazed shyly down into her glass. His features were so perfectly proportioned it almost hurt her to look at them, maybe because she knew she would never be able to capture them on paper; she could never do justice to the haunting poetry of his bone structure. And his eyes… his eyes were such a clear blue she almost experienced a strange vertigo looking into them, as though the sky was falling in on her…

'Please, Maia,' he urged quietly, 'I would very much like to hear you describe one of your paintings.'

'Well, they're a bit strange,' she admitted, glancing up at him, and his seriously attentive expression encouraged her to go on. 'I haven't shown them to anyone, not even Carol... she's my aunt. I live with her.' She shifted anxiously against the deep cushion she was sinking into in such a way she was afraid she wouldn't ever want to get up... yet she absolutely had to go home later, she couldn't possibly stay here all night with a total stranger... 'I should call her and tell her I won't be home for supper tonight. She'll be expecting me.'

'I'm sorry, Maia, I don't have a phone.'

'Oh.'

'Don't worry about it, just drink your wine, she'll understand. And I promise, you won't go hungry. In fact, you can have anything you like here.'

'Except a phone,' she pointed out.

He smiled as he took another sip of wine, apparently waiting for her to comply with his request and describe one of her paintings to him.

She bit her lip, but curiosity was too much for her. 'What I really want is for you to tell me what you were doing at the standing stones last night,' she blurted.

'I could show you,' he offered quietly. 'We could drive there after we finish our wine, if you like, it's going to be a full moon tonight.'

His response to her query was so unexpected she started in surprise and embarrassingly bloodied the front of her dress with the delicious vintage. 'Oh my God!' she cried, so upset by the sight of the red stain spreading fatally across the pure white fabric that she didn't realize she had dropped her glass until she heard the fine crystal shatter against the floorboards. 'Oh my God,' she repeated helplessly and closed her eyes, unable to face the disaster she had made of such a promising evening. When she felt him gently grasp both her arms, part of her stiffened in dread, not so much of his intentions as of her own humiliating lack of self control.

'It's all right,' he whispered soothingly, 'I'm here, Maia.'

She sank willingly back against the cloud-deep cushions, knowing that her breathless whimpers as he lifted her dress sounded more like soft exclamations of pleasure than modest protests, and so did the way she moaned when he grasped both her slender thighs with his strong craftsman's hands and quickly spread her legs wide.

'I want you to live for me, Maia,' he whispered passionately in her ear, 'Don't fight me. You're so beautiful!'

She was shocked that he didn't bother to kiss her first. He simply ripped off her panties with a violent skill that dazed her, and swiftly slipped two fingers up inside her. For an instant his sudden penetration hurt so much she wanted to cry out in protest, but almost at once the firm, knowledgeable way he began exploring her as his thumb pressed on her mound just below her clitoris made her breathless with pleasure. It almost felt too good to believe the way his fingers flicked gently back and forth deep inside her sex.

'You're so beautiful, Maia. I want you to live for me, sweetheart, do it for me...'

She wanted to tell him that the slow, exploratory penetration of his fingers felt almost too good to bear, but she couldn't seem to find her voice. It had been wonderfully obvious to her from the moment he lifted her dress up out of his way that she was in a real man's hands at last. He was saving her from the crude pawing of the mere boys she had dated whom she had known from the beginning could never handle the depth and intensity of her feelings and win her heart or even her desire. Finally, she felt her body being used as it had always longed to be, and she was so excited she had to keep her eyes closed to endure it.

'Come on, baby…' He thrust his hard fingers even deeper into her tender, clinging pussy.

She felt her inner juices flowing shamelessly into his hand as she gasped and moaned and writhed against the cushion, shifting her hips as if compelled to escape the excruciating delight, but the actual effect of her sensual squirming was to shove her sex willingly up into his hand. He hadn't even kissed her and yet already he was finger-fucking her. She couldn't believe it, this wasn't the way a gentleman behaved on the first date, and yet the truth was his rough possessiveness aroused her like nothing else ever had. Then he gave the mysterious seal of approval to her budding ecstasy by pressing his mouth lightly against hers. He kissed her chastely at first, keeping his lips sealed as her tender pussy lips bloomed open around the digging stamens of his fingers, then at last his tongue reached for hers and began dancing with it, leading hers around and around and making her aware of the climax forming like a whirlpool deep in her hole. Her clitoris had found a magical harbor between his thumb and forefinger and a hot joy was flooding her body as it never had before, much more intensely than it did when she played with herself in the privacy of her bedroom. She had been afraid no man would ever know how to touch her the way she knew how to touch herself, and she was thrilled to experience him killing this fear inside her once and for all. The orgasm cresting between her thighs had all the devastating power of a tidal wave about to wash away everything she knew about sex like a frustratingly small town as it exposed the wildly beautiful landscape of all her fantasies. But right now it was too much for her the way his tongue kept playing with hers while his fingers plunged relentlessly in and out of her wet pussy, cradling her clitoris in the caressing folds of skin between his thumb and forefinger as he thrust his rigid digits up inside her body as far as they would go. She wanted to wait for his cock to come, but she couldn't take anymore; she had to surrender to the pleasure and climax in his hand, moaning breathlessly and gratefully up into his mouth thinking that at last she had found a real man, or rather that at last he had found her.

CHAPTER THREE

Carol Wilson's entire body ached and psychologically she was feeling black-and-blue with fear and guilt. She had been driving the car in which Maia was injured, and the truth was she would rather have died herself than hurt her beloved niece. Peter and Stella had forgiven her, naturally, pointing out that the accident was in no way her fault, but she was finding it much more difficult to forgive herself. Yet it had all happened so fast; there was nothing she could have done to get away from that falling tree.

'Oh doctor, it was terrible!' She closed her eyes, but that only made her see the hellish scene even more vividly on the dark screen of her inner eyelids. 'There was this blinding flash of light in which I saw everything so clearly for an instant... the wet road shone like a silver snake winding between the trees... then it was as if the Devil's own pitchfork was flung straight in our path! I've never seen anything like it before in my life, doctor, and I hope I never do again! Three bolts of lightning, one right after the other, cut through that huge old tree like a knife through butter!'

'Don't keep dwelling on it, Ms. Wilson,' Eric urged, yet he had to admit the old woman painted a disturbingly sinister picture. 'Try and forget about it,' he insisted without much conviction.

Carol's eyes snapped opened. 'How in God's name can you ever forget something like that?' she demanded.

'I don't know. You just have to.' He was still trying to get up the nerve to tell her that her lovely niece had paid for her life with any she might have hoped to conceive in the future.

'My brother tells me you've stayed by Maia's side day and night, doctor. We all appreciate your help more than we can ever express, but you really should get some sleep, young man.' She knew his blue eyes were staring at her so intensely not because she was anything worth looking at anymore, but because he was on the verge of collapsing from exhaustion. 'If you don't get some rest you'll need a doctor yourself soon.'

'I'll be fine,' he replied a bit gruffly, haunted by two long nights spent watching over 'Sleeping Beauty', the nurses' inevitable nickname for Maia. He was growing both attached to, and angry with, the lovely, unresponsive body, and neither emotion was in any way respectable or productive.

* * *

Maia felt completely wiped out. She had never experienced such an intense orgasm in all her life, not even in her wildest dreams, and even after her heart stopped pounding and her blood stopped racing down her veins, resuming its normal pace coursing through her body, she couldn't seem to move. She was also reluctant to open her eyes because then she would have to face her incredibly wanton behavior, and the inevitable dimming of respect in Christopher's eyes as he regarded her in a less serious light. She was afraid how easily she had succumbed to his advances, not to mention how quickly and intensely she had climaxed, would make him think less of her.

'Maia, look at me,' he commanded gently.

She had no choice but to open her eyes, yet it cost her an immense effort of will to do so. She did not want to see her ruined dress or the shattered glass at her feet, and the memory of the intense pleasure she had suffered in his hands was still smoldering in her womb in a way that felt almost like the ghost of pain.

'What's wrong, Maia?' Her silence seemed to be upsetting him. 'Talk to me.'

She found the courage to meet his eyes, and the tender concern in them amazed her because it was a universe away from the sharp cynical glint she had expected to see as he planned to keep taking advantage of her easy virtue. 'Nothing's wrong,' she whispered, holding on to his expression as though it was a life raft in the turbulent sea of her feelings. She needed to know he approved of her intense sensual nature, and wouldn't respect her less for not holding anything back from a total stranger. 'It's just… it's just that I've never done anything like this before.'

He smiled as he gently brushed the hair away from her face with one hand. 'You've never done anything like what before, Maia?' His other arm was wrapped around her shoulders where he sat as close to her as possible on the yielding cushion.

'You know…' she hedged shyly, avoiding the sight of her ruined dress still hiked shamelessly up her thighs, but for some reason she didn't feel like pulling it back down modestly; she liked the fact that he could see her pouting pussy lips and feeling vulnerably open to whatever he might desire to do to her next. It excited her that he was still fully and elegantly dressed while she herself was a weak and helpless mess in his arms.

'You're not still a virgin.' It wasn't a question; he had probed her sex deeply and thoroughly enough to know her hymen had been ruptured before tonight.

'No, I'm not,' she admitted, 'but I've never… I've never come like that before.' She gazed earnestly up into his eyes, silently pleading with him to understand that she had barely known him two hours yet already he had made her experience sensations no other man had ever come close to arousing in her. 'And I've never accepted a dinner invitation from a total stranger, much less gone home with him,' she added fervently, praying he would read between the lines and hear what she was telling him – that he was special and she had started falling in love with him from the instant his features rose out of the darkness in the graveyard.

His contented smile deepened as he insinuated the tip of his thumb between her lips. 'You're being a very naughty girl tonight, aren't you, Maia?' he teased quietly, gradually forcing her to accept his whole thumb.

She moaned and sucked on his hard and slightly salty digit like a baby. It made her try to picture his cock still buried in his black slacks, and his penetrating stare told her he knew what she was thinking and that it both amused and pleased him. And the longer he made her suck on his thumb while staring down into her eyes, the more she longed to reach into his lap and feel the hard-on she hoped was waiting for her there, but for some reason she couldn't bring herself to touch him so boldly. She was grateful when he took the decision out of her hands by grasping one of her wrists and resting her palm against his crotch. She gasped with pleasure at the rock-hard erection filling her grasp through his silky-soft pants.

'Would you like to feel me inside you, Maia?' He slipped his thumb out of her mouth so she could answer.

'Oh yes,' she whispered.

He laughed softly and stood up abruptly.

The suddenness of his motion made her catch her breath, then whimper in alarm as he grasped both her hands and pulled her to her feet. She was afraid of slipping on the wet floor, made even more treacherous by shards of broken glass. Red wine seeping into the wood looked disturbingly like freshly spilled blood, and she suddenly suffered a vivid flashback of the car's broken window through which tree branches thrust unhindered and cold rainwater poured into the front seat where she lay pinned down beneath the rough old arm...

He swept her up into his arms and carried her away from the wreck she had made of his living room. She wrapped her own arms gratefully around his neck and gazed trustingly up at his face. She could scarcely believe he was real, and it both thrilled and worried her to know that any moment now she was going to see his penis for the first time. Everything around her told her he was as talented and creative as he was physically attractive, yet if she didn't like his cock, if it wasn't big enough to satisfy her fantasies as well as her flesh, none of his good qualities would matter as much. It was terrible, yet it was true, and the suspense came close to killing her as he strode across the room with her cradled against him. She had thought he was going to carry her upstairs to his bed, but she discovered he had other plans for her when she felt a hard edge against her backside as he set her down carefully. He spread her legs and stood directly between them. 'Lie back,' he said.

She obeyed him, but moaned in disappointment that he wasn't going to undress her. It hurt her that he didn't want to see her naked body and couldn't be bothered to prime her for his penetrations by caressing her a little first. Then she stiffened against the hard wooden surface when she realized how wrong she was. 'What are you doing?' she gasped. 'No!'

'Relax, Maia, I'm not going to hurt you.' He gripped the edge of her dress over her chest, and began slicing through it with the small knife he had pulled out of his pants. He lifted the material away from her skin as he cut it all the way down to where it was crumpled around her thighs, then quickly reached up to nip through the spaghetti straps on her shoulders.

She learned in those moments that mixing dread and desire was seriously intoxicating as her body went limp and her pussy got so hot for him it burned straight through her ability to think. He peeled her dress open, fully exposing her curving, naked body to his eyes as he unzipped his fly. She lifted her head slightly, and literally held her breath in desperate anticipation as he pulled his cock out of his slacks. Her dark eyes widened as she absorbed the length and girth of his hard-on, and unconsciously she spread her legs even farther apart where they hung off the edge of the table. His penis was everything she could have hoped for, and there was as much relief as desire contained in her cry as he slipped his hands beneath her thighs and raised them forcefully up around him.

Suddenly, Maia couldn't believe what was happening, but even as her prim and proper mind closed itself to the shockingly wicked way she was behaving tonight, her pussy willingly opened up to the experience. He didn't make a sound as he penetrated her so patiently she thought it would drive her crazy even as she loved every overwhelming second. First he tormented her with the fullness of his head spreading her labial lips open around it and making her achingly aware of how empty she was without his cock filling her up. Then finally he began pushing his way into her, and her pussy seemed to weep with joy at how good his erection felt, as though the dimensions of his desire had been made especially to fulfill hers. He possessed her so slowly, she was aware of every nerve ending in her tight cleft clinging to his dick, and sensing that his pleasure was as breathtakingly acute as hers mysteriously burst the last proper dam inside her.

'Oh God, just fuck me!' she begged. 'Fuck me, please!'

His cool scrotum kissed her hot vulva as he lodged his enormous erection all the way inside her tight little pussy. 'Say my name,' he commanded, squeezing her thighs where they rested in his hands but otherwise not moving a muscle.

'Oh God, Chris, please…'

'Please what?' he teased cruelly, squeezing her thighs again.

She gasped as the slight pain intensified the tormenting pleasure of his erection kissing the mysterious heart of her flesh and nearly killing her with longing to be stabbed by him over and over again. 'Please fuck me, Chris, please!'

He pulled out of her.

She whimpered in distress at how empty she suddenly felt.

He thrust back inside her.

She cried out from the overwhelming satisfaction and continued crying out softly as he banged her mercilessly. The few young men she had been with until then had pumped awkwardly against her and come in a matter of minutes, but not Chris, and blended with her intense pleasure was joy and amazement at his virility mixed with the exciting fear that she wouldn't be able to handle it. Her heart and thoughts racing, she suspected the climax he had offered her as a gift before fucking her had served another purpose besides rendering her even more malleable to his will; it had made her sex wet and pliant enough to accept, and thoroughly enjoy, the onslaught of his almost painfully big cock making her aware of her innermost flesh as never before. No other man had made her so aware of the silky passage of her pussy clinging to him even while blooming open around his relentless penetrations. How beautiful he looked as he possessed her selfishly, almost violently, inexorably deepened her yielding ecstasy, which was mysteriously stoked by the intent expression on his face as he concentrated on driving his rigid penis as deep into her flesh as possible faster and harder. Yet his eyes were on her face and holding hers in a way that made her want him even more as she seemed to feel him thrusting deeper and deeper. Her breasts bounced wildly up and down beneath his onslaught and her lips parted as she panted in sympathy with his approaching orgasm. She had never truly enjoyed the taste of cum before, but gazing up at him as he approached his peak she was sure it was only because she had been eating in all the wrong places...

'Oh Maia,' he said breathlessly, and abruptly pulled out of her eagerly straining hole.

She moaned as he pumped his erection fervently over her body, tossing his head back with a groan as a stream of foam bathed her belly and formed a milky pool in her navel. She was grateful to him for not coming inside her since she had not told him yet it didn't matter; she could never get pregnant.

CHAPTER FOUR

L et's see what we can prepare for this special young man,' Carol said cheerfully.

'I have no idea how old he is, auntie. He's so beautiful, he seems ageless.'

'Dear, when you're my age, everyone else is young.' The old woman's good-natured chuckle evoked a seasoned hen laying yet another egg.

Maia smiled fondly up at her aunt from her usual place at the kitchen table. Carol had filled her life with stories in which the nourishing yoke of a moral was always inevitably concealed in the round-about way in which she told the tales.

'You say he built his own home and everything in it? He must be amazingly talented and creative.'

'Yes, he is.' Maia stared down into the murky depths of her tea. 'I'm nervous about tonight,' she confessed.

'Why in heaven's name should you be nervous, dear? I'm doing all the cooking. Shall we have rack of lamb or a beef roast, what do you think?'

She shrugged indifferently.

Carol glanced at her in alarm. 'He's not a vegetarian, is he?'

'I don't know.' She remembered the violent way he had stabbed her with his erection as she lay naked across his kitchen table, the white peel of her dress spread open around her. 'No,' she shook her head, 'I really don't think he is.' She wished she could share her tumultuous feelings with Carol, but the poor old dear would be too shocked; she would be absolutely stunned to learn that her usually well-behaved niece had made love with a complete stranger last night, a man she didn't know at all, except in the biblical sense now. It had not been like her to do what she did, but then Chris was like no other man she had ever met. He lived deep in the woods in a house like a hollowed out tree trunk and his blond hair was so soft and luminous it made her think of spun sunlight. She would almost be more surprised if he actually showed up at her house for dinner tonight than if she never saw him again. She half expected him to vanish forever like an enchanted being in a perverse fairytale after offering her a teasingly cruel glimpse into the mythical kingdom of great sex. What she had experienced with him last night was worlds away from the clumsy, groping frustration she had so often suffered in the front seats of cars after a mind-numbingly boring date invariably consisting of a disappointing dinner and a mediocre movie. She had wondered if getting her own flat would improve her love life. Maybe her life would miraculously become more exciting if she moved out of her aunt's house and got a place of her own. But the truth was that none of the men she had dated truly excited her, not mentally or physically, and if she stopped splitting the bills with Carol she would be obliged to seek full time employment at the solicitor's office where she was now fortunate enough to only work half days. This left her enough time and energy to paint, never mind that she would probably never be able to make a living off her strangely surreal and sensual landscapes. That wasn't important, all that mattered was the fact that art, at least, enabled her to experience a sense of magic and a mysteriously profound fulfillment sadly lacking from her day-to-day reality, not to mention her love life. She kept recalling the wonderful moment last night when she had felt her heart knight Chris her true love as he knelt before the wooden cabinet containing his spirits. She didn't want to dwell on what had happened on his love seat, and then later on his kitchen table, not while she was in the same room with Carol. She would think about it all again later upstairs in her bed...

Maia's thoughts felt like a car's windshield wipers in a downpour powerless against the rush of emotions this man aroused in her. He had asked her to spend the night with him, but had not insisted she do so when she told him Carol would be seriously worried about her if she didn't come home, and since he didn't have a telephone there was no way she could let her aunt know she was safe. He had not argued with her, he had simply unbuttoned his shirt, shrugged it off and slipped it on her tenderly, gently lifting her arms and turning her around as though she was a life-sized doll. The dark-red shirt had been wonderfully warm from resting against his skin, and there had been something very comforting about the soft, cozy way it embraced her all the way home when she was alone in her dark little car again. She had not needed to ask him to give her directions back to the main highway; he had led her back there in his own car, and she had felt as though her heart was vanishing into darkness when he turned back onto the narrow, tree-shrouded roads winding confusingly back to his home. Fortunately, Carol had been asleep when she let herself in and so had not seen her niece wearing a man's shirt and nothing else except high-heels.

'Maia, sweetheart, where are you? You've been lost in day-dreams all morning,' Carol observed as she limped efficiently around their small kitchen. 'Christopher isn't like all the other lads, is he?' Her voice betrayed a mixture of hope and concern. 'You're really taken with him, aren't you?'

I was taken by him all right, Maia thought, and yet again a debilitating desire flashed like lightning in her belly. 'Carol, do you remember our accident?' The question was rhetorical since every step her aunt took reminded her of that dreadful night. 'I still don't know what actually happened. I remember it was thundering and lightning and-'

'It doesn't matter now.' Carol said quickly, closing the refrigerator and leaning back against it. 'Go upstairs and get some rest while I straighten out this mess.' She glanced at the wreckage of dishes in the sink.

Normally, Maia would have offered to help, but this morning she simply rose, abandoning her cup of tea untouched, and climbed the stairs up to her room, where she lay back across her bed to once again relive the unbelievably naughty way she had behaved last night, and how much she had enjoyed it.

* * *

Dressed to receive their guest in a short red cotton dress with a V-neck and matching high-heels, her dark-brown hair falling in gentle waves half way down her back, Maia rejoined Carol later that evening. 'Can I help with anything?' she asked belatedly. Her aunt had apparently spent most of the day in the kitchen, but since Maia knew she loved to cook it didn't make her feel guilty.

'Well, let's see… you can break three eggs into that bowl for me, dear, that would help. I'm baking your favorite buttermilk biscuits.'

'Oh great, thank you.' She selected three eggs from the carton, then rested the fragile spheres on a green pot-holder so they wouldn't roll off the counter. She carefully cracked open the first one. 'Oh look,' she exclaimed, 'it's a double yoke!'

'Well, so it is, dear. That seems like a good omen for tonight, wouldn't you say?'

'Yes.' It meant Chris was her soul mate, he had to be, there were no other possible candidates in Stoneshire and he had made her feel things last night she had only fantasized were possible. 'But now I don't feel like scrambling them...'

'Oh they won't mind,' Carol replied brightly, 'not as long as you beat them together.'

Maia reluctantly picked up a fork and attempted to impale both yokes at once, but they kept slipping and sliding away together, so she was forced to decide which one would go first. Soon they were a single flowing whole, their liquid saffron cloud reflecting the vivid sunset outside the kitchen window, its dying luminosity scrambled by a lacy white curtain. She picked up another egg and, suddenly, she became disturbingly conscious of all the unknown forces surrounding the fragile illusion of their cozy little home just as her fingers gripped the delicate shell... it made her aware of how hungrily she was holding on to every instant of her life...

The doorbell rang just as she cracked the egg against the edge of the bowl. 'Oh my God, he's here,' she cried. 'He's early!'

'Indeed he is, but there's no need to panic,' Carol scolded her tenderly. 'Just rinse your hands off and go let him in.'

The countless possible greetings Maia had rehearsed all day vanished like shadows beneath his smile, forcing her to use her arms' silent sentences to tell him how relieved and happy she was to see him again. She felt as though they could have stood embracing in the dark foyer forever, but somehow they managed to separate into two bodies again and walk hand-in-hand into the dining room.

'Why did you leave me last night?' he whispered, giving her hand a reprimanding squeeze. 'Today was centuries long.'

* * *

'You sit here, please, Christopher.' Carol was at her most formal this evening.

He smiled as he obeyed her. 'Call me Chris.'

'Of course. It was very nice of you to bring a bottle of wine, Chris.'

'Can I help with anything, Carol?' Maia was compelled to ask before she seated herself on Chris' right side at the circular table.

'No thank you, dear, I have it all under control. There's tomato soup to start with and homemade buttermilk biscuits. I won't be a moment.' She pushed through the swinging wooden door dividing the kitchen from the dining room.

Chris immediately grasped Maia's hand, and laid it beneath his on the white table cloth. 'You wanted to say something to me before she walked in?' he prompted.

'I'm not sure… I forgot what it was…'

'Tell me.'

'Chris, please, you're cutting the circulation off in my fingers,' she whispered, glancing in the direction of the kitchen. 'You don't know you're own strength.'

'I know it very well, Maia.' But he released her hand in order to caress the knife at his place setting as though admiring the craftsmanship.

Watching the tip of his index finger stroke the full length of the silver, she was reminded of how devastatingly skilled it was. Never before had a man made her come with only his hand…

'Here we are.' Carol returned carrying a heavy steaming bowl she quickly placed in the center of the table. 'Help yourselves while I go get myself a glass of water and pull the biscuits out of the oven.'

Chris reached for the ladle. 'It smells divine, Carol.'

'No, thank you.' Maia covered her soup dish with one hand as he prepared to serve her.

'Why not?' he asked, smiling as though he knew the answer but wanted to hear it from her.

'I just don't want any... I haven't felt like myself all day, really.' She stared down into her empty bowl, studying the colorful wreath of flowers decorating the rim of the white stoneware.

'Maia is being a bad girl,' Chris informed Carol when she returned. 'Your niece doesn't even want to taste any of your delicious soup.'

'Why not, dear?' Her aunt sounded concerned. 'You love my tomato soup.'

Maia cried out when a cold wave of water suddenly drenched her breasts as her limping aunt inadvertently tripped on a warped wooden floor board.

'Oh my dear, I'm so sorry!' Carol set the tray of biscuits down on the table along with her now empty water glass. 'I've completely soaked you. You'll have to go upstairs and change, you can't eat in that wet-'

'It's all right, Carol, sit down, please, I'm fine,' Maia assured her, but shivered uncontrollably as Chris began drying her off with his white cloth napkin.

'You really should change your dress,' Carol insisted, hovering over her in concern and frowning slightly at the familiar way Chris was stroking her niece's pert breasts with the napkin. 'You'll catch your death...'

'I'm fine!' Maia snapped at her without meaning to. 'Now sit down, please, auntie,' she said more kindly.

'You see, Carol,' Chris dropped the napkin and quickly rose to pull his hostess's chair out for her, 'it's destiny that you partake of some wine this evening.'

'I suppose it is.' She politely twisted her shaken frown into a smile as she seated herself across from him.

'Let's light the candles to help dry Maia off,' he suggested, and proceeded to do so with the pack of matches he slipped out of his pocket. He was clad in a forest-green button-down shirt and dark-brown slacks that made him look even more handsome than Maia remembered him, if that was possible. Glad to put the embarrassing moment behind them, she rose to switch off the overhead light as he lit the candles, but when she resumed her seat, it dismayed her that Carol's lovingly prepared soup looked very much like a sinister cauldron of blood with three flames pulsing around it.

'Does it remind you of something?' Chris asked her, uncannily reading her mind as he began pouring them all some wine, beginning with her glass.

'Yes,' she admitted, feeling inexplicably somber.

'You see, Carol,' he said again as he proceeded to fill her glass, 'your niece and I have met before.'

'That's more than enough, thank you, Christopher… you mean before you helped her get her car started in the graveyard last night?'

'No, another time I helped her into the graveyard.'

'Excuse me?' Carol brought a wrinkled hand up to her right ear. 'My hearing isn't what it used to be. I don't think I heard you correctly.'

'Never mind.' He smiled indulgently and raised his glass. 'Cheers,' he said, and took an appraising sip of the dark-red vintage.

'Well,' Carol cleared her throat as though something was sticking in it, 'since Maia's not having any soup, I think I'll pass on it as well and go get the lamb out of the oven.' She rose again with difficulty. 'Excuse me, I won't be a moment.'

Maia impatiently watched her leave the room. 'What did you mean by that?' she demanded of Chris as soon as her aunt was out of earshot. 'I never saw you before last night. And why are you trying to scare her saying things like that? It sounded like you said you helped me into the graveyard, not in the graveyard. Why-?'

'Baby,' his tone was infinitely patient as he picked up her glass of wine and handed it to her, 'drink.'

Upset as she was by his behavior, which although oddly sinister was faultlessly polite, she could not resist obeying that tone in his voice or the look in his eyes reminding her of what he could make her feel... she sipped her wine obediently.

'You have to realize, Maia, that you were just now symbolically baptized for sacrifice when Carol spilled water over you and I lit fire to help dry you off.'

'What are you talking about?' Her chest was suddenly so tight she could scarcely get the words out. 'You're starting to scare me, Chris.'

'You say there are standing stones in all your paintings, which means that whenever you drive by them you can feel the energy stored inside them, can't you, Maia?'

'I think so,' she agreed, desperately hoping he was going to explain his strange comments so she could feel good about him again and not be afraid of the power he already had over her.

'There's a Celtic saying, he who defies the spirit of reason places himself within reach of salvation.'

As if in a dream she heard herself add, 'But also exposes himself to the dangers of the sword-edge bridge.' The words welled out of her unbidden; she had no idea where they came from. The only explanation she could think of was that she had read them somewhere once and forgotten she knew them until he triggered her memory.

'Very good, Maia.' He leaned over to gently kiss her forehead. 'We've already started across the sword-edge bridge together.' He sat back in his chair again looking in the direction of the kitchen. 'Now we just have to get you out of here. You're coming with me tonight, sweetheart, and you're going to stay with me. After dinner I want you to go up to your room and pack a suitcase with all your essentials. We'll collect the rest of your things some other time.'

'But, Chris…'

'No buts, Maia.' He picked up his silver spoon and took a sip of the blood-red soup. 'Mm, this is wonderful.'

'Chris, I can't just leave with you tonight,' she protested in a conspiratorial whisper, glancing in the direction of the kitchen where Carol was taking her sweet time.

'Why not?' He held her eyes, the expression in his at once tender and challenging. 'You feel the connection between us, don't you, Maia?'

'Yes, Chris, but-'

'Then why waste time? You know perfectly well you want to leave here with me, so why not tonight?'

'If it was just up to me, Chris, I wouldn't hesitate, but Carol…' She glanced at the dividing wooden door again. 'Carol will be shocked.'

He shrugged, and concentrated on his soup again. 'Sometimes shock is a good thing,' he said lightly, and paused to swallow another hot red mouthful before adding, 'it wakes people up.'

'But what about my art supplies?'

'You'll bring those with you, of course. They're the most important thing you own, much more important than clothing. You won't really be needing that.' He smiled and winked at her.

She laughed even as her heart gave an anxious flutter. 'But I have so many canvasses and brushes and paints, not to mention my easel…'

'Maia,' his tone and the way he set his spoon down made it clear her hesitant attitude was beginning to make him impatient, 'it's only stuff, and my trunk is bigger than it looks. We'll take everything you need with us, and Carol will deal with it. It's not the end of the world, just of your life together, but you'll be beginning a new adventure with me. Isn't that what you want?'

'Yes,' she replied fervently, 'more than anything!'

He slipped his hand beneath the table and stroked her bare thigh. 'The sword-edge bridge is a fascinating place to be,' he stated cryptically, and squeezed her flesh possessively. 'You'll see.'

CHAPTER FIVE

Maia stared up at the full moon through the small window in Chris' proportionally small bedroom. The sun's clinging satellite was slowly sinking in a silky-black sky perspiring with stars as it gazed amorously down at his naked back where he lay sleeping beside her. It was strange how the marble-white light carving out the deep shadows of his muscles made his arms and shoulders look thicker and broader than they actually were. The earth's one and only moon was perched in the heavens cool as a queen surrounded by her court; all the stars visible at the edges of her royal-blue aura sparkled like infinitely wealthy lords and ladies covered from head to toe in jewels. Maia couldn't see her lover's face because it was turned away from her on his pillow, which he had bunched passionately up around his head like a cloud, and she found herself wondering at how inexplicably dark his hair looked in the otherworldly light that seemed to be forging the muscles in his body just for the pleasure she took in gazing down at them…

She concentrated on the moon's infinitely calm face in order not to remember Carol's politely concealed distress when her niece left the house with a man she had met only twenty-four hours ago, taking with her two suitcases and a large duffel bag full of art supplies. And as Maia stared at the moon without blinking, its luminous sphere became the bottom of a polished silver chalice into which the sun passionately poured its boundless energy without ever filling her... then she blinked a few times and the full moon struck her as the ghostly negative of a fingerprint belonging to every beautiful woman who had ever lived impressed on the universe at the moment of her birth, the shadow-lined sphere the soft round end of her own pale, mysteriously unique fingertip...

Maia realized she must have fallen asleep while gazing out the window because suddenly she was standing in front of her parents' tombstone, only it had grown much taller than she remembered it and sprouted a protective dome like a massive mushroom. She was rather pleased by its transformation, yet she hesitated to approach the narrow black opening in the solid white stem. The mushroom's head glowed like a perfect half moon, so she wasn't surprised to discover there wasn't really a door, only an impenetrably dark portal. Then she thought she glimpsed the soft glow of her mother's red hair inside, and the sight gave her the courage she needed to enter the hauntingly organic mausoleum.

The woman in whose body she had shaped herself lay beneath a stone sheet, the cold weight of which didn't seem to bother her because she was smiling peacefully, her head slightly raised by a marble pillow carved in the shape of a large open book, its blank pages dimly illuminating the circular room. All around Maia the shadows were thick and heavy as black velvet curtains slowly rising in whichever direction she focused, then swiftly falling again when she looked away. Glancing into one corner of the pitch-black crypt, she briefly made out smiling figures painted on the wall, their clothing impossibly bright in the absolute gloom. And then, just beside her to her right, appeared an exquisite little prayer room very much like the kind found in Medieval Cathedrals containing a beautiful statue of the Virgin Mary perched on a gilded globe of the world.

'Oh mummy,' she sighed, bending over to rest her head for an instant on the cold stone breasts of Stella's effigy. She longed to be comforted and loved without question, to know that no matter how badly she behaved her mother would always care for her. The tiny prayer room did not vanish even when she turned away from it, and looking back at it curiously, she realized the black serpent imprisoned beneath the Virgin's white toes was alive. With one upraised hand the Mother of God blessed the world while with the other hand she wantonly raised the hem of her sky-blue dress, smiling with secret pleasure as the evil serpent began sliding slowly up her shapely leg.

'Father!' Maia cried in horror.

'It's all right, sweetheart, don't be afraid, you're not alone....' A man's voice spoke directly in her head as she felt a reassuring warmth envelop her and safely cradle her within it, giving her the courage to watch the serpent twist eagerly up to a snowy thigh. She held her breath, waiting for cruel fangs to pierce the Virgin's infinite tenderness and for red rivers of blood to run, but suddenly a passionate faith in the Lady's power possessed her as she felt her cheek pressed against an invisible yet mysteriously benevolent chest. Mary's blue skirt and white shift were the daylight sky filled with soft clouds, and as the serpent rose eagerly up into this heavenly atmosphere, she gasped in the throes of a sensation such as she had never known; a sensation that intensified almost unbearably when the tip of the black tail shuddered a victorious defeat between the Virgin's thighs and disappeared inside her...

Maia woke with a cry of mingled ecstasy and alarm as Chris rolled over and unconsciously pinned her down with a heavy arm. She couldn't move and the moon was no longer visible outside the window.

She was having very strange dreams lately, but this last one had been particularly vivid. She could still see her mother's red hair rippling like fire across the cold marble bed, and the Virgin letting herself be possessed by the serpent coiled submissively beneath her delicate white feet... She should have found the images rising out of her subconscious disturbing and shocking, but instead she realized with a soft groan of shame that they had made her pussy so warm and wet the pressure of Chris' arm across her breasts was seriously tempting her to wake him. In the morning, she would try and paint the scenes she had seen in the mushroom-shaped mausoleum of her dream, but right now she wasn't interested in symbols and metaphors; what she wanted was the undeniably real pleasure of Chris' cock inside her. They had only made love once so far, yesterday evening when he spread the feast of her naked body across his kitchen table, and carved her hungrily up with his erection as the hot juices of her pleasure flowed helplessly around him. When they arrived at his little house tonight with all the essentials she had been able to bring with her at such short notice (and with all her beloved art supplies, naturally) she had been expecting him to take her passionately in his arms and have his way with her as he had not been able to do in front of her aunt Carol, but he hadn't even kissed her. Leaving her possessions in his living room, he had simply taken her hand and led her upstairs. His unlit narrow stairway seemed to spiral up and up for longer than seemed possible judging by the house's physical dimensions, and his bedroom had been just as impenetrably dark. She had been about to ask him to turn on a light when he told her to take off her clothes. She heard him doing the same, and had been too hurt and disappointed by his indifference to complain as she slipped casually into bed beside him as though they had been together forever.

Long after he fell asleep after a quiet 'Good night, Maia' she lay awake gazing restlessly up at the moon tormented by the awareness of his naked body lying so close to hers, and now her haunting dream was somehow making her want him even more. 'Chris?' she whispered, feeling it would drive her crazy if he didn't wake up and fuck her. 'Chris,' she repeated a little more loudly.

'Mm,' he said, his voice muffled by her hair. His face was buried in the side of her neck as he slept, but suddenly it slid purposefully down to one of her breasts.

She gasped when his lips latched on to one of her nipples, and moaned in delight as his tongue lapped her stiffening peak, suckling it like a sleepy baby. The pleasure traveled directly from her breast down to her sex as inexorably as a lit fuse smoldering in her pussy, and she was so aroused already, she knew all it would take was a few hard strokes of his cock for an orgasm to explode between her thighs and wipe out all the night's frustrations.

'Mm...' he said again, sounding more awake now, and she cried out hopefully as he fervently transferred his attentions to her other nipple. His insatiable hunger got the tips of her tits so rigid she felt the beginnings of a climax lick deep inside her belly like a hot forked tongue as he gently bit one.

'Oh Chris,' she breathed, 'please, I need you...' She wondered if he was going to make her beg him to fuck her again, and her mouth had opened to say the words when he abruptly slid beneath the sheet and thrust his whole body between her legs. Before she knew what was happening he had buried his face between her thighs and transferred the skilled attention of his tongue from her nipples to her clitoris.

'Oh yes,' she sighed gratefully, reaching down to lightly grasp his head in her hands. His hair was so soft it made her almost morbidly aware of the contrasting hardness of his skull. She was desperate to feel the rending length of his erection fully opening her up around it, yet the sensation of his features imprinting themselves on the yieldingly moist warmth of her labia was so sweet she didn't mind waiting.

In the past she had never taken much pleasure from oral sex, either in giving or receiving it, but she had been right to suspect that with Chris everything would feel miraculously different. The awkward, unfocused licks and uncomfortable groping fingers she had come to expect were tonight replaced by a concentrated yet effectively indirect attack on her clit. The flicking tip of his tongue and his suckling lips almost made her vaguely ashamed of the way her hot juices began pouring helplessly into his mouth, but she couldn't help herself; her sensual slot had never felt so bottomless, so in need of him to fill it, even if it was only with two of his fingers.

'Oh yes, yes…' she breathed, flinging her arms up over her head and clutching a pillow as she gently gripped the sides of his hard head with her soft thighs. She shifted her hips against the bed, seeking to position his penetrating fingers and orbiting tongue in just the right elusive spot that would send her hurtling along the blinding course of a climax. But he was teasing her; every time she felt her flesh poised on the speed of orgasmic light about to dissolve in timeless flashes of heart-pounding ecstasy, he shifted the stimulation of his tongue slightly and altered the rhythm of his fingers plunging into her cunt, cruelly delaying her release.

'Oh God, Chris, please,' she begged, 'I want to come, please…' She forgot about her lust for his cock; all she wanted now was to catch the pure joy cresting between her legs on the warm wave of his tongue and ride it to its crashing end in her blood.

He didn't respond to her plea verbally, but respond he did by suddenly pushing all her right buttons, sliding his fingers in and out of her pussy just hard and deep and fast enough as his tongue concentrated its assault on her clitoris, keeping her escalating ecstasy relentlessly on course. She lay breathlessly still on the soft launch pad of the mattress as her pleasure soared, then at last her body took off and she wasn't aware of anything anymore except his face between her thighs and the sound of her cries as she climaxed more intensely than she ever had in her life. She didn't just come the way she did when she touched herself alone in her room; she came and came and came, her pussy juices rushing into his mouth as though he had struck the elixir of life with his digging fingers and determined tongue, making her orgasm feel eternal. It almost scared her how long he was able to prolong her ecstasy as she self-ishly rode his mouth, until she was thoroughly exhausted by the pleasure's unbelievable staying power.

It was a relief when he finally slipped out from beneath the sheet and lay down beside her again. He took her utterly relaxed body in his arms, and pulling her over onto her side, he held her close that way for a long time, until they fell asleep together.

* * *

Peter was offended by how much Drew appeared to be enjoying his breakfast, the yokes of his fried eggs bright as suns that had no place in the curtained dimness of a dining room where only black tea had been served for the last forty-eight hours.

'May we ask if you made any progress last night, Merlin?' Peter had decided this was an appropriately sarcastic nickname for someone whose command of the Dragon's Breath was exercised only through the poisonous smoke of cigarettes, a clear sign of physical weakness rather than of spiritual power.

'Dear, that's quite enough,' Stella said quietly but firmly. She had made her own decision – not to wear black anymore. After all, her daughter was not dead, she was merely sleeping, therefore, in an effort to reflect her positive attitude and her growing hope that Maia would make a full recovery, she had donned a form-fitting knee-length violet dress with long sleeves and a plunging neck-line.

Peter thought his wife's garment positively indecent considering the circumstances. 'Going to a party, love?' he asked her contemptuously, feeling oddly chastised by the beautifully smooth coolness of her deep cleavage.

She flinched at his tone even as she told herself it was only a temporary mix of fear and grief that made his eyes seem to glitter hatefully. 'Unlike you, dear,' her smile was strained as she paused to sip her tea from a cup decorated with colorful wreathes of flowers, 'I am attempting to maintain a positive attitude. You know perfectly well how I feel about the color violet, and I am not about to stop applying my beliefs when we need them most!' The porcelain saucer chimed defiantly against its matching plate like an urgent bell rung in the kingdom of the Fairies punctuating her faith-filled statement. The high-pitched sound was followed by the charged silence of an emotional storm brewing, and Drew added a sinister hissing sound to it as he lit a match.

'Aren't you afraid of getting lung cancer?' Peter demanded, and awaited a platitude on the negative nature of fear in response he could enjoy shooting down.

'It crosses my mind now and then,' Drew replied amiably, blithely continuing to ignore the tension in the room as he enjoyed a cigarette after his meal. 'I'll quit eventually,' he added wistfully, 'if I don't die first, of course.' A smile touched his lips. 'But in answer to your first question,' he sobered up, 'yes, I believe I connected with Maia last night, very briefly, but it was a definite beginning.'

Stella's left hand flew up to her slender throat and clung to it as though this was the only way she could control the desperate anxiety in her voice as she spoke. 'How is she?'

Drew caressed the crescent-shaped scar below his lip. 'I can't very well tell you she's just fine,' he admitted, 'but she's definitely... active.' He studied the cigarette's slender form caught between the slightly rough tips of his fingers. 'Her soul feels much older than her twenty-three years... her essence is very deep and powerful.' He leaned towards Peter over the table even as he held Stella's eyes. 'What I'm saying is that, psychically, you can add at least two zeros to Maia's age. She's an old soul, and she's right at home in another dimension. I'm going to have a hell of a time convincing her to come back.'

CHAPTER SIX

Maia lay in bed, comfortably propped up against some pillows, staring at the scaled down silhouette of a tree Chris had carved as a kind of bas relief into one of the oak walls in his bedroom. The shower hissed loudly inside his tiny bathroom. Listening to it, she was strangely aware of the water pipes coiling behind the walls like supple metal serpents, their fangs thrusting out in the handles of his sink, which she had seen for herself earlier were minimalist slivers of metal. She could not help but be impressed by a man who had designed every little detail of his home himself. Objects she herself had always taken for granted – the fixtures of a bathroom sink, for example – in her lover's house assumed intriguing organic qualities that were naturally aesthetic. There was so much she wanted to ask him about how and why he had built everything the way he had that she hadn't been able to figure out where to start.

Last night, her bare feet had relished the thick green carpet she hadn't been able to see in the darkness, but when she woke this morning and was confronted by the bare black arms of a tree's silhouette, the sight unsettled her so much she almost hadn't been able to enjoy it when, murmuring with sleepy lust, Chris rolled over into her arms and began exploring her naked body. Nothing had come of it, however, as she desperately needed to empty her bladder first, and when she returned to the bed, he declared it was his turn and disappeared into the bathroom. Now he was taking a leisurely shower while she studied his bedroom. It was very small and almost perfectly round; it could actually be a hollowed out tree trunk. The ceiling was so high, it was lost in darkness even with the bedside lamp turned on and with the humidly tarnished silver light of an overcast day failing to penetrate into the room through the small window. Half the wall space was hidden behind tall bookshelves he must also have made himself because they conformed perfectly to the curving architecture, which had an odd effect on the leather-bound volumes, thrusting some out farther than others. Gazing at the spines, Maia verified her initial impression that most of her lover's books appeared old and worn enough to be first editions. She could make out texts on Astronomy and Physics and Biology on the top shelves, with poetry anthologies as well as works by individual poets just below them. Underneath the poetry were rows of novels, countless fictional realms sitting over heavy tomes on history and ancient cultures, with one whole bottom shelf devoted exclusively to Celtic culture and the legend of the Druids.

She would not have been so impressed by her lover's apparent erudition if it had not been so uniquely coupled with his skills as a craftsman (which also struck her as unusually artistic) not to mention with his physical beauty and with how skilled his hands were in other ways... his tongue was also extremely eloquent...

She sighed and stirred contentedly yet also restlessly against the deliciously comfortable feather pillows. It was so gray and gloomy outside she felt even less inclined to rise. She must have done something right in her life, because the universe had rewarded her with Christopher Thorn, a totally unique man who transcended even all her fantasies of the perfect lover.

She frowned gazing at the black bas relief of the tree directly across from her. She told herself it didn't matter that he could be strangely cold and detached sometimes, like last night, for example, when he had gone to sleep without even kissing her. Of course, he had more than made up for it later when he gave her another intense climax by going down on her. Still, she would have liked for him to cuddle her a little this morning before spending such a long time in the shower by himself, especially since she had believed he was only getting up to relieve himself as she had; she had expected him to come back to bed.

She sighed again, pouting. Didn't all new lovers shower together in the morning? Yet it was silly and superficial of her to expect Chris to behave normally when that was precisely the last thing she wanted him to do. So far, normal had bored her nearly to death in men. Therefore, she had to take the good with the bad and consider herself lucky, which she definitely was to have met someone like him in dreary old Stoneshire.

At last she heard the water shut off in the bathroom.

'Well, what do you think?' Chris emerged almost at once followed by a cloud of steam drying his water-darkened blond hair with a light-blue towel.

Maia stared at him, wide-eyed. He was completely naked and the perfection of his body aroused the artist in her even more than the woman. He looked like a Renaissance sketch of the ideal man fully fleshed out by the strokes of a master, a master whose brush had been slightly tainted with red paint; his pale skin had been beaten into an unnatural rosy hue by the hot shower. 'Think about what?' she asked lamely. His cotton bed sheet was decorated with blazing autumn leaves. She pulled it shyly up to just beneath her naked breasts and they looked cool and white as snow against the vivid colors.

'What do you think of my bedroom?' He lowered the towel and shook his wet head over her like a puppy coming in out of the rain. 'Wake up,' he commanded, wrapping the wet towel around his lean hips.

'I love your room,' she said fervently. 'I love your whole house. I feel like I'm inside a giant tree.'

'I know.' He sat on the edge of the bed beside her. 'That's what I want it to feel like.'

'How did you do that?' she asked, looking over at the bas relief of the tree.

'It's a different kind of wood from the rest of the house.'

'I can see that, but how did you do it?'

'It wasn't easy, believe me; it involved lots of exact measurements. I built the whole room around it, not the other way around. The wood came from an oak that was struck by lightning three time in one night, and obviously I used only the charred pieces of wood.' He stood up and approached the branching silhouette.

Maia watched him thinking how his blue towel looked like a fragment of the sky and wondering when he was going to kiss her good morning. Once again she found his behavior disappointingly casual and friendly. She would have liked for him to be more passionate and loving. She felt the need to be reassured that she had done the right thing essentially moving in with him after only knowing him for twenty-four hours.

'It's my closet,' he announced.

She gasped in astonishment when he casually pushed open the trunk of the tree and a row of shirts and pants appeared that gave the silhouette a disturbingly impressive depth.

'You see, Maia, I believe my soul has worn as many bodies as this.' He smiled at her over his shoulder as he stood proudly in front of his considerable wardrobe.

'I don't doubt it has,' she agreed, very pleased with his comment, for she had always thought of her body as a dress her ageless soul would slip off at the end of her life's long day.

He stepped into his sinister closet, and emerged a moment later holding a short-sleeved button-down shirt the same color as his towel, and a pair of stiff blue-jeans. 'I think we can expect a visitor soon,' he said, tossing his clothes onto the bed.

'A visitor?' she repeated, feeling like a queen spotting an invader on the horizon; she was loath to surrender her sensually rich and fledgling intimacy with him.

He walked over to her again. 'Don't be so distressed, love.' He mussed her hair affectionately. 'Our guest won't stay long. He's just dropping in to see my work.'

'Well, if he doesn't like it, he has absolutely no taste,' she declared.

He laughed. 'Your faith in me will not go unrewarded, young lady.' He unwrapped the towel from around his hips again and let it fall to the floor. 'I think my baby needs her bottle.' He held her face with one hand while with the other hand he gently insinuated his soft penis into her mouth. 'There you are, drink your protein like a good girl. It tastes good, doesn't it?'

She moaned and the bed sheet slipped down into her lap as she sat up to eagerly align her face with his hips.

'Yes, that's a good girl, it's all yours, Maia, so suck on it, suck on it and make it hard… that's it, I want you to have every last drop.'

No man had ever talked to her before while she went down on him, and she discovered now that words excited her as much as the possessive way he stroked her hair with both hands, smoothing it away from her face so it wouldn't interfere with the smooth passage of his stiffening cock sliding in and out between her soft, full lips. She had never really enjoyed giving head before, and she closed her eyes with a slight grimace expecting not to like the taste of his semen. His dick was getting so big and rigid between her soft lips she had to keep opening her mouth wider as she adjusted his burgeoning dimensions against her tongue. She moaned again, this time anxiously when she realized he was casually reaching for her throat as though it, too, had been made especially to caress and please him. She knew she was not very good at fellatio, much less at deep-throating, and opening her eyes again she tried to tell him this with a desperate, pleading glance up at his face.

'It's all right,' he slipped the fingers of both hands through her dark hair to take control of her head, 'you can handle it, Maia. Not only can you handle it, you're going to love sucking my cock, trust me.'

It amazed her that she believed him, maybe because the flavor of his pre-cum was so clean and subtle there was nothing about it she found distasteful, and this was such an intense relief her jaw relaxed around him, giving him full entry into her inexperienced orifice.

'Oh yes,' he whispered, managing to get his erection all the way into her mouth for an excruciating moment that made her squeeze her eyes closed again as they watered from the effort she had to make not to gag on his swollen glans. 'Mm, that's good, Maia, very good,' he praised her even as he had mercy on her by slipping almost all the way out of her mouth.

She sucked gratefully on the tip of his shaft, grasping it with one hand for the purpose of stroking it, but also to keep it out of her throat for the moment. She pumped him passionately in her fist while twirling her tongue around his head, feeling a bit self-conscious about her oral skills or lack thereof. It made her wonder how many women had been in her position, and she was afraid most, if not all, of them must have done a better job at pleasing him this way than she was doing.

'You have a lot of energy and enthusiasm, Maia,' he said, sounding insultingly unaffected by how hard she was working on his penis, 'the skill will come later with practice, and believe me,' his chuckle was intensely sexy, 'I'll let you have lots of practice.'

Already she both loved and hated the way he seemed able to read her mind as she concentrated on the challenge of properly stimulating and intensifying his erection. The pleasure she took in her efforts was different from his, and this morning she imagined her satisfaction was even greater than the one he experienced fucking her mouth simply because he had enjoyed himself this way before but she never had; this was the first time she felt an inexplicable but very real sense of fulfillment going down on a man. Until now it had always seemed like a lot of effort for nothing, but the sensation of Chris' hard-on sliding gently yet relentlessly in and out of her inexperienced mouth was mysteriously stoking her pussy too, making her receptively warm and wet between her legs.

She was growing tired from the subtle strain of this novel exertion even as she relished the exercise, which would have been made somewhat easier if he had let her know how she was doing, but he was silent as a standing stone towering above her. He didn't make any sounds of pleasure, but his rock-hard cock told her she must be doing something right. She wondered if he was planning to get off in her mouth and was a little worried about how she would deal with that honor if it came. She had never brought a man to his climax with her lips and tongue and so had never been forced to swallow frothing mouthfuls of cum. She needn't have been concerned, however, for Chris slipped out of her abruptly and mussed her hair affectionately again as though her devoted licks had merely been those of a naïve kitten. 'That's enough for now,' he said like a school teacher addressing a student. 'You need to shower and dress. Our guest will be here any minute.'

* * *

Sir Eric Wolfson looked slowly around the living room, and his luminous gray eyes brought the overcast day's cool depths into the small space. They alighted on Maia, and remained fixed on her as he peeled off his black leather gloves one by one. He then gracefully draped them both over one slender but muscular thigh, revealingly clad in skin-tight black leather. 'Lovely,' he said, his quiet, lazy voice a seductive contrast to the thick brown hair waving passionately around his fine-boned face.

'What's lovely?' Chris asked, smiling. 'Are you referring to my work or my girlfriend, sir?'

'Both, naturally,' was the languid reply as he kept his eyes on Maia the whole time.

'Have a seat, please,' Chris said briskly, 'and I'll pour us some tea. Maia, dear wait for me upstairs, please, I won't be long.'

Eric turned and walked slowly over to the love-seat, his apparent lethargy actually only enhancing his obvious fitness and almost cat-like grace. 'Must she leave us?' he asked as he dropped onto a cushion, his knee-high leather boots looking even blacker against the light-blue cloth.

'I'm afraid she must,' his host replied sternly. 'We have business to discuss and she would only distract us.' Chris looked over at her, and then glanced significantly at the steep little staircase leading up to his bedroom.

'I beg to differ,' his guest disagreed politely, crossing his legs and resting his limp gloves over his crotch. 'To say that beauty can distract is to imply there is something better worth doing than enjoying and appreciating it.'

'It was a pleasure meeting you, Sir Wolfson,' Maia said quickly, and ascended the steps with her pulsing fluttering like a bird's wings as she obeyed the invisible current of Chris' will. She did not find his dismissal humiliating, on the contrary. It was extremely flattering to know her presence affected him enough that he was obliged to ask her to leave so he could concentrate. The way two highly attractive men had determined her actions between them, as though she had absolutely no say in the matter, might have offended her if it had not made her feel so beautiful and desirable. The moment he walked through the door, Eric Wolfson's wicked aura of fame and fortune made her feel as nervous as a mouse spotted by a dangerous black cat. He was so intensely sexy, her heart caught in her throat looking at him, another reason she did not mind leaving the room. It disturbed her to realize she had been staring at him the whole time instead of at Chris, her wonderful new lover who until a few seconds before she had never dreamed could be rivaled by any other man in Stoneshire or beyond.

It was impossible to resist the temptation to crouch in the grass-green carpet at the top of the stairs in order to listen to what was being said downstairs. As she held her breath and strained her hearing, both hoping and strangely dreading they might still be talking about her, all the unpolished wood surrounding her felt like the roots of an ancient tree...

'Vines and serpents it is then,' she heard Chris say, and his voice seemed to be coming from deep underground. 'How many bottles would you like it to hold, sir?'

'A great many,' Eric replied laconically. 'As many as possible.'

'That's not very specific.'

'Specifics bore me.'

Suddenly ashamed of eavesdropping, Maia stood up and stepped into her lover's bedroom, where she dove restlessly onto the bed and crushed handfuls of painted leaves in order to smooth them out again. She frowned, burying her face in the mattress and restlessly kicking her feet as she fought the nearly irresistible current of her curiosity. Finally, she couldn't stand it anymore and she found herself perched at the top of the stairs again listening.

'Naturally…' Eric drew the word out languidly. 'Now, may I at least bid farewell to that lovely creature you're foolishly attempting to hide from me?' The heel of a boot struck wood as she pictured him rising from the loveseat, and the sound kicked her heart out of Chris' orbit for an exhilarating yet also terrifying moment. She could scarcely believe this intensely sexy man wanted to see her again when it was obvious from his attitude that he could have any woman he wanted.

'No, you may not bid her farewell,' Chris replied.

'You can't keep her from me forever,' Sir Wolfson warned mildly.

'The hell I can't.' Her lover almost sounded amused by his quest's arrogance. She couldn't be sure, but she thought she detected a confident smile in his voice.

CHAPTER SEVEN

'Dear, I never wanted to tell you this, but I only belong to this... this cult to indulge you.' Peter's thick silver hair gleamed like armor against his skull as he smoothed it firmly back with both hands away from a face nobly scarred by the years.

'What?' Stella was literally beside herself where she stood before an ornately framed mirror in a corner of their library. She clutched the back of a large chair upholstered in burgundy leather as though needing to steady herself against the shock of her husband's revelation.

'I didn't see any harm in it at first,' he added morosely from where he sat slumped in his favorite chair, 'although Carol certainly didn't approve of my becoming involved, even when I told her that some of the rites are quite lovely...' He stared down at the red and gold rug embroidered with stylized dragons that had been his aesthetic pets for years, yet ever since Maia's accident he suddenly saw them for the fierce ugly creatures they actually were.

'Peter,' Stella said desperately, 'look at yourself… this isn't the man I love, this isn't-'

'No, the man you really love is upstairs, isn't he?' He glared up at her. 'Isn't he?' he repeated, surging angrily to his feet. 'But he doesn't want you, Stella, he wants our daughter.' He grabbed both her upper arms and shook her roughly, as though trying to dislodge all the pagan ideas in her head by way of physical force since reason had failed. 'He wants Maia, do you hear me, that's why he's here, that's why he's helping us, because he wants her for himself afterwards!'

'Let go of me!' she gasped as strands of hair escaped the fiery ball at the nape of her neck. Static electricity from the rug made them cling to her pale cheeks, where they resembled a pattern of very fine cuts inflicted by her distress. 'Peter!'

'I'm sorry,' he breathed, and suddenly gentle, he urged her to sit down in the chair she had been holding onto. 'Please forgive me, Stella,' he begged miserably, sinking to one knee before her.

'Oh my love, why are you fighting me?' she asked wearily, gently resting one of her hands on his tormented head. 'I didn't do this to our daughter. I'm not responsible for her accident and neither is Drew. Maia isn't being punished by God because her parents belong to a pagan cult, as you put it.'

'But you heard what he said.' He stared up at her imploringly. 'You heard him!'

She sighed. 'Would it make you feel any better if there was absolutely no mystical reason for what happened to Maia?' She sat back in the chair as he stood up. 'Would it make you feel better to think that she's completely unconscious, trapped in a lifeless, mindless coma? If Drew is right, then at least there's some hope he can bring her back to us.'

'Oh yes,' he scoffed, 'it's quite magical that Maia is lying in a hospital bed now, not to mention that she'll be barren for life. We'll never have grandchildren, do you realize that?'

'She was struck across the womb by the branch of a centuries-old oak tree just after it was struck by lightning three times,' she reminded him patiently, as though it was a word-problem they were both assigned to solve in a class on metaphysics.

'It truly distresses me, Stella, how easily you can accept the fact that Maia was perhaps chosen by natural forces as some sort of sacrificial victim to appease the world's violated soul. Isn't that how he put it?' Peter now avoided his favorite chair like the throne of a kingdom in the throes of a bloody battle where rational strategies were completely useless. 'Maia is an embodiment of the modern world… that's essentially what he said, isn't it? She's innocent in herself, but born of poisoned roots, unable to conceive life in her body now just as our technology-worshipping society keeps taking and taking from nature without giving anything back. We're incredibly honored to be her parents, don't you think, since according to that fire-breathing dragon upstairs our daughter … please, what was it he said?'

Stella gripped the arms of her chair as though it was moving at the speed of light and only appeared motionless. 'He said that Maia has the power to appease nature's violated forces with her profound sensuality…'

'That's it!' He laughed bitterly. 'Oh I love that, that's rich.'

'She's a grown woman now, not just your daughter,' she reminded him, folding her hands in her lap now and sitting straight-backed as a Victorian matron, but her chest heaving with emotion brought to life the marble-white perfection of her cleavage.

'I know she's a grown woman. That is not the issue here.'

Her face was hard. 'Yes it is.'

'For Christ's sake, Stella' he gripped the fireplace mantel with both hands and leaned forward with his arms fully outstretched, 'have you taken leave of your senses?' He stared down at the cold gray hearth.

'No, I have not taken leave of my senses, but I also haven't merely been playing an eccentric game as you apparently have been. I know we can't really call ourselves Druids since there aren't any written records describing what their rites were actually like, but the rituals we do practice mean something to me and nature is my church, not some-'

'You're grasping at straws, love,' he cut her off, 'straws that come straight from the wicker man. What was it your chain-smoking high priest said about love being the only thing that can save Maia? In heaven's name, Stella, if my love can't bring her back, the love of a father for his only daughter, what makes you think she'll respond to some strange man's crude psychic pawing? You're letting him run around in some other dimension with our little girl doing-'

'You see, that is the issue here.' It was her turn to interrupt him angrily. 'I think you would almost prefer it if Maia died and took the sweet Virgin by the hand. You hate the idea of her naked energy joining with Drew's so he can help her slip her body back on like a dress. You hate thinking of his feelings caressing hers and of his thoughts penetrating her desires, you hate-'

'Forgive me for being so dense, dear.' He straightened up, but continued gazing down at the cold hearth. 'I think I understand now, please correct me if I'm wrong. What this twaddling bastard means is that Maia's soul is mysteriously making love to the sacred spirit of the oak tree that nearly killed her, and that she's having such a bloody good time she doesn't feel like zipping back into her body just yet.'

'It's not that simple and you know it, Peter,' his wife said desperately.

'No, it isn't that simple,' he echoed, staring at the woman he loved as though he had never seen her before in his life.

* * *

A faint cloud of smoke hovering above him, Drew Landson tucked his head into the crook of his arm and wiped an intangible perspiration of concentration from his brow. The white wicker chair that matched the delicate glass-top dresser was stronger than it looked, for it was managing to hold his weight without the slightest whine of pain.

Avoiding his reflection in the oval mirror, he picked up Maia's brush with his free hand. Dark strands of hair wound between the black bristles in a maze of tangles that made absolutely no sense; they lacked the purposeful order of a loom or the precise hunger of a spider's web. Nevertheless, he found that holding the brush helped him untangle some of the threads in the mystery surrounding its lovely owner.

He set it down again after a moment, and caressed the long crack running down the dead center of the egg-shaped mirror-glass dividing his reflected face in half. An intrigued smile lit the five-o'clock shadow surrounding his lips. This young woman had more power than he would ever have believed possible, more power than he cared to admit to her mother, much less to her totally distraught father. From the terrible tangle of her feelings at the accident on that stormy night, Maia had fashioned such a tight imaginative knot that even his fine comb of metaphysical logic was having a tough time with it. He was beginning to realize that unless he was a firm as he was gentle with her in her dream, there was a good chance she would end up cutting off her whole life by never returning to her body.

He hoped Stella would be able to keep her husband under control long enough for him to do his work. He had been about to drive home to pick up some of his things when he discovered that he could not just slip casually out of Maia's personal space. He had taken possession of her bedroom with the intention of guiding her back into her body as swiftly as possible, yet now he found himself inclined to linger with her in another dimension…

He smiled at the reflection of her blue-and-white comforter flowing at the level of his gaze in the mirror's frozen surface, his imagination gliding like an ice-dancer as his mind warmed to its arousing choreography. Even Stella might turn against him if she grasped the full nature of his intentions. He couldn't risk slipping up, yet her parents should have realized his head-on battle with unknown forces would inevitably have serious consequences if he succeeded in winning Maia back for them. If he helped Maia's soul back into her body, she would be his forever.

The bedroom door opened silently behind him, but he pretended not to notice as he gazed into the cloud of smoke veiling his features from the cigarette hanging languidly between his lips.

'Drew?'

'Mm?' He shot Stella's reflection a look that would have burned through her heart if he had exposed her to it directly.

'Do you know what Peter just said to me?'

She sounded unnaturally calm and he noted that her lovely face was even more pale than usual. As always, he had to resist the urge to take her in his arms because the way he desired to make her feel better would only make them both feel worse in the end. 'What is it, Stella?' he asked gently.

'Peter says he only belongs to indulge me, and he called it a cult!'

'Leave him,' he suggested lightly.

'What?'

He half turned towards her on the wicker chair, resting an

elbow on Maia's glass vanity while idly stroking a denim-wrapped thigh with the back of her hairbrush.

'Stop that,' she snapped, the tide of her grief receding beneath a violent wave of jealous guilt.

He obeyed her, and added yet another butt to the ashtray's crude stone altar. 'I have to go now.' He stood up.

'Where? Where are you going? You're not abandoning us, are you?'

'Of course not, Stella.' He paused before her to gaze tenderly down at her frightened face as he slipped on his jacket. 'I'm just going home for some of my things. I'll be right back.'

'Oh… thank you.'

'Don't worry about Peter. You know he's not himself right now.'

She frowned. 'I'm beginning to think he's more himself right now than ever.'

'He's battling all his demons at once, Stella. His contentment's castle is under siege and he either surrenders to all the doubts and fears in his subconscious moat, so to speak, or he wins a greater understanding and mastery of himself. You can only do so much to help him. After all,' he caressed fiery strands of hair away from her cheek and lowered his voice, 'you have your own weaknesses to fight.'

She closed her eyes as he moved past her on his way to the door. 'Hurry back!' she sighed.

* * *

Maia dreamed that Chris gave her two large tombstones as gifts, but they were really bookends, and she chose the summit of a hill as her shelf. She placed the tall stones a few yards apart to make sure the sun would set between them, and then sat down at the base of a tree, leaning comfortably against the trunk. She was enjoying the spectacle of the twilight when a man she vaguely remembered having seen somewhere before strolled into view. He was walking up the steep hill wearing a black leather jacket staring down into his cupped hands as though he had just caught a butterfly. He looked up as he released his invisible captive, and he didn't seem at all surprised to see her sitting in the grass beneath the deep shadow of an oak tree. She gazed up at him in curious wonder, unable to understand why she felt she knew him. Suddenly, one of the tree's dark limbs came to life and slithered down towards her in a menacing way. She could not find her voice to cry out, but she did not need to. The handsome stranger grasped the threatening branch firmly in one hand, and she watched in grateful amazement as in his grip it transformed into an ornately carved sword tarnished by centuries. She tried to sit up, but all she could manage was to catch her breath as he pierced the flesh directly over her heart with the sharp point of the ancient blade. A perfectly round drop of her blood ascended against gravity towards the sky and merged with the glowing red sphere of the dying sun perched on the horizon. The man then reached down for her hand, and pulled her to her feet beside him. A row of dark coffins standing upright were now neatly arranged between the tombstones like books.

'Maia,' he whispered.

She felt her pulse flutter strangely beneath the warm breeze of his breath, and she was more than willing to let his lips rest against hers for an instant in the lightest kiss imaginable.

'Come back with me,' he urged.

'No,' she said stubbornly, tilting her face up and closing her eyes in the hope that he would kiss her again. 'You stay here with me.'

He did not respond.

CHAPTER EIGHT

Maia opened her eyes and for some reason was intensely disappointed to find herself lying beside Chris in his bed. The moon was gazing possessively down at him again tonight, and his nocturnally muscular body looked strangely unreachable in the ghostly light.

She had just been dreaming about a man she had never met. This was not unusual; she often dreamed with people she did not know, but he felt different, she was sure she had seen him somewhere before... in fact, it might even have been his body lying beside hers right now, his dark hair and broad shoulders illuminated by the moon's romantic reflection of the sun's often disenchanting clarity. It was truly strange how different Chris' naked body looked at night, thicker and more muscular, and with the sheet caught around his thighs, she could see the tight white cheeks of his backside tempting her to caress them...

She bit her lip in frustration. Was she going to have to wake him up every night so he would pay attention to her sexually? After

Eric Wolfson left, he had called her back downstairs, but only to tell her he was off to his workshop for the day. 'Make yourself at home,' he instructed, then added with a teasing glint in his eye as he kissed her good bye on the cheek, 'and feel free to play around in the kitchen later.' Maia still could not believe he had gone to work on their first day living together. She kept telling herself she was being unreasonable. A man could not be expected to totally rearrange his schedule just because he was in love… if he was in love. They had only just met. How could they really know if they loved each other or not?

She turned restively over onto her side and deliberately closed her eyes. She had to stop waking up in the middle of the night. She had to stop letting the moon illuminate all the disturbing thoughts lurking in the dark depths of her emotions, which seemed so much more straightforward and positive during the day. The moon had millions of years of experience gazing down at men and women and so couldn't help being somewhat cold and cynical about the concept of love. From the moon's perspective, one human soul's attraction to another was no more eternal than the minds and bodies that fell into sexual orbit around each other and thought of it as a special, magical thing called love…

The cool silver light kissing her eyelids inevitably forced them open again. Sighing, and giving up on sleep for the moment, she gazed pensively out the window again. The moon was not the best friend a hopeful young woman could have; she knew too much. Maia suspected the moon was also mysteriously jealous of the human body's ability to feel and touch. The moon made naked skin look so good beneath her caressing light because she wanted this sensual experience for herself…and in the end, all lovers become a part of her timeless desire… for if there really is such a thing as life after death, flesh absorbs and reflects the spirit's energy just as the moon is made visible and tangible by the sun...

Maia sighed again and rolled over onto her other side, turning her back on the window and the earth's disturbingly eloquent satellite. At least this way she could enjoy the sight of Chris' moonlit skin arousing her even while taunting her with its unavailable proximity, because he was fast asleep. She had prepared them a wonderful supper of Prawns sautéed in white wine and garlic, accompanied by a large garden salad. He opened a light red wine to go with it, and they ate informally in his tiny but well equipped kitchen. She felt wonderfully happy as he told her about the various projects he was working on for a handful of private clients like Sir Wolfson, yet her appetite had been somewhat compromised by how much she was anticipating what would happen afterwards when they left the kitchen...

Nothing had happened. Out in the living room, he opened another bottle of wine and sat beside her on the loveseat, where he regularly refilled his glass but not hers (she had had more than enough to drink with dinner) while he talked and talked about everything under the sun. She thoroughly enjoyed listening to him, she could not deny that. He seemed to know so much about everything, not just boring facts but the intriguing details of how things worked and were related to each other. He kept jumping from subject to subject as she did her best to keep up with him mentally, trying not to feel increasingly stupid because she could not think of anything to add to what he was saying. She was flattered he was opening up to her, yet also a little annoyed that he did not seem to care whether she added anything to the conversation or not. She felt peculiarly exhausted by the time he set his empty glass down and, grasping her hand, led her up to his bedroom. Yet it had been just like the previous night – they undressed in absolute darkness and then slipped into bed together like an ancient married couple.

'Is everything all right, Maia?' he asked her as he kissed her forehead good night.

Wanting to scream in frustration, she was afraid of saying too much. 'Yes, everything's fine,' she lied, too shy to beg him to make love to her; to prim and proper to beg him to fuck her as hard and selfishly as he had their first night together on his kitchen table...

Even though she was lying perfectly still beside him, Chris suddenly lifted his head from the pillow and looked at her. 'What's wrong, Maia?' he murmured.

She was impressed by the fact that her turbulent emotions had awoken him. 'I need you,' she whispered.

He rolled over onto his side and drew her gently into his arms. 'I'm here, baby.'

'That's not... that's not what I mean,' she dared to murmur against his chest.

'You want my cock, is that it?' He sounded wide awake now.

'I... I didn't say that, Chris.'

'Not in so many words,' he thrust a hand between her thighs, 'but your pussy doesn't lie.' He gently dipped the tips of two of his fingers into her sex. 'Does it?'

'No,' she sighed.

'Mm, you have such a sweet, tight little pussy, Maia.'

'Oh God,' she whispered, tilting her face up towards his lips, 'please make love to me, Chris.' She longed for the feel of his cock thrusting up between her legs as his tongue thrust between the lips on her face, totally possessing her and filling her with his desire.

'But I have been making love to you, Maia. We're living together, we're sleeping in the same bed together, we had dinner together, and afterwards we talked for hours together. Our lives are becoming one, and that's all part of making love, isn't it?'

'Yes,' she breathed, suddenly ashamed of herself for being so...

so superficial, wanton, slutty… there was no end to the bad names she could call herself for craving rough sex more than the tender love she had been so miraculously blessed with. Here was a real man who cared for her and she was pouting and figuratively stamping her foot because he did not take enough advantage of her physically.

'But I suspect that's not what you meant by making love, is it?' He flung the sheet off them and spread himself on top of her. 'Be honest with me. We're never going to get anywhere if you conceal your true feelings from me. You don't just want me to make love to you, do you?'

'But it is what I want,' she protested weakly, spreading her legs for him.

'No, it's not.' He raised himself on his arms to separate his body from hers.

She moaned in sweet torment as the head of his erection kissed her labia and cruelly teased her with its firm fullness, making her sex lips ache to bloom open around his full length.

'Tell me what you really want, Maia,' he insisted quietly.

'I want you to fuck me!' she confessed abruptly, the words escaping her tense moral control as though mysteriously lubricated by her juicing pussy.

'See, that wasn't so hard,' he said, and entered her with a swift, hard thrust.

She gasped, 'Oh yes!' and gripped his firm ass with both hands as she raised her legs up around him, trying to shove his erection even deeper into her body.

Burying his face in her hair and neck, he pumped fiercely in and out of her, groaning with pleasure as her hands squeezed his tight buttocks and her pussy squeezed his cock.

She moved her hips up and down in rhythm with his, positioning her pussy in just the right place for his hard-on to sink into her as deeply as possible every time he rammed her with it. 'I want you to come inside me, Chris!'

He moaned and his body tensed against hers as his climax inexorably approached.

'Oh yes, come inside me!' she begged. 'Please, come inside me hard!'

He didn't interrupt his rhythm to ask her if it was safe; he simply reached down with one hand to grasp one of her soft ass cheeks for leverage as he relentlessly stabbed her tight slickness with his swelling cock faster and harder, pounding into her with all his strength as he ejaculated. Then he ruthlessly continued rending her open around his pulsing length as he milked every last drop of cum and pleasure from his cock with the fervent embrace of her innermost flesh.

* * *

'If I fail to observe my pledges to thee, may the sky fall and destroy me and the sea overflow and drown me, Maia dear.' Chris was quoting Celtic sayings to her in an academic tone that, in her opinion, deprived them of their profound poetic power.

'You've never mentioned your parents,' she said, wanting to know more about this man she could not resist, a man she occasionally found frustratingly cold and detached, but he was also capable of giving her the most intense pleasure she had ever experienced in her life.

'That's because my father was a mighty oak tree and my mother a vine of mistletoe,' he replied matter-of-factly, 'so there's not much to talk about.'

She frowned to herself in growing annoyance. He was being so deliberately evasive about his personal life that it was like playing tennis with a god who hit the ball so far she could not even try to run after it. 'Did you have a falling out with them?' she persisted.

'Yes,' he laughed, 'I definitely fell out of my mother!'

'Oh stop it,' she pleaded, but couldn't help laughing. The beautiful sunny day was cutting strangely into her vision as the bright sunshine outlined every leaf and blade of grass in breathtakingly sharp detail. It was also making her lover's blond hair almost blindingly bright, impressing upon her the fact that ever since she met him she could not seem to see anything except how much she desired him... or was it that she desired the incredible things he could make her feel? 'Are yours parents like mine, Chris, I mean... are they dead, too?' The words felt like black bugs crawling out from between her lips.

'No, they're not, and neither are yours.'

'What do you mean?' She rose restlessly from the blanket they were sharing in the middle of his backyard, a small clearing surrounded by trees. But then she didn't know what to do with herself and so merely stood beside the blanket ripping a blade of grass apart.

'Maia, there are endless wings in the Mansion and in one of them your parents are probably planning the next voyage together during which they can once again indulge in their love for each other. Yet instead of packing suitcases they're fashioning bodies and checking into hospitals as babies, so do them a favor and don't anchor them with your grief. They were given a great gift when they died together; they were allowed to enter the next world as one. What more could they have asked of Fate?'

She gazed down at his beautiful face in amazement, stunned by his logic. Ever since her parents' accident, she had perceived only her own terrible loss – a dead-end set up by the laws of reason she hadn't the profound courage to break.

Closing his eyes, Chris lay back across the blanket and flung his arms open at his sides.

She continued looking down at his slender body expectantly, but he was apparently through talking for the moment. She walked over to the nearest tree and yanked a leaf off a branch. She studied its veined body morosely sensing her lover falling asleep on her again.

'Hello.' Eric Wolfson suddenly strode into view, walking around the house from the front where he must have parked his car, obviously an extremely expensive vehicle with a nearly silent motor.

She was so surprised to see him she accidentally ripped the leaf in half as she echoed, 'Hello!'

'Is he asleep?' Eric whispered, treading as softly as a cat around Chris' inert body. Then he gracefully curled his long legs beneath him and sat cross-legged on one edge of the dark-red blanket. 'Come here...' He continued whispering as he patted the blanket between him and her sleeping lover. 'There's plenty of room for the three of us.' His gray eyes were so pale in the sunlight they appeared absolutely expressionless.

She tossed the leaf away and approached him, yet she couldn't just sit casually cross-legged beside him because her favorite cotton sundress decorated with tiny violet roses was much too short. Yet she also didn't want to stretch her bare legs out for his eyes to wander over casually, which meant she was forced to sink awkwardly to her knees beside him. Eric leaned back on his arms and closed his eyes, concentrating on absorbing the sun for a few long moments during which she was able to study his face unobserved. Faint lines branched around the delicate eggs of his eyelids like the imprint of crow's feet in his winter-pale skin, and a ghostly trace of long-ago acne on his cheeks made her think of a fragment of the moon impossibly fallen into the sunny yard. 'It's beautiful weather,' she said inanely, clutching the blanket on either side of her wondering how long she could tolerate kneeling like this.

'Yes, it is.' He sat up again and wrapped his arms around his knees as he stared over at her. His eyes narrowed, but whether it was due to the bright sunshine or to what he was thinking it was impossible to tell. 'I want you, Maia,' he informed her quietly.

She felt as though he had whipped out a knife and stabbed her in the heart merely to test the sharpness of his blade, and her helpless blush must have satisfied him she was vulnerable to him moving in for the kill.

'Well, hello there.' Chris woke up abruptly. 'May I ask what you're doing here, Sir Wolfson?' In his white cotton shirt and pants he evoked a ray of light alongside Eric's entirely black outfit – black leather sandals, black jeans and a sleeveless black silk T-shirt.

'I came to ask you for another piece.'

'I'll bet you did. Excuse me a moment.' He sat up by stretching his arms straight out before him as though he was diving up into the sky. 'As the mystics say,' he leapt lithely his feet, 'I must empty myself. I'll be right back.' He mussed Maia's hair affectionately (and it seemed to her reassuringly) as he walked away towards the house. She had no idea if he had overheard Eric's declaration and she wasn't sure whether she hoped he had or not. If he really had been asleep, then he was innocent of the position he was putting her in by leaving her alone with this dangerously sexy client of his...

'I have a proposition for you, love,' Eric informed her when they were alone with all the birds and insects working industriously but invisibly around them.

'A proposition?' she repeated blankly, her fingers embracing each other anxiously in her lap.

'How would you feel about starring in a music video, Maia?'

She glanced anxiously over at the house. 'A music video?' she echoed lamely, still not fully recovered from his blatant declaration of lust. 'You're a musician?'

'Yes, and it's the video for my latest hit song about the Druids and their fondness for human sacrifice.'

'Not today.' Chris was back again suddenly. He handed her a darkly glistening bottle of ale, keeping one for himself and rudely not offering his guest anything to drink.

'Eric wants me to be in his new music video,' she informed him, needing to know what her lover thought about it before she dared feel anything about it herself.

'Does he now?' He sat cross-legged beside her on the edge of the blanket.

'It's a video for a song about the Druids,' she added, anxiously studying his profile as he sipped his beer.

He gave her a sideways glance. 'Which means you'd be the lovely sacrifice?' he asked lightly, but his eyes and lips weren't smiling.

'It might be fun,' she heard herself say. 'Um, I really don't want anything to drink right now…' She offered her cold bottle to Eric. 'Would you like it?'

'Don't mind if I do,' he said, taking it from her, and the warm caress of his fingers was a delicious contrast.

'Well, I say we finish our drinks,' Chris declared, 'and then all go for a little walk in the woods to discuss this video.'

CHAPTER NINE

As they walked, Maia kept glancing up at the vein-like branches of the trees above them hoping to catch a glimpse of a cardinal's swiftly beating heart. She felt self-consciously sandwiched between two men who could not have looked more different except for how attractive they both were in their own way. Even their personalities clashed in an amiable but also seriously challenging way that made her feel they were both holding invisible swords. Chris made more cutting remarks than Eric, which she thought was understandable since he was on the defensive; he was defending his claim on her. She knew her lover was more than intelligent enough to sense the wealthy musician's personal interest in her, yet she also suspected he was confident enough not to feel too threatened by it. With her hand safely nestled in his as they walked, she was filled with feelings for Christopher Thorn – admiration, respect and gratitude – even while she found herself half hypnotized by the sound of Eric Wolfson's quiet voice as he described his creative project to her.

'What makes a good music video,' he was saying, 'is part planning and part chance, and in my opinion it's usually all the unexpected elements that crop up during filming that end up making it truly interesting.' He had tied his shoulder-length hair loosely back away from his face with a red band, exposing his beautiful high cheekbones. 'There's no reason for you to be nervous about it, Maia.' He gave her a brief, respectful glance. 'The production will be very intimate, involving only a few special friends I have in the industry.'

'What exactly will happen in the video?' she asked him, but it was Chris she looked at because his permission was the most important thing to her.

He squeezed her hand as though he approved of her dependence on his opinion and answered her question before Eric had a chance to. 'I imagine Sir Wolfson is planning to re-create his fantasy of a Druid sacrifice, Maia, and I say his fantasy because there really is no way to know what Druid rituals were like. They didn't leave behind any written records, much less an official sacrifice manual.'

'We'll be shooting a great deal of raw material and editing it all together later,' Eric elaborated without offering anymore information on the video's actual plot and content. 'Intimate,' he stressed the word, 'low-budget productions are often the most powerfully atmospheric.' Chris' skeptical attitude didn't seem to bother him in the least.

'In my opinion,' her lover's mild tone paradoxically stressed how important his opinion was, 'you should focus on the experience of her soul after the sacrifice, not on the gruesome bloody details.

"And how would we manage that, pray tell?' The musician followed Maia's eyes up into the trees. 'It's an interesting suggestion, but impossible to capture on film since the soul is invisible.'

'To the physical eye it's invisible,' Chris elaborated in his usual reasonable tone, 'but just because certain energies are invisible to the light receptors in our corneas doesn't mean they're insubstantial and formless. If you think of the soul as color and motion, as the human imagination turned inside out so feelings and desires manifest in a kaleidoscopic dance, so to speak, then you have a lot to work with. Magical transformations are relatively easy to express by way of visual metaphors. I'm sure you could find inspiration for your video in one of Maia's paintings, for example.'

Chris was the only person on earth besides Carol she had shown her work to, and his reaction to her surreal sensual landscapes had been much more gratifying then her aunt's. Seeing her paintings through his eyes had not only made her appreciate her talent more, it had showed her how profoundly erotic her vision was.

'I'm thinking especially of her painting of a woman lying across an altar,' her lover went on. 'Her arms are raised towards the heavens as they merge with the slender trunks of trees as her long red hair pours down the back of her stone bed and flows across the ground into the blazing sunset on the horizon. It's a powerfully sensual image I feel would work very nicely in your video.'

Eric gave her another narrow-eyed glance. 'She's an artist,' he said shortly, as though that explained everything.

'The video could visually express the mysterious fact that her soul is supernaturally the earth's body,' Chris added intently.

'Why do I get the feeling you want to direct the whole thing yourself?' Eric accused him mildly.

'I would love to.'

They came full circle along a path winding between the trees and leading them neatly back to the clearing behind Chris' house. He spread himself across the blanket again on his back, gently but firmly pulling Maia down beside him as Eric stretched out on his side facing her, behaving as innocently as a domestic cat the size of a black panther. She would much rather have sat up, but if Chris wanted her lying beside him she was not inclined to argue, even if she did question the wisdom of exposing the full length of her body like this to another man who was uncomfortably close to her. She bent one of her legs and rested her hands awkwardly over her womb as she turned her head towards her lover on the red cloth, but he was gazing serenely up at the heavens oblivious to any discomfort she might be feeling, in any sense. So, inevitably, she turned her head in the other direction.

Eric met her eyes boldly, and her breath caught as if his sharp stare had sunk like ruthlessly experienced fangs into her emotional jugular. She had no doubt that all she was to him was entertaining sexual prey, yet a blindly feminine part of her could not help but be flattered he found her desirable enough not to be deterred by the fact that she would be very hard for him to get his hands on since she was already taken. Turning her head again to stare neutrally up at the clear blue sky, she wondered if Eric knew she and Chris had only been together three days.

The three of them lay silently on the blanket for a while, and Maia found herself wondering at the ability of a perfectly beautiful day to empty the mind, as though thoughts had their origin in adversity and if the body could always manage to be happy and comfortable no concepts would ever be born at all…

Through the corner of her eye she was relieved to finally see Eric rolling lazily onto his back; his fixed regard had been making her extremely uncomfortable. He raised his arms over his head, and the skin beneath them struck her as vulnerably pale and tender in contrast to his black silk T-shirt, making her think of a beached whale with a shiny oily back and a white underbelly. Then a faint buzzing sound told her to watch out for a bee headed towards one of her leg's smooth runways. She denied it permission to land by gently shooing it away, but she remained very much aware of the sexy and intriguing musician lying beside her. A quick glance at Chris told her his eyes were closed, which made her feel free to turn her head fully towards Eric again. She was fascinated by the way his sinewy muscles clung so tightly to his bones, like snakes wrapped tenaciously around tree branches, and suddenly she knew that her attraction to him could easily prove fatal to her newborn relationship.

He sat up without warning and yanked off the elastic band holding his hair back. He shook it loose around his face, glanced back at Chris, and gave one of her legs a swift, appraising caress from her ankle up to her knee.

She sat up in an instinctive effort to hide another man's caress from her lover, but now the singer's mouth was only a dangerous breath away as his eyes locked challengingly with hers. She had bent both her legs as she sat up, so it was easy for him to reach beneath them and squeeze one of her calves. She bit her lip to keep from crying out not sure whether she should stand up or lie back down again. As a result, she remained where she was, caught between a chilling fear and an insidiously warm excitement threatening to melt her cautious tension.

'I'll expect both of you at the small party I'm throwing Friday night,' he said.

'We'd be delighted to attend,' Chris replied, reaching up to idly stroke her back. 'Wouldn't we, Maia?'

'Yes...' she agreed uncertainly.

'Well, what is it you want?' Chris finally demanded of Eric, sitting up. 'You said you came to ask me for another piece, some original artwork to adorn your walls, perhaps? You would love Maia's paintings. She brought them all with her when she moved in with me, so perhaps you'd care to take a look at them and make her a generous offer on one or two.'

'It would be a real pleasure,' Eric declared, his eyes on her legs.

'But you might not like my paintings,' she protested shyly, somewhat embarrassed by all the attention she was getting in every sense.

Chris laughed as though he found her modesty amusing. 'You know he'll love them,' he said, kissing her earlobe gently as he added in a private whisper, 'Use him!'

'I would love to look at them now,' Eric declared.

She blushed as though he had just asked her to strip for him. He and Chris were both ostensibly talking about her art work, but somehow she felt it was her body, and even her soul, they were discussing. 'I don't know…'

'Unfortunately, however, I have to run,' he added, surging gracefully to his feet. 'I'm already late for another appointment. But I'm very much looking forward to seeing your work, Maia. And remember, I'm expecting you both at my place Friday night.'

'How small is this small party of yours going to be?' Chris inquired.

'Oh it's to be a very intimate affair, only two-hundred of my best friends are invited.'

'Two-hundred?' she gasped.

'Yes, but never fear, you will be the most beautiful woman there, Maia.'

'Oh please, I doubt it.' She was a little annoyed by the excessive compliment, which implied she was either incredibly vain or insecure about her looks.

'Never doubt,' Chris whispered in her ear again, and then said in his sternest voice, 'Good afternoon, Sir Wolfson, we'll see you Friday night.'

* * *

'A rich and famous musician is probably going to buy one of my paintings, Carol, can you believe it? He might even buy more than one.'

'Certainly I can believe it, dear, they're... err, they're very interesting.'

'Chris said I could ask hundreds of pounds for each one, but I-'

'Speaking of pounds, dear, the solicitor's office called to ask when you would be going back to work.'

Maia stared at her aunt's face as though the woman had just spoken another language she had to make an effort to translate in her brain. 'When I plan to go back to work?' she repeated blankly, and then shivered as shock drenched her psyche like an ice-cold ocean wave. 'I forgot all about my job!' she cried in disbelief. 'Ever since I met Chris, I haven't been able to think about anything else... I mean... I mean...' But it was no use, there was no sane excuse for how completely she had forgotten about something that been part of her life every Monday through Friday for nearly four years; it was impossible her job could have slipped her mind so completely if she wasn't losing her mind... she wasn't even sure how many work days had she missed... 'Oh my God, what did you tell them?' she asked desperately.

'I told them you hadn't been feeling well,' Carol replied calmly, 'that you had a very bad case of the flu. I apologized for not having called them, and said you would be back as soon as you were feeling better.'

'Oh God, thank you! I... I just don't know how...'

'Maia, dear, sit down, please, you're wearing me out pacing back and forth like that, not to mention what you're doing to my nice antique rug.'

'But auntie,' she dropped onto the edge of the couch, 'I completely forgot about my job!'

'It's all right, dear,' Carol patted her hand reassuringly, 'that young man has swept you off your feet, that's all. When you're in love, you're in a whole other world and it's easy to forget mundane things.'

Maia shook her head. 'Yes, I know, but-'

'Don't trouble yourself about it anymore,' the older woman said firmly. 'I took care of it. You rest up for a while and go back when you're ready, although sooner would be better than later as you don't want to try their patience too much.'

'But it's going to be such a long drive from Chris' place to the office,' she mused out loud, so utterly disturbed by her mental lapse she couldn't bring herself to truly face it.

'You should have thought of that before you moved in with him,' Carol replied tartly, but then added soothingly since she could see her niece was seriously distressed. 'I'm sure you'll work it out. The important thing is for you to come back to work soon and not dally too long in idleness. You know what they say about idle hands.'

'Maybe I don't need to... maybe I can start making a decent living off my artwork. If I can get at least seven-hundred pounds for each painting, and Chris says I definitely can, then-'

'Don't be foolish, Maia.' It was Carol's turn to look disturbed. 'You can't quit your day job! Please don't even think of it, dear, not yet.'

'No, I guess not...' She glanced out the window. 'But at least I'm not shy about my paintings anymore, not now that two other people besides me are interested in them.'

'Two other men, you mean,' Carol pointed out as mildly as she could bring herself to, 'one of them an eccentric carpenter, and the other one, God help us, a wealthy rock star.'

'He's perfectly nice,' Maia defended the sexy musician, 'a perfect gentleman.' The honest way he had declared his intention to seduce her could, she supposed, be interpreted as the act of a gentleman.

'Oh I'm sure he is,' Carol declared skeptically; Maia might as well have insisted the neighbor's dog was a brilliant scholar. 'I wonder...' She turned her head in the direction of the window and sunlight streaming in between the drawn curtains cruelly revealed countless wrinkles etched deep into her skin.

'You wonder what?' Maia stood up and began moving around the small living room again in an effort to assuage her restlessness; she hated being separated from Chris.

'I wonder why no one around here has ever heard of Christopher Thorn. Your charming carpenter seems to have sprung straight out of the ground like the trees he likes to cut up.'

'Carol, you've been gossiping about us? I thought you liked him!'

'Oh I do, dear, don't misunderstand me.' She rubbed her injured knee. 'I only wish you had gotten to know him a little better before you moved in with him, that's all.'

Maia went and stood by the window. The driveway looked achingly empty without Chris' bright red car parked in it. 'His house is very isolated,' she reasoned out loud, appreciating how patient and understanding her aunt was forcing herself to be with her. 'And we wanted to be together more than anything, so what was the point in waiting. Life's too short.'

'You only feel that way because you're young, Maia. Life is quite long, actually, and it's also like a recipe – you can't skip certain steps and ingredients and expect everything to turn out just the way you want it to. Well, perhaps no one in the neighborhood has heard of your handsome carpenter because they can't afford him. All his clients appear to be quite wealthy. You know, dear,' she tried to laugh, but failed miserably, 'if I didn't know better, if I hadn't seen Christopher with my own eyes, I could almost believe you were making all of this up, wealthy art patrons and music videos, indeed, all in quiet little Stoneshire! You always did have a marvelous imagination.'

'You and daddy thought it was a bit too marvelous sometimes,' Maia reminded her.

'Yes…' Her fond smile as she remembered dimmed sadly. 'I'll admit, I was a bit worried about how you'd turn out, but Stella always assured me you'd be fine.'

Maia perched on one of the couch's old arms. 'Chris is making frames for all my paintings, auntie,' she announced excitedly.

'Dear,' Carol avoided her eyes, 'has he mentioned marriage at all?'

'We're going to be together forever,' the young woman vowed fervently. 'I know we are. He's my soul mate, I felt it the moment I saw him in the cemetery.'

'Oh Maia, I wish you wouldn't…'

'Carol, please stop.' She leapt to her feet again impatiently. 'What's the matter with you today? I've never seen you worry so much. You can't deny how wonderful Chris is. I mean, you've met all the pathetic sods I had to put up with before him. Chris is in a whole other class. He's the best thing that's ever happened to me. I've never been so happy.'

Carol winced. 'Please don't yell at me, dear.'

'Well then stop being so suspicious. I'm happier than I've ever been before,' she insisted. 'Can't you see that?'

'Yes, dear. Would you like some tea now?'

'Please, that would be lovely, but I'll make it. You stay here and rest.'

Carol sighed. 'I get frightfully bored if I'm not busy doing something,' she protested.

'Isn't there a book you're reading?' Maia glanced around the small living room. 'I'll fetch it for you.'

'You know I've never had the patience for books. I like to keep busy.'

'Oh all right, you make the tea if it'll make you happy.' She grasped both the old woman's hands and helped her up off of the couch before falling back across it herself. She was exhausted from the weight of minutes chaining her down while she waited for

Chris to phone and tell her he was on his way over. It upset her she didn't know where his workshop was and that she had no way of reaching him there.

She was just drifting off to sleep when the phone on the table beside the couch rang suddenly, shocking her back into consciousness.

'God, I miss you,' Chris whispered in her ear.

'It's your fault for not taking me with you,' she retorted, because his sexy voice reaching her through the serpentine miracle of telephone wires was an agonizing tease. 'Are you on your way over now?'

'Yes. I'll be there in a flash.'

She sighed, 'Please!'

'Make some excuse for me. I don't feel like hanging out with your little old aunt this evening.'

'All right,' she agreed, and hung up only after she heard the clicking sound of the receiver being put down on his end. Then she got up and hurried happily into the dining room. Carol had just finished laying out tea. 'Chris is coming to pick me up now, auntie. He says he's terribly sorry he can't stay for tea, but one of his clients just called him and we have to go meet him somewhere.'

Carol looked distressed. 'Well, I hope you have time for at least one cup.'

'Of course.' Maia quickly sat down at the table. 'Oh, cucumber sandwiches, my favorites.' She poured the tea for them.

'The great oak is just a nut that held its ground,' Carol mumbled as she seated herself with a grimace of pain.

Maia laughed. 'What made you say that?'

'Dear,' there was a determined note in Carol's voice, 'it's time you knew something.'

'Knew what?' she asked with wary curiosity, somewhat worried by the intensely sober look darkening the old woman's eyes.

Carol took a deep breath. 'It's time you knew that your mother never really grew up, God rest her soul, and your father loved her so much he indulged her to the very end even though he never took the whole thing seriously himself. They might still be alive if...' Her lips set and she stared at the silver teapot as grimly as if was an urn containing her brother and sister-in-law's ashes.

'What...' Maia swallowed a lump in her throat. 'What are you talking about?'

'Peter kept assuring me it was all perfectly harmless,' Carol went on slowly. 'He knew I disapproved, and that the neighbors gossiped about it.'

'Gossiped about what?'

'Your mother was the priestess of a modern group of Druids that meets at the standing stones every week!' Carol blurted as though it was the only way she could get the truth out. 'There,' she sighed, 'now you know!' She carefully picked up her teacup between two gnarled fingers and took a long sip of the hot, fragrant liquid as if to get the strange taste of the words she had just uttered out of her mouth. 'Stella told me once that she believed in Christ,' she went on less urgently, 'but I never saw her enter a proper church. I suppose there was nothing wrong with her beliefs, and yet it was on their way to one of those pagan rites she was so fond of that they were killed at that intersection. It was such a horrible death, Maia, to be burned alive like that... like witches at the stake.' She shuddered and took another heartening swig of hot tea.

Maia was stunned, but before she could absorb what she had just learned, the warm bass note of Chris' car horn sounded outside, melting some of her shock and enabling her to get up. 'I love you, auntie, but I have to go now.' She needed to get away from the unbelievable fact Carol had just unearthed after all these years. Anger at the way her parents had kept her in the dark about their secret life was already spreading a thorny vine of hurt feelings and confused thoughts inside her she couldn't deal with just yet. 'We'll talk about this later.' She kissed the old woman's parchment-dry cheek. 'Thank you for telling me, it was the right thing to do,' she added, and then literally ran out of the dimly lit dining room into the afternoon sunlight's much more positive wavelength.

CHAPTER TEN

With the slowly setting sun playing in his hair and transforming his eyes into bottomless lakes, Chris looked much too good to be innocent of some kind of sorcery. The skin of his face and arms washed smooth of flaws by the fervent light of early evening, his profile resembled a molten hilt forged over the straight sword of his spine resting on the black leather seat. She could hardly wait to slip him inside her pussy's tight sheath.

He glanced at her, narrowing his eyes shining fragments of the sky. 'I'm going to fuck you blind when we get home,' he warned quietly, 'so be prepared.'

'Mm,' she said, and caressed one of his hard thighs happily.

'Don't get me going.' He removed her hand from his leg gently. 'Not yet. Right now I want you to tell me what's troubling you.'

'I don't want to talk about it,' she said tightly. 'It's too unbelievable to even mention.'

'Tell me,' he commanded quietly.

'You're not going to believe it,' she warned.

'I said tell me, Maia.'

'Carol just informed me, after keeping it a secret all these years, that my mother was the high priestess of a modern group of Druids that meets at the standing stones every week!' She got it all out in one breath thinking it curious how such a momentous discovery could fit into one casual sentence.

'Is that all?' He rested his warm hand on one of her cool thighs and pushed her dress up out of the way. 'Modern Druids are harmless enough. Their so-called rites are child's play, really; there's nothing truly ancient about them, but at least most of them are avid environmentalists. God knows this planet needs as many environmentalists as possible these days.'

Maia stared at him in consternation. 'You're not at all surprised, are you?'

'No.' He glanced at her. 'Should I be?'

'Why aren't you a Druid since you're so interested in the standing stones and Celtic culture? I've seen all those books in your bedroom.'

'I don't belong to a group of Druids because all such contemporary cults are sanitized and essentially neutered, their beliefs and rituals conveniently and safely packaged for the modern sensibility, meaning there's nothing truly holy or pagan about them. They're like de-clawed cats that don't threaten to rip open the cozy fabric of the respectable, conventional life everyone is so deathly fond of nowadays.'

'Oh so you'd prefer it if they still practiced human sacrifice and things like that?' she challenged as a joke, but then gazing at his luminous profile she suddenly felt breathlessly worried.

'There are other much crueler ways of sacrificing people day in and day out, thousands, millions, at a time, Maia.'

'I don't know what you're talking about,' she declared, panicked by how sinisterly calm his voice was. She was appalled to feel herself close to tears, overwhelmed by everything she was discovering about her parents and now about her lover all at once.

'Relax, Maia.' He reached over to cradle her pussy possessively in his hand, pressing his hard palm against her soft panties as though this would help steady her emotionally. 'You're with me now.' He skillfully maneuvered his forefinger beneath the elastic of her skimpy undergarment and casually penetrated her with it, forcing his rigid finger up between the tenderly moist folds of her labia into her tight yet also welcomingly slick passage.

'Stop,' she protested even as she slouched lower in the seat so he could slip his finger even farther up inside her. She clutched the dashboard and closed her eyes as it wormed around in her hole stirring up all sorts of subtle sensations. 'Stop,' she whispered again, 'please...'

'Are you sure you want me to stop, Maia?'

She moaned.

'That's right, you don't want me to stop.' He deftly added another strong and eager digger to her moistening shaft at the same time that his other hand turned the wheel sharply.

She grasped his wrist. 'Deeper...' she begged softly.

'That's it, sweetheart, give it to me, I want to hear you come.'

'Oh Chris, I can't, not so fast...'

'Yes you can, just relax...'

His confident encouragement stoked the climax simmering in her nerve-endings with miraculous swiftness. She ceased to feel the shell of the car around them as she pressed the heel of his palm directly against her clitoris and rubbed herself furiously, taking possession of his wrist as though it belonged to her. 'Oh yes!' she gasped as the pleasure ascended between her legs with devastating intensity. She spread her thighs as far as she could on the leather seat and shoved his fingers even deeper into her clenching pussy. Yet it was the heel of his palm rubbing back and forth against her vulva's throbbing little heart that inspired her senses to rise up amongst the powerful trees flanking the road as she climaxed... the soul of her flesh soaring on the single wing of his hand with his fingers rooted deep inside her...

Her pulse beat gradually down to earth again as the car slowed to a stop.

'That's my good girl,' he said, slipping his fingers out of her panties and smoothing her skirt back down. 'You shouldn't doubt yourself, Maia.' He switched off the engine and the pregnant silence of the forest at twilight descended over them like a rich green cloak.

'What do you mean?' she asked languidly, open to anything he might have to say; to anything he might have to tell her about herself that would enable her to come like that again and again.

'I mean,' he held the keys in his hand where it rested between them on the seat, 'you're a sensual being. All you have to do to experience unimaginable pleasure is just let yourself go.'

She looked out at the trees. 'That's easier said than done... what exactly does it mean to let yourself go?'

'It means having faith in your divine nature and not letting doubts and fears clip your wings.'

'What exactly do you mean by my wings?'

'You spirituality and your sensuality. You literally can't get off the ground if they're both not working together.'

She looked at him, and his smile struck her as mysteriously luminous in the deepening dusk. 'Oh Chris,' she bent over and kissed the back of his hand, 'you're so wonderful.'

'I'd like to keep you here with me forever,' he said quietly, 'but whether you stay, or whether you go back, is entirely up to you, Maia.'

She sat up. 'I'm never going back.'

'It's your life,' he replied mildly. 'Now let's go have some wine.'

* * *

The following morning was dismally overcast and the sky opened up after Chris drove off to his workshop, leaving her alone in his home again.

Maia had no idea what she was going to do about her job. She never wanted to go back to the excruciatingly boring solicitor's office. It was very tempting to hope that from now on Chris could support her... and even more appealing was the dreamy possibility that she could make enough money to live selling her paintings, at first to some of his wealthy clients, and then perhaps to some of their friends, and their friends, until she was rich herself... the fantasies she indulged in while lying lazily in bed were endless. At first it was wonderful not having anything to do except daydream, but after she finally got up and showered and dressed, the day started crawling by more slowly than the occasional snail the pounding rain drove out of its murky lair. By the time she had gone down to the kitchen and fixed herself a cup of tea, the hours she had to wait for Chris to return in the evening already felt like a chain she was dragging around with her as she went and opened the front door in order to stand out on the small covered porch.

In the depressing downpour, amorphous fears she had been avoiding surfaced in her mind like worms rising out of the muddy ground, the relentless drumming of the rain on the roof echoing her own anxious thoughts clamoring for attention.

Her physical attraction to Eric Wolfson was just too much for her to handle right now. Her cup had been full with Chris, but now it was overflowing dangerously since there was a chance she could lose everything if she gave into the intoxicating lust the sexy musician aroused in her.

Then there was the skeleton Carol had unearthed in what she had believed was her parents' eternally locked closet. Learning about their secret life as Druids had ripped the healing scab of the years off her grief. Yet on the other hand, she no longer suffered that terrible, sinking despair when she remembered their coffins being lowered into the earth. When she pictured them now, they were walking hand in hand through the woods. Carol hadn't said as much, but Maia suspected it was her father who had forbidden Stella to involve their daughter in pagan pastimes. She wondered what the rites of this modern group of Druids was like, and found it impossible to picture her otherwise perfectly normal parents wearing formless white robes while chanting up at the moon.

At one o'clock in the afternoon the rain finally stopped for a little while as the sun's rays shoved the clouds away with slender but powerful arms. Maia gratefully watched them emerge from the sky's heavy gray cloak admiring the way they made the wet trees around Chris' home glimmer with gold.

She ached for a telephone to call him with. Her longing to communicate with him was so intense she felt it should at least take the form of a subliminal ringing in his ears.

She stood in the open doorway again for a long time inhaling the fragrance of wet grass and leaves and sipping yet another cup of tea. She sighed, wondering what she could do to keep herself from getting bored and depressed. No activity seemed able to contain her mood lately. Ghosts weren't bed sheets you could wash the soil off and rationally bleach away their darkly haunting nature. Ever since Carol's revelation, she couldn't seem to stop thinking about her parents. It was strange that her relationship with Chris had begun in the cemetery on the anniversary of their death. And she did not even want to remember how completely she had forgotten about her job at the solicitor's office. It was hard to believe, everything that had happened to her since her car stalled on her that night in the graveyard. Thanks to Chris, she was so unexpectedly fulfilled and excited about her sexuality and the future that the very atmosphere felt lighter. Yet it was impossible to deny her sexual attraction to Eric and that it threatened her new-found happiness like the veritable serpent in Eden.

'Oh God,' she muttered, caressing her long hair away from her face, too lazy to go back upstairs and brush it. Her hair provided an agreeably warm mantle in the winter, but it became unruly and tangled as the thriving foliage in summer.

Maybe if she pulled out a blank sheet of paper and stared at it long enough a drawing would take form and help her make sense of her emotions. She had all her art supplies with her; there was nothing stopping her from expressing herself creatively… nothing except the fact that she couldn't seem to focus here in Chris' home, not the way she had been able to apply herself to her artwork in the privacy and comfort of her own room. Yet she didn't want to go back to her old bedroom, not really…

She stood there a while longer gazing down at the dark dregs of her tea as though trying to read her future. She was about to turn back inside when the distant hum of a motor threaded itself through the sound of the renewed downpour. A moment later, she spotted Chris' small red car speeding towards her down the narrow road lined with trees like sentinels guarding the approach of their lord and master. She watched breathlessly as he pulled up, leapt out of the car and ran up onto the porch. Even though he was drenched, he smiled at her cheerfully. 'You called?'

* * *

She was feeling a little better. Chris had promised to come home and have lunch with her everyday, unless it was absolutely impossible for him to get away from the shop. This meant she would not be quite so lonely, because they had also discussed the matter of her position at the solicitor's office and decided there was no need for her to go back.

'I can find buyers for your work, Maia,' he assured her, sipping the hot tea she had made for him when they came inside. His hair and clothes were wet and she was afraid he would catch cold. 'You should concentrate on your creativity and stop wasting time in a dull little law office. You're immensely talented, there's no reason you can't devote yourself to your paintings from now on if that's what you feel like doing.'

'But Chris, it's not so easy,' she protested reluctantly, because in truth she was already seduced by his logic.

'Why not?' he countered, stoking the flames he had just brought to life in his tiny fireplace, brightening the cold gray day with warmth and color.

She shrugged, thinking she could have lit a fire for herself, but it would not have felt the same without him there. Nothing felt the same without him; everything felt different when she was alone, less uncomplicatedly beautiful and positive.

'You look great in my shirts,' he told her, setting down his empty tea cup. 'I love looking at you in my clothes.'

'I was too lazy to get dressed,' she murmured, gazing shyly

down at her lap. She was wearing one of his long-sleeved forest-green button-down shirts, a pair of his black woolen socks, and nothing else.

'Come here.' He urged her to lie down beside him on the colorful Oriental rug softening the gray stones of the hearth.

Maia was distracted by the pleasure of his embrace as she wondered where she had seen this rug before with its vicious-looking stylized dragons...

'Come here,' he repeated gently, slipping one arm beneath her and pulling her onto her side so he could press the full length of his body against hers.

She sighed at once restlessly and contentedly. He was much taller than she was so her face was on a level with his chest. His damp slacks pressed against her naked thighs, and she shivered slightly as she reached up to caress his still wet hair before running her hand up the strong slope of his shoulder, her other arm pinned uselessly between them. He was a stimulating contrast of temperatures and textures – cold and warm, hard and smooth, tender and unyielding. She had never realized before how arousing a man's body could be whether fully dressed or naked.

He kissed the top of her head. 'I can't stay long,' he whispered, 'so I'll give you a choice. Either you fix me so lunch or you let me eat you. After all, a hardworking man needs his nourishment.'

'Mm,' she murmured, 'I think I'm feeling too lazy to get up.'

'Not a problem.' He released her and she rolled languidly onto her back as he positioned himself between her legs. The fire crackled eagerly beside them, sending warm, caressing shadows across her pale flesh as he shoved the shirt she was wearing all the way up to her neck, exposing her sex, her belly and then her breasts, apparently too pressed for time and too hungry for her pussy to patiently unbutton it.

She raised her head slightly and gazed down the length of her fire lit body at his golden hair setting between her legs. Her breasts were pert mounds crowned with big puffy aureoles and long nipples begging to be licked and bitten. It was a sweet suffering that he concentrated exclusively on her clitoris and labia, his hands resting lightly on her inner thighs to hold them open around his intent face. He didn't caress her or penetrate her. All he did was lick her, deliciously tormenting her with everything else he wasn't doing to her while subjecting her to the sweet pleasure of his devotion to the heart of her pleasure, which he knew from experience was not easily seduced. Her clit had never before been treated with such respect and skillful consideration, and she realized her body's sensitive little button was very much like a queen who could not be approached directly, rather his tongue had to seek obsequious audience with her surrounding skin, first rousing her interest. He worked her up to a point where her clitoris was aching to grant his mouth a full, exclusive audience, and it felt almost too good when he at last focused all his attentions on the mysterious seed of her ecstasy. Her hips began writhing on the dragon-embroidered rug as she fondled her own breasts hungrily, her nipples longing for the same attention he was giving her pussy, but he was cruelly forcing her to choose between them. Then suddenly he penetrated her with his tongue, thrusting its surprisingly hard muscle as far into her juicing slit as it could reach, and its flicking thrusts stoked the delight smoldering between her thighs into an orgasmic fire.

'Oh God, yes,' she breathed, vaguely wondering why she could never think of anything more original to say as the need to climax inexorably possessed her. Yet what more was there to say? Once he brought her this far, it felt like a matter of life and death to her flesh to achieve the release hovering so tantalizingly on the horizon of her nerve-endings. She simply had to come now, so when he abruptly sat up, abandoning his skilled tending of her growing ecstasy, a wordless wail of disappointment escaped her. Only the sight of him quickly opening his pants assuaged her disappointment. Then his thick and rigid cock was in his hands and all she could think about was how much she wanted to feel it stabbing her between the legs. But all he did was tower over her on his knees as he held his pants open with one hand and with the other hand swiftly stroked himself. She watched in frustrated fascination as the thick tip of his erection slipped in and out between his fingers, the sweet cleft in its head glimmering with semen.

'Touch yourself, Maia,' he commanded. 'I want to watch you pleasure yourself, and then I'm going to come all over you.'

'Oh Chris, please fuck me,' she begged. 'I want to feel your cock inside me, please.'

'You can feel it inside you later,' he teased soberly, 'right now I want to see you touching yourself. I want to see you enjoying your body.'

It was not what she wanted, but the tone of his voice and the look in his eyes told her she had no choice, so she decided to make the best of it... and discovered there was indeed something perversely enjoyable about teasing each other like this as he pumped his hard-on with increasing fervor, never once taking his eyes off her, and she fervently rubbed her clitoris with the fingertips of her right hand as her other hand played with the soft mounds of her breasts and pulled on the almost painfully stiff, rosy nipples crowning them. All she had to do to push herself over the edge was imagine his big hard dick sliding up inside her... she bit her lip to keep from crying out shamelessly as a climax broke between her thighs at the same time that he groaned and ejaculated, spraying her belly and breasts with the white foam of his cum.

CHAPTER ELEVEN

'You want me to tell you all about myself, don't you, Maia?' Chris asked her casually when he came home from the shop again later that evening.

'I do,' she admitted eagerly.

'Then let's have dinner out tonight,' he suggested. 'Go put on a nice dress for me.'

'All right,' she agreed happily. 'I'll go get ready.' She ran upstairs and emptied her bladder in the tiny bathroom toilet first, but she could not do the same with her heart, which felt almost uncomfortably full. Standing at the seashell-shaped sink, she cupped cold water in her hands and gazed down into the tiny pond formed by her palms for a contemplative moment before splashing it over her face. She dried herself off, ran a brush through her thick hair a few lazy times, and needlessly pinched some color into her cheeks. She had been blessed with a flawless complexion, long black eyelashes that never called for mascara, and her full rosy lips defied the need for lipstick. She was a little disappointed Chris did not appear to be into kissing, but he was definitely into fucking and that was more than enough for now. She had had her fill of necking in the front seat of cars; her new lover's confidence and sexual sophistication were infinitely more exciting and if kissing was the price she had to pay for his otherwise devastatingly thorough attentions, then so be it. At least that's what she told herself; she had too much on her mind to add one more uncertainty to the list.

Back in the bedroom, she slipped out of his shirt and socks before kneeling beside her suitcase to search for just the right dress. She had not yet unpacked her clothing; she was feeling remarkably lethargic these days. Also, she did not really care to admit it, but Chris' closet frightened her a little. She was not yet ready to hang all her clothes up across from his in that sinister space guarded by lightning-blackened oak wood. She spotted a simple, sleeveless red cotton dress at the bottom of the suitcase, wrested it out from the heavy pile of material on top, and wriggled into it, not bothering with a bra. She did, however, snatch up a pair of black bikini panties, also made of soft breathable cotton, and slipped them on before sitting on the edge of the bed to fasten a pair of black strap high-heeled sandals to her bare feet. She had never been so conscious of every part of her body; being with Chris was heightening all her senses to an almost unbearable point. Right now she was delightfully aware of her labial lips clinging moistly to her panties almost as if they resented being bandaged up like that, and her nipples also felt strangely confined where they poked against her dress, a sight she was sure her lover would appreciate.

He was already outside leaning against the car waiting for her by the time she hurried back downstairs. The sun was beginning to set behind the trees and she looked forward to enjoying the drama of the twilight on their way into town, which would take them right past the standing stones.

They rode in silence for a while, and during that time she determined that her mind would not be a courtroom in which her lover's history would be judged when he finally began telling her about himself. Her heart had to be the perfectly loving space in which all his past trials were soothed away.

When the standing stones came into view, he slowed the car down to give them both time to admire the dramatic tableau. The nine phallic pillars stood parallel to the sun that was descending amongst them like nobles at the bedside of their dying lord, some of them leaning forward slightly as though bowing respectfully. It occurred to her then that she had first experienced Chris (if not actually seen him) the evening he had been parked on the hill at exactly this time of the day. His red car had gleamed in the dying light like a bloodstained modern suit of armor protected by the small but powerfully concentrated force of the ancient stones...

'That's right,' he said abruptly as though reading her mind.

'That's right what?' she asked lightly, but for some reason she didn't dare look at him. Instead she leaned forward in her seat to gaze up at the deep blue color of the sky at the zenith peacefully ignoring the blazing passion of light and color on the horizon, where clouds had gathered like noble lords clad in richly dyed cloths accompanied by ladies wearing lovely pastel veils. And their undisputed sovereign the sun was a perfect drop of blood just as in her dream, the dream in which a mysterious dark-haired man had pricked the skin directly over her heart with the point of an ancient sword...

'The moon is our physical life,' Chris remarked matter-of-factly, 'the sun is the soul of experience, and our eternal being is the darkness itself. Matter is God's flesh, don't you think?'

'Yes, that makes sense,' she agreed casually, having entertained similar thoughts herself, thoughts she strove to express in her paintings. 'But I thought you were going to tell me about yourself Chris, not discourse on metaphysics.'

'What's the difference?' He smiled, his eyes fixed on the empty road.

The sun vanished behind the earth at last and Maia found herself wondering if the death of a loved one was a similar illusion. Wasn't it ignorant to believe that merely because the dead disappeared from view that they were lost in darkness? The sun kept burning and sustaining her life even when she could not see it, and in a similar sense she still felt some of her parents' love with her even though they were gone forever.

They didn't speak again for a while and she didn't suspect until too late where he appeared to be taking her. It wasn't until he had made disturbingly familiar turns down the streets of Stoneshire that she exclaimed without thinking, 'I don't want to go to The Phoenix!'

'Why not?' he asked, yet he didn't sound surprised by her passionate reticence.

'Because my parents and I ate there every Sunday night until they died. We have to go somewhere else, please.'

'No,' he said shortly. 'You have to face things, Maia. It's the only way to see where you're going.'

'Right now all I see is where I'm not going!' She crossed her arms defiantly over her chest feeling on the verge of a tantrum. 'Why are you being so cruel?' she begged to know, a sob catching in her throat.

'You should honor your parents with a visit to their old haunt, Maia, excuse the pun. After all, you've just discovered something fascinating about them, something which leads me to believe they wouldn't appreciate such appetite-suppressing grief on your part.

I imagine they find your sorrow much more distressing than being dead, a state of being that might be more enjoyable than you can possibly imagine.'

'Chris, please…' She felt helpless against his logic, which rolled over her like one of the ancient standing stones crushing any possible arguments against it.

'We're eating at The Phoenix tonight, Maia, and that's final.'

'I thought you were going to tell me about your life, Chris, not go back into my past!' She was furious with him now.

'Here we are.'

* * *

As ever, the intimate restaurant was only half full. She could scarcely believe it, but nothing had changed after all these years except for the waitress – a thin young creature who looked as though she never ate anything herself who darted from table to table like a robin in her brown-and-yellow uniform.

Maia seated herself in the chair Chris pulled out for her, and then stared at the candle burning steadily in the center of the small round table avoiding his eyes, not sure whether to be angry with him or grateful. The flood of memories overwhelming her was like sitting at the edge of a rushing river as vanished moments hit her chest directly over her heart like a cold spray… the red dress her mother had worn one night so similar to the one she was wearing herself now… her father discoursing on the fate of the candle flame… there seemed no beginning and no end to the nostalgic flow.

'See?' Chris winked at her over the black menu.

She raised her own menu in order to hide behind it.

'Not speaking to me, are you? Well, if you don't behave you

might just find yourself in the kitchen helping with the dirty dishes.'

'I'll just have soup,' she stated, setting the menu down indifferently. If her appetite was a person, she would soon have to report it to the authorities as suspiciously missing.

He raised an eyebrow. 'Just soup, when you can have absolutely anything you desire?'

'All I want is for you to stop teasing me.'

'It's Eric who's teasing you, love.'

She was speechless for a guilty moment. 'I think he'd do a lot more than tease me if I let him,' she finally retorted.

'He'd only dump you in the end.' Setting his own menu down, he leaned over the table towards her, his face suddenly more intently beautiful than ever. 'He's nothing but a blind and selfish collection of hungers!' he whispered fiercely.

The waitress passed their table bearing two large grilled steaks on a platter.

He glanced in the direction of the fragrant meat. 'The only thing that motivates Eric is hunger for flesh!' He drew the word out in a disgusted hiss.

'Maia…' She felt a light touch on her shoulder and knew she had not only imagined hearing her name spoken. 'Maia Wilson, I believe.'

* * *

She stared at the man seated at the table with her and Chris. It was uncanny how clearly she remembered him even though she had glimpsed him only briefly years ago here in this very restaurant. Yet somehow it felt like yesterday as she re-lived her restlessness that evening, and then her disappointment when he got up to leave dressed all in black leather like the embodiment of her oddly pleasurable melancholy. She had watched the handsome stranger walk away as her father continued discussing the fate of the candle, not sensing the flames waiting to take both him and his wife into their violent embrace by way of a car crash only a few days later...

'But if you knew my parents,' she asked the man, 'why didn't they say hello to you that night?' She didn't want to sound suspicious, but she felt her self-control slipping. Too much was happening too fast and she was learning more than she had ever wanted to know about the past.

'Our friendship was not an open one,' Drew replied, gazing soberly but serenely at her face.

She noticed his eyes were the same deep blue color the sky had been tonight above the passionate sunset on the horizon. Then her awareness perched expectantly on his lips as she waited for him to say something more, and her pulse fluttered in a strangely wonderful way when he smiled slightly.

'Do you want the truth, Maia?' he asked, raising one hand to his heart as though about to swear on his honor. She didn't know whether to be relieved or disappointed when he merely extracted a pack of cigarettes from inside his black leather jacket. He had unzipped it but not bothered to remove it even though the temperature inside the restaurant was ideal.

'Yes, of course I want the truth,' she declared.

The skeletal waitress arrived to take their orders.

Maia still couldn't locate her appetite, but she quickly looked over the menu again compelled by Chris' pointed expression to order something other than soup.

'You're running out of time,' her lover warned her beneath his breath, and then smiled civilly at Drew. 'Can you give her any suggestions?'

'I'll decide for myself,' she said uncertainly.

Chris cheerfully addressed the waitress, 'We'll start with a carafe of the house red, please, love.'

'Very good, sir,' she chirped. 'I'll go fetch it and be back to take your orders.' She darted away, but not before smoothing her short skirt over twig-like thighs while holding Chris' eyes just a little longer than necessary.

'You were saying?' Maia addressed the dark-haired man even as she pretended to continue concentrating on the menu, yet the truth was that none of the entrees appealed to her.

'You wanted the truth,' he reminded her quietly.

'Yes,' she insisted, sensing he was giving her time to prepare herself for it, which made her nervous wondering what to expect.

'Maia,' Chris hooked her attention again, 'I suspect Mr. Landson here was part of your parents' secret life.'

She had already suspected as much herself. 'And my father didn't want me to know about it,' she mused out loud, 'so he pretended not to know Drew that night.'

'It was wrong of him to keep her in the dark, don't you think?' Chris asked.

'He had his reasons.' Drew leaned back in his chair and cradled his right elbow in his left hand to more easily draw the smoke from his cigarette. 'Does it bother you, Maia?'

'That my father-?'

'No, my smoking.'

'Daddy called them cancer sticks,' she informed him sternly.

'Yes,' a smile softened his firm mouth again for an instant, 'and he never stopped harassing me about my filthy habit.'

'And yet here you've outlived him by years,' Chris commented. 'Amazing irony, isn't it? Ah, we're saved.' The wine had arrived. 'Bless you, love.'

The girl preened. 'Are you ready to order now?'

'Maia?' Her lover's eyes commanded her to pick a dish whether she wanted it or not.

She quickly made a decision. 'I'll have the onion soup and a mixed green salad, please.'

Drew said he would have the same as the lady.

Chris suffered a peculiar lapse of imagination and ordered fish and chips. He then caressed Maia's knee beneath the table. 'It seems she's going to be hard to hold on to,' he remarked, and gave the other man an openly challenging stare.

'So you were a Druid too?' she asked quickly, and laughed a little from a build-up of tension, not because she thought the idea was silly. She fervently hoped Drew realized that.

'Were?' His lips puckered around the word as he stared at her with one of his dark eyebrows forming an incredulous arch at her choice of tense.

'Oh I'm sorry…' Her clumsy apology tripped over his sudden smile. 'You are a…' She found it impossible to bring the mysterious ancient term of 'Druid' into the casual present.

Drew gently killed his cigarette while Chris occupied himself with the wine's body, raising his glass and frowning when he discovered it had absolutely no legs.

'Is it all a secret,' she persisted, 'or can you give me some idea what-?'

'There's a time and place for everything, Maia,' Chris interrupted her. He had given up on the wine's body and was settling for the ghost of a bouquet. 'I'm sure Mr. Landson would rather not get into it right now.'

Drew fingered another tobacco shroud. 'It's not all a secret, Maia.'

'I feel I have a right to know… thank you.' She accepted a full glass of wine from her lover without taking her eyes off the other man.

'Yes, you do have a right to know.' Drew's low-pitched voice was almost hypnotically quiet, yet its timber made every word he said ring in her head. 'I'd like to tell you everything,' he added, continuing to hold her eyes.

'I'm sure you would,' Chris said agreeably. 'She'll hear the so-called truth about the Druids from you, and get to experience all the sensational fantasies about them through Eric Wolfson. A famous musician who recently commissioned a wine rack from me wants Maia to be in a music video he's producing that will essentially recreate an ancient sacrifice.'

When Drew abruptly glanced in the direction of another table, Maia realized it was the first time he had looked at anyone besides her. 'The standard sacrifice scene?' he asked.

'I assume so,' Chris replied, 'although we might be able to save it from total banality if he lets me direct the video. I doubt he will, however.'

Drew contemplated the flame of the match he lit before raising it to the fresh cigarette dangling between his lips, and watching him, Maia imagined an Indian woman tightly wrapped in a white shroud about to be burned with her husband. 'How do you feel about it?' he asked her, meeting her eyes again.

She felt as though he was inhaling her soul while he waited for her response. Looking down at the table, at once unnerved and reassured by his steady regard, she followed the snow-bound trail of a fold in the cloth with her little finger, which trembled slightly as she spoke. 'It might be interesting…'

'She's dying to say yes,' Chris rephrased her tentative reply.

Drew focused on Maia's restless hand. 'Maybe you can arrange for me to have a talk with Mr. Wolfson,' he suggested. 'After all, music videos are a powerful medium.'

She looked up again and was caught by the small silver earrings he wore, then by the thin silver chain describing a wide ark across his black shirt as her awareness seemed to fall into orbit around it…

CHAPTER TWELVE

Maia had always considered pubs to be somewhat seedy places, but tonight she felt herself to be in an alchemist's basement where exotically labeled bottles and glasses of all different shapes gleamed an aura of dangerous enchantment... where the deep shadows seemed to orbit Drew's body sitting beside hers, intensifying his gravitational pull and making it difficult not to lean even closer to his mesmerizing voice.

After dinner, the three of them had walked a few blocks to a pub to continue their strange conversation, which couldn't seem to properly take off in the restaurant's more conventional atmosphere. But now, with countless bottles of spirits lined up before them like levers in a magical control panel, ideas could soar in any direction.

Maia took such comfortable root on her stool she almost grew fond of it. She began seeing it as a stem on which the full blossoming of her feeling depended, all the concepts contained in her mind like petals unfurling.

Chris had disappeared for the time being. Apparently, he had a number of casual acquaintances scattered around the pub's dim domain and he seemed intent on greeting all of them. She also suspected he was deliberately leaving her alone with Drew, which would have surprised her if she had expected her lover to behave normally. Whatever Chris' reasons, it suited her to have Drew all to herself for a while, and not only because she wanted to question him about her parents' secret life as pagans. He was dividing his attention between her and his drink, staring down into it as he spoke, and then up into her dark eyes as though to savor her reaction to his words. At first he leaned against the bar, but gradually he turned to face her, and she unconsciously reflected his movement like pure metal following the irresistible pull of a magnet.

'Are you confused?' he asked her.

'Yes,' she admitted.

'Why?'

Even in the dark space she could make out his vivid blue eyes. 'Because, just the other day I was wondering if anything exciting was ever going to happen to me…' She glanced down at the dark hill of his lap, and a sudden impulse to bend over and bury her face in it de-railed the train of her sentence for a breathless moment. 'Because my life was so drab and predictable,' she started over, 'and then all of a sudden so much is happening to me that my head is spinning!' She found herself relaxing as she could never remember doing with anyone before, not even (especially) with Chris. It was very nice the way Drew listened to everything she had to say, as if he had already guessed the words about to pass between her lips and yet still cared to hear her express them herself. He also seemed to enjoy watching her mouth as she talked. 'I mean,' she found herself looking down at his lap again, 'I met Chris in a cemetery. Can you believe it?' She laughed self-consciously, and then absorbed a little more courage by taking a quick sip from her glass of red wine. 'I drove to the graveyard to visit my parents' grave and my car stalled just a few yards from the gate,' she went on matter-of-factly, her casual tone striving to belie the strangely sinister event. 'I panicked. I don't know a thing about cars and I was out in the middle of nowhere. All I could think of to do was turn on my emergency blinkers, and before I knew it Chris had miraculously pulled in to help me. Yet there wasn't anything wrong with the engine after all, oddly enough.'

'No, there wasn't.' He touched her knee gently, but almost before her senses could register the warmth of his fingers, they were resting lightly on his glass again. 'I'm very fond of your mother, Maia,' he confessed, gazing down at the golden pool of his drink.

'You mean you were very fond of her.'

'No, I mean I am very fond of her. No one ever really dies,' he met her eyes, 'and I think you know that.'

Suddenly, all her hope of immortality seemed to hang from his silver earrings. 'Do you really believe that, Drew?' she asked him fervently, staring fixedly at his profile as he took another sip of his scotch 'Chris says he does, but do you, really?'

Once more he looked directly into her eyes. 'Absolutely.'

She felt more than heard his response, his whisper a gentle breeze in the pub's dark atmosphere storming with dozens of much more lively conversations than theirs. 'I'm so glad,' she whispered, and realized after it was too late that her hand was resting on one of his thighs.

Smiling, he spread his own warm fingers over hers. 'Do I feel familiar to you, Maia?'

'Yes,' she admitted, grateful to him for being able to sense how she felt. 'I don't know why, but you do.'

'That's what I have to talk to you about. You remember your

accident, when an oak tree was struck by lightning three times and collapsed across the car you were in with your aunt?'

'Of course I remember. That's not the sort of thing you ever forget.'

'I helped bring you back.'

'What do you mean you helped bring me back? You mean you found our wrecked car and called the rescue and helped them-?'

'No, that's not what I mean. Someone else found the wreck and called for help. You're aware of the fact that you were unconscious for an entire month afterwards.' He added as if by way of an arcane explanation, 'For one full cycle of the moon.'

'I know I was,' she sounded impatient because she was getting nervous, 'but I still don't understand what you mean when you say you helped bring me back.' She knew, however, what it meant now when she saw him reach for his heart. 'Please don't,' she requested.

'You want me to stay, don't you, Maia?'

'Are you telling me you would get up and go because I don't want you to smoke?' She refused to believe he could be so rude and selfish.

'Trust me.'

Her heart burned with indignant disappointment when he lit the cigarette against her wishes.

'You see, to put it simply,' he went on, exhaling smoke across the bar away from her, 'you were having an amazingly good time away from your body.' He met her eyes again with this remarkable statement. 'You remember when you were a little girl playing in the yard how you resented going back inside when your mother called you in for supper, because you were in the middle of a really great game and you didn't want to stop playing?'

'Yes!' She laughed. 'All the time.'

'Well, you weren't listening to your mother or your father begging you to return to consciousness after your accident, therefore,' he tapped ashes into his empty glass, 'they asked me to run out and get you, so to speak. Although I'm afraid your father wasn't too happy with how I went about luring your soul home.'

* * *

Maia was amazed and enthralled by Drew's story. Strangely enough, it had never occurred to her to wonder why she had awoken from her month-long sleep in her own bedroom instead of in the hospital, which is where they normally kept people in comas. She was still disturbed by the fact that she had lost an entire month of her life, yet for her the time had gone by in the blink of an eye. Afterwards, her parents had done everything in their power to help her forget the unnerving experience as quickly as possible. Now Drew had given her an enigmatic sketch of physical facts merged with supernatural events in which possible and impossible merged like light and dark in his penetrating stare, and somehow the effect was realistic.

Chris finally returned to the bar to claim her, and she walked out of the pub pensively, as though her emotions were slippery stones emerging from a river she was being forced to cross in the dark, its dangerous currents the rushing sound of traffic on the street. It distressed her how hard she found it to part from Drew, a man she had only just met, and it was an effort not to let Chris see how she felt about her parents' old friend. The slight pain when Drew forcefully gripped her arm and whispered in her ear, 'We'll talk again soon' was the sweetest sensation ever.

CHAPTER THIRTEEN

During the long drive back to his house from town, Chris said, 'You fancy him.'

She quickly attempted to deflect his mild accusation with a revelation, 'He told me something I'm finding very hard to believe, and yet I do believe him, for some reason.'

'Maia,' his tone was indulgent, 'a woman always believes the man she desires no matter what he says.'

This blunt statement rendered her speechless for a long moment in which her guilt was loud as a scream. Chris was the man of her dreams, yet in the handful of days she had known him, he had already inadvertently introduced her to two other highly desirable men she found herself helplessly attracted to. 'I'm sure that's something you take full advantage of,' she retorted quietly, finally managing a swing at him, but her heart was heavy. What Eric aroused in her was uncomplicated lust she could get a reasonable grip on and fight against, but the feelings Drew inspired in her were at once too intense and too subtle for her to resist, at least not yet, she needed to see him and to talk to him again.

'Maia, I care about you very much.' Chris raised his left arm invitingly, steering with one hand so she could snuggle up close to him. 'What did he tell you, dear, you seem upset?'

'Oh Chris,' she sighed, taking comfort from his warmth and the already familiar feel of his slender yet muscular body. 'I can't believe that only a few days ago I didn't even know you! And now all this about my parents being Druids… that was hard enough to believe without everything Drew just told me.'

'There, there,' he murmured, 'you've been hit with a lot at once, but you don't have to think about it all right now. Relax and just let me hold you. Everything will be all right, trust me.'

'But I have to think about it,' she protested. 'I want to think about it.' She attempted to slip out from beneath his arm, which suddenly felt more like an oppressive weight than a comforting embrace.

'You want Drew, not an explanation, Maia, desire is all you understand.'

'Let go of me, please.'

'As long as you realize you're already mine,' he let her slip away across the seat, 'I'll let you have your fun.'

'I think maybe I should move back in with Carol,' she said numbly.

'You're not going back, Maia,' he insisted pleasantly. 'You don't really want to. You know we were meant to be together, you felt it from the moment you saw me, didn't you?'

'Yes,' she confessed even though she was so distressed she couldn't think straight; she was too busy trying not to cry.

'And I can give you anything you desire, even other men, if that's what you want sometimes.'

'Oh God, no…' She suddenly wanted to die. How could he possibly love her if he felt that way?

'It's all right, Maia, I'm not the jealous type, and there's a world of difference between love and lust. I can give you everything,' he promised again gently. 'There's no need for you to go back to work. I want you to concentrate on your painting.'

His excessive generosity filled her with despair and threw her into a mysterious panic. 'But Chris, if I don't work-'

'I can give you anything you desire,' he insisted, 'there's no need for you to work.'

'But I have to earn a living for myself,' she said desperately, 'and I have no idea if my paintings will sell.'

'You can't worry about that, Maia, you just have to follow your heart no matter what.'

The car sped around a sharp curve in the road and suddenly the standing stones rose up against the star-filled sky.

The awe-inspiring sight smoothed out her passionately tangled emotions like a hauntingly pleasurable caress. Impulsively, she rolled down her window and the cold night wind roared in like a black dragon impaled on the car's headlights – straight golden swords piercing the darkness, which seemed to emit a climactic scream of pain as Chris burned rubber to swerve off the road onto the grass.

'What are you doing?' she gasped.

'We're going for a little moonlit stroll.'

'But I'm tired,' she protested half-heartedly.

'I'm sure you can make it up the hill.' He turned off the engine, plunging them into darkness as he switched off the headlights. 'You won't be tired for long,' he promised in an almost reverently hushed voice. 'More energy than you can ever use is stored in these stones, Maia. All you have to do is open yourself up to it and let it fill you.' He reached over to squeeze her leg just above the knee. 'You're good at that.'

Maia felt herself becoming excited by the absolute stillness surrounding their small vehicle. Yet the darkness outside was also alive with the singing of crickets, a high-pitched energetic sound that seemed to communicate with the vibrant pulsing of the stars overhead. There wasn't a cloud in the sky. The moon was holding full glorious court in this once sacred place. She knew the luminous disc had to be gradually waning, she had been communing with it for several nights now, but so far the earth's shadow had not encroached upon it at all...

'Have you ever made love beneath the stars, Maia?'

'I've had sex in a car beneath the stars,' she replied tartly.

'That doesn't count.' He opened his door. 'Come on.'

She followed him out into the cool night air. The grass felt prickly against her bare toes and didn't inspire her to remove her high-heeled sandals even though it would have been easier to walk up the hill barefoot.

'Keep your heels on,' he instructed, as ever seeming to read her mind as he took her hand.

She let him lead her quickly up the steep slope. She had driven past the standing stones her whole life yet she had never stopped to walk amongst them, and it felt strange to be there now, as though she was crashing a party to which she had not been invited; a gathering of spirits and forces beyond the comprehension of her excessively rational modern mind, which no longer knew how to understand this passionately simple language of nocturnal insects singing and of wind rustling through the grass. The stars were so bright, a part of her almost felt they were screaming at her on a frequency too high for her physical ears to register, but it was as though her soul could hear the cosmic symphony so that she didn't feel alone with Chris. It was as though they were entering an infinitely exclusive place very few people knew about or could gain mysterious admittance to.

When they reached the summit, he let go of her hand and she stumbled on the uneven ground as the full presence of the stones overwhelmed her. Now that she was amongst them, she could truly appreciate how tall and broad they were as well as how much individual space there was between them, each phallic column possessed of a private aura as it held its own special position in the group. The moon was intensely interested in Chris' white button-down shirt, which made him wonderfully visible to her as he strode into the open space between the stones. She thought about following him, but then decided not to. She didn't share his bold familiarity with the place and the pillar closest to her had captured her in its orbit. She found herself walking towards it as though it had silently commanded her to approach and reach out and touch its rough stone skin...

'Maia,' her name resounded amongst the stars and the moon suddenly seemed to be gazing exclusively down at her, 'take off your dress. I want you naked.'

She glanced self-consciously down the hill at the road, but there were no cars approaching from either direction. Part of her wanted to obey him, yet she hesitated to expose herself and not because it was a chilly night, but because she felt surrounded by timeless elemental forces that would all be attracted to her vulnerable mortal flesh. She felt surrounded by ghosts, not so much of people as of the centuries themselves... if she took off her dress she would be exposing herself to the cold dark fingers of long-vanished decades to which her precious individual life meant nothing...

'I said take off your dress and your panties as well, Maia.'

It was impossible to resist her lover's command coming from

the heart of an ancient stone circle. She grasped the hem of her cotton garment, took a bracing breath, and pulled it swiftly off over her head. She immediately felt her nipples harden beneath the wind's coldly moist lick as it forever blew between the erect columns of stone, and the way it wafted against her pussy as she slipped off her panties was almost too stimulating. Shivering, she abandoned her undergarment to the grass as she held her dress protectively over her breasts, thankful for the long hair cloaking her shoulders. Then she shivered again as Chris strode purposefully towards her.

He wrenched the dress out of her hands and flung it carelessly onto the ground behind him. 'Turn around,' he commanded. 'Brace yourself on the stone.'

She turned back towards the dark shape looming over her and bent at the waist to rest her hands on the rough surface, preparing herself for his thrusts. It turned her on how intensely aware she was of her warm pussy fully exposed to the cold night air. How vulnerably available her tight little hole was intensified her appreciation of the phallic columns surrounding her, and imagining Chris' erection reflecting them thrilled her to the core as she felt him step up behind her. She didn't need to see him to know he was still fully clothed and that he was pulling his cock out like a weapon to stab her with. Then, waiting for his penetration, she suddenly caught herself thinking about Drew... picturing the way his dark-brown hair flowed back away from his high forehead and then curved gently around again to fall almost to his shoulders... remembering the cigarette burning between his firm lips and the crescent-shaped scar below them luminous in his unshaved chin as he looked into her eyes, listening... The napkin on which he had written his phone number down for her was folded carefully inside her purse resting on the front seat of the car. She hoped no one would steal it, but that seemed highly unlikely out here in the middle of nowhere…

She gasped when Chris clutched her hips with both hands, digging his hard fingers into her tender skin like a predator sinking its talons into unresisting prey. She thought of asking him to loosen his grip on her, but she didn't; she liked being roughly possessed like this by a man who knew what he wanted and wasn't afraid to take it. She moaned expectantly when he insinuated the full head of his erection between the moist folds of her labia, and bit her lip as she endured the exquisite tease of him just resting there for a moment. She could feel the breathtaking length and girth of his hard-on poised at the entrance to her flesh ready to sink into her body's yielding depths, and she both loved and hated the way he made her wait for it, making her whimper and arch her back even more deeply to push her pussy back towards him invitingly. Without either of them saying a word he was making her beg him to fuck her. And the whole time she waited for his thrust, she was aware of the moon looking down at her like a haunting reflection of the tiny satellite of her clitoris needing his penetrating energy to come alive…

'What are you thinking, Maia?'

'I'm wishing you would fuck me.'

'Very good.' He shifted his hands down to her ass cheeks and squeezed them approvingly. 'You're learning to be more honest with yourself. A few days ago you would have said you were waiting for me to make love to you.'

Drew would make love to me, she thought, and then it was too late to take the feeling back and pretend she was really alone with Chris. Her heart began racing, but there was no way she could escape the conviction that Drew would be able to fuck her just as hard but that he would also make love to her.

'Mm, you're even more beautiful in the moonlight, Maia.' Chris ran his hands slowly up and down her back, his thumbs pressing into the sweet dip where her firm spine merged with her soft hips. 'I know you're thinking about that Druid priest. He's too late, of course, you're all mine now, but if you want to think about him, I don't mind, whatever turns you on, baby.'

Protests perched on her lips, but somehow she never got around to uttering them. She couldn't quite reconcile how guilty she felt with how turned on she was until Chris at last condescended to stab her with his erection. He sank deliciously deep into her pussy, but then just rested there with his balls kissing her sex lips, tormenting her in another way; suspending her in a whole new dimension of mingled fulfillment and frustration. It seemed an eternity before he began driving his stone-hard cock swiftly in and out of her, slamming his body against hers as he banged her in rhythm with her soft cries of pleasure. She closed her eyes and braced herself for all she was worth against the stone, forgetting all about the moon and the stars, aware only of the earth beneath her sandaled feet as she dug her heels into it, keeping her legs perfectly straight so her hole was offered perfectly up to his filling thrusts. In this position he sank so completely inside her she almost couldn't bear the overwhelming nature of the fulfillment, and yet she also loved it more than anything. His rigid shaft stroking her most intimate depths felt better than anything, better even than his tongue teasing and licking her clitoris or her own fingertips crushing her body's little seed so she could enjoy the beautiful sensation of an orgasm blooming between her legs. When he was fucking her like this she didn't care at all about coming; the overwhelming experience was an end in itself with psychological roots too profound to analyze, and in any case, it was impossible to think when he was ramming himself to the very soul of her flesh like this…

But it wasn't impossible to fantasize… there seemed no difference between her imagination and her skin while she was possessed by a handsome virile man, so even though it was Chris' hard-on in her cunt, she also felt as though Drew was there making love to her… as though he was watching her and appreciating her long legs and wantonly arched back and trembling breasts … she could almost feel his penetrating regard mysteriously embracing her…

She knew when Chris began climaxing because the pleasure became almost devastating as he pulsed and swelled inside her clinging passage, relentlessly opening her up around him, and her cries of ecstasy rose to the heavens where stars glimmered like divine sperm as he ejaculated deep in the dark space of her sex.

CHAPTER FOURTEEN

Maia felt as though all her turbulent emotions had become audible in the rumbling of thunder around Chris' little fairy-tale tree house. Images and events from the past few days flashed with a sinisterly vivid quality through her mind as she lay in bed without even the moon for company tonight. She could not shake the impression that the storm had its origin inside her, the almost continuous flashing and rumbling the generator of her own imaginative powers. She couldn't possibly sleep through it, yet Chris had drifted off peacefully a long time ago, essentially leaving her alone on the bed sheets' leaf-strewn shore even though his body was still lying beside hers. She could almost sense his adventuring sub-conscious floating somewhere in the night around her, anchored by his naked body. He lay on his side with his back to her, and the lamp she kept on for company evoked the setting sun at twilight behind the steep slope of his shoulder, smooth and warm as a desert dune.

Outside, lightning kept striking with a dangerous undiminished passion as the sky kept groaning…

She thought of Drew's black leather jacket, about the way it had gleamed beneath a street lamp like wet asphalt as he watched her walking away, disappearing into the darkness with Chris...

Careful not to wake her lover, she got up to use the bathroom and to attempt to relieve herself of fantasies for a few moments, fantasies that were at once exciting and tormenting. She told herself it shouldn't matter to her that Chris was just a bit odd. Everyone had quirks. Nobody was normal, not really. She had also read somewhere that nothing is known, only imagined, and lately she was feeling the truth of these words acutely. In any case, normal was synonymous with dull and she wanted no part of a mundane life.

She accidentally tugged out a long white carpet of toilet paper as a deafening clap of thunder made her jump. Her lover's house was surrounded by large old trees and she knew from experience how attracted lightning was to them.

As always, after washing and towel drying her hands, she paused to gaze at her face in the little oval mirror hanging over the seashell-shaped sink. Her sense of self perched proudly on the lovely branch of her smile, and then her pulse soared at the thought of Drew lying in his bed somewhere not too far away. If everything he said was true, they had somehow met in another dimension years ago when he succeeded in the haunting task of luring her soul back into her body. Was this why his slightest gesture was almost too intense for her, because the supernatural intimacy they had somehow shared still had a devastating effect on her sensual wiring even now?

Maia finally switched off the light in the tiny bathroom and slipped back into bed beside Chris. Even though she could scarcely wrap her brain around it, she had to admit part of her desperately wanted everything Drew had said to be true. Disturbing as his story was, she was determined to see him again and get all the details about their supernatural encounter. She also very much wanted to ask him about this modern group of Druids he belonged to, and why her father had not been at all happy with him even though he should have been grateful to Drew for awakening his sleeping daughter…

Reality was torn violently in half as a blinding bolt of lightning struck directly outside the window followed instantly by the deafening sound of the atmosphere being ripped open.

Chris rolled towards her and opened his eyes with a smile on his face…

She screamed as the night of her accident came back to her in full force recorded by the storm's photographic flashes in terrifying detail that made her relive all the shock and pain by way of a series of swift images flashing like a movie on her desperately closed eyelids… then dimensions closed up again just as abruptly and there was only the sound of the rain drumming on the roof and beating on the leaves of the forest and generally soothing the world…

'Lightning struck one of the trees outside,' Chris murmured sleepily, 'that's all, there's no reason to be afraid.'

She crossed her arms over her chest trying to breathe normally as she told herself she was only imagining the cramp-like pain in her womb, yet she suddenly couldn't understand what she was doing in this totally unreal bedroom. During the storm's endless eerie winks, the silhouette of the tree in the wall seemed to open all its dark arms just for her, and suddenly the sense of being trapped inside a huge tree trunk was more than she could bear. She flung the sheet off her gasping, 'I have to get out of here!'

'What's wrong with you, Maia?' Chris gripped her arm and effortlessly prevented her from rising. 'It's just a bloody storm.'

'Everything's wrong!' She almost hated him for not understanding how she felt. He knew her accident had happened on a night like this. She wanted Drew, he would understand. She needed Drew. She needed to talk to him again…

Chris sat up abruptly, and took her in his arms. He held her tightly, but to her horror the bed had transformed into the front seat of a car again from where she watched with hopeless fascination as the lightning's silver sword defeated the mighty oak tree's centuries-old armor with three swift slashes…

'Maia, what's wrong, sweetheart? You're trembling.'

She moaned and tried to push him away the way she had struggled to push open the car door, but there was no time. Sinisterly determined to get to her, the tree's gnarled old arms swooped possessively towards her and cracked the roof of the car as easily as an eggshell. One of the heavy limbs struck her directly across the womb, and then she was only vaguely aware of her body writhing beneath its weight like a fledgling fallen from its nest as the sky wept over her, mourning the death of the tree while baptizing her entrance into another world as her eyes closed…

* * *

The warm and comforting kiss of sunlight on her eyelids woke her to the loud hissing of the shower.

She lay staring up at the faraway ceiling impatient for Chris to leave for his workshop so she could drive to Carol's house and use the phone there. Once again she looked over at her small snakeskin purse where it sat on his desk. Last night it had swallowed the napkin with the mysterious nourishment of Drew's phone number written on it and the hunger to get in touch with him was the only thing motivating her this morning.

Chris held her in his arms for a long time after rousing her from her nightmare. Her dream had felt so real she believed herself to be awake. Strangely enough, it was the first time she had ever dreamed about her near fatal accident and she sincerely hoped it was the last time. She had no desire to suffer through it again in such excruciating detail.

Her lover emerged from the bathroom with wildly towel-dried hair and his fine skin beaten rosy by the hot water. 'How are you feeling?' His usually smooth brow furrowed with concern as he gazed down at her.

'I'm okay, I guess.' Her gaze was irresistibly drawn down to his crotch. Even in repose his penis was impressively thick and long nestled against his scrotum. She had never realized before how luxuriously attractive a man's sexual organ could be, especially when framed by a tall and ideally proportioned body.

'That was quite a nightmare you had last night,' he commented, turning his back on her on his way to the closet.

She admired the way his broad shoulders tapered down to slender hips and the tightest, sweetest little ass she had ever seen on a man, but then again she hadn't seen all that many naked male buttocks.

'Do you often dream about that night, Maia?' His question was muffled by the contents of his closet as he chose his outfit for the day.

'No, I don't, thank God.' She was trying to find the energy to get up and shower, but she had become lazy as a cat lately, lying around all day waiting for Chris to come back and doing nothing useful in the interim. But today would be different. She was going to call Drew, and she was going to see him again, she had to.

Chris stepped out of the closet tugging on a pair of tight black jeans and she wondered at how nicely he always dressed just to go to his shop, where he never seemed to get dirty. Come to think of it, she had never seen him come home with even a speck of sawdust on his shirt...

'So, what are your plans for today?' He smiled brightly at her over the black T-shirt he slipped on.

'I'm going over to Carol's,' she replied, and guilt at her lie propelled her out of bed.

'Paying the little aunt a visit, eh?'

'Yes... I'm going to shower now.'

'Hey.' He grabbed her as she attempted to walk past him, and pressed her naked body against his fully clothed one. 'Don't I get a kiss goodbye first?'

He seemed to be looking down at her sadly, but she told herself it was only her guilty imagination imbuing his expression with such profound regret. He could not possibly know she was planning to call Drew, and even if he did know, all she wanted to do was talk to him again... She quickly reached up on tiptoe to kiss him on the lips, and as usual they were coolly unresponsive. 'Have a lovely day,' she said sweetly, wondering how Drew's mouth would respond to hers. She was sure he would kiss her back.

'Be good, Maia,' Chris said, letting go of her, and his quiet voice paradoxically rang in her head all through her shower, and as she dressed, and during the drive to her little old aunt's house.

* * *

'Maia, darling!' Carol looked infinitely relieved to see her. 'I should never have told you about your parents being Druids,' she chided herself. 'I should have left well enough alone and let them rest in peace and not broken their confidence since they obviously wanted to keep it a secret...'

'Carol, relax. You can't possibly be serious? Of course you did the right thing in telling me. I should have been told a long time ago.' She slipped into her usual seat at the kitchen table and carefully unfolded the precious napkin neatly stained with ink – the vital row of numbers that would enable her to get in touch with Drew again. She wanted to wait until at least ten o'clock to call her parents' old friend in case he liked to sleep late. 'Auntie,' she could make use of that time, 'did you ever meet a man named Drew Landson?'

Carol swiftly made the sign of the cross and nearly collapsed into a chair. 'How...?' She put a wrinkled hand over her eyes.

Maia couldn't help but be gratified by the dramatic effect her simple question had. 'I met him last night,' she added casually.

Her aunt looked at her in weary confusion. 'Last night?'

'At the restaurant where-'

'Oh my word!' She looked up at the blank white ceiling as though it was a Cathedral painted with angels who had all betrayed her.

'Then you have met him.'

'Oh no, I never actually him!'

'But you know of him, obviously,' Maia insisted.

'Yes, unfortunately I do.' She rubbed her bad knee fervently.

'Carol, what happened? He says that-'

'Don't listen to him, Maia, please.' She sounded a little calmer now and yet somehow even more desperate. 'Whatever you do, don't fall under his spell like your mother did.'

'Mummy was...?' Her stomach suddenly felt queasy; secrets were definitely not the best thing to have for breakfast. 'Mummy didn't-?' She could hardly think it much less say it.

Carol's eyes widened in horror. 'Never! How could you think such a thing about your own mother?'

'I didn't… Carol, remember when I was unconscious for a month after our accident?' She spoke carefully, afraid of further shattering her aunt's peace of mind with her hunger for information on the past, which had not been the normal domestic nest she had believed it to be. 'Drew said he helped bring me back… I mean, he said he helped wake me up from my coma. Is that true?'

'That's what he wanted your parents to believe, but as far as I'm concerned, it was that wonderful doctor who saved you, Dr. Christianson, Dr. Eric Christianson, a very handsome, hardworking young man he was. He stayed with you night and day, never left your side. The poor boy nearly died of exhaustion. All Drew ever did was sleep in your bed and fill your room with his foul cigarette smoke!'

'Really?' Maia realized she was smiling at the thought of Drew in her bedroom.

'And then…' Carol angrily caressed her bad knee again. 'To this day I cannot believe your father permitted it!'

'Permitted what?' Maia asked breathlessly, glancing up at the clock. It was ten o'clock. If she called Drew now there was still a chance she might wake him (he looked like the sort of man who liked to stay up half the night and sleep in) yet she didn't think she could stand to wait much longer and there was always the chance she might miss him…

'He asked,' Carol went on tightly, 'or rather he commanded that you be taken out of the hospital and brought back to your bedroom.' She shook her head, her disbelief and disapproval still as sharp now as they had been at the time. 'Even Stella finally hesitated to do as he said, but in the end she obeyed a relative stranger, simply because he called himself a high priest, instead of listening to her own husband. How she managed to convince Peter I will never know.'

Maia said in wonder, 'I do seem to recall a funny smell in my room when I woke up…'

'I'm sure there was.' She snorted derisively. 'That man smoked like a chimney.'

'Then it's true, he did somehow manage to bring me back.'

'Nonsense, you were in Doctor Christianson's hands for weeks and you were with that charlatan for one night. You would have come around in the hospital if Stella hadn't somehow convinced Peter to move you. It was only a coincidence you woke up when you did.' She frowned, and then blurted out the fact at the root of her indignation, 'You woke up in that man's arms! Thank God the neighbors never had any idea what your parents had permitted. I was even more thankful you didn't remember anything of the affair yourself.' She paused, looking more distressed than angry now. 'I shouldn't even be telling you any of this…'

'Oh please, Carol, go on, I have a right to know.'

'Hmm… well, he said to Stella that you opened your eyes for a moment at around three o'clock in the morning and smiled at him, but that you didn't come around completely for another three hours. Yet in my opinion, if it wasn't for that man none of it would have happened, not the accident, not any of it.'

'But Carol, how can you say that? It can't possibly be his fault that a tree was-'

'Oh yes it can.' She looked down at her bad knee as she intoned somberly, 'To this day I believe that man somehow had a hand in that storm!'

CHAPTER FIFTEEN

It was unusually cold for May, but the sun was shining as it rarely ever did in Stoneshire. However, Maia's conscience was nowhere near as clear as the sky. She was afraid Chris knew exactly what she was up to today, and she had always been a terrible liar. One way or another, she was destined to confess her indiscretion to him later, but she simply had to see Drew again, so here she was sitting in the front seat of his car.

His black vinyl jacket was mesmerizing, but everything about him seemed to have that effect on her. Swift silver snakes of light kept slipping up his arms and around his chest her eyes enjoyed following all over him as the sun played on the shiny material. It was only eleven o'clock in the morning, but he looked dressed for a nightclub in black wrap-around sunglasses. Even when his profile was turned towards her she couldn't see his eyes; all she could see was the reflection of trees flowing swiftly down a dark and narrow channel. Despite her shy efforts to concentrate on the colorful world flowing by outside the windows, she ended up staring at him most of the drive. She kept waiting for him to say something, but he seemed content to concentrate on the road. Like Chris, he paid absolutely no attention to the speed limit. They were going so fast, she was having a hard time holding on to any particular thoughts in the emotional rush and couldn't think of anything to say herself.

'You know, Drew,' she spoke up finally, 'my aunt is terrified of you.' She could still scarcely believe Carol's morally paranoid fantasy that Drew magically helped orchestrate the storm which caused their accident that stormy night when lightning felled an old oak tree. The idea was so ridiculous it was almost exciting.

'I know she is,' he replied placidly. 'Stella told me how Carol felt about me and about the strange idea she got in her head that I had something to do with that storm, but I'm not Zeus or Thor, Maia. I can't command lightning.'

'I read somewhere once about a man who was struck by lightning years ago and hasn't worn a coat since then because he doesn't feel the cold anymore.'

'Lucky bastard.'

'Oh I don't know, I think it would be dull not to be able to experience contrasting sensations.'

'You're right, it would.'

She laughed. 'Make up your mind.'

'I made up my mind a long time ago never to make up my mind. A room that's too neatly arranged isn't lived in.'

'That makes very good sense, Drew.'

'You're a delightful young woman, Maia.'

'Thank you, but I wasn't fishing for a compliment. Where are you taking me?'

'I'm not taking you anywhere. We're both going somewhere together. Or do you prefer the idea of being taken?'

'I think most women do,' she confessed on behalf of her entire gender so it would seem less like a personal revelation on her part.

'I thought a picnic would prove a pleasant outing on such a beautiful day.'

'A picnic? You should have told me, Drew, I would have brought something...'

'I've taken care of it. We've got all we need in the trunk. Your aunt's opinion of me notwithstanding, I'm actually a pretty cool guy.'

'I believe you,' she murmured.

'Why?' he asked just as quietly.

'I don't know... I just do.'

'How do you know you're not just feeling what you want to feel about me?'

'I don't know,' she repeated, biting her lip uncertainly. She had been wondering that herself lately about Chris, the beautiful stranger who had saved her from spending the night in a graveyard and whom she had consequently knighted her true love as he knelt before the beautifully carved cabinet containing his spirits. She had only met Drew last night, yet already he was making her wonder if she was only imagining Chris was the prince of her dreams because he was like no other man she had ever met before... because he fucked her like she had never been fucked before...

'Think about it, Maia. How do you know when you're actually sensing what a person is like,' he sounded rather like a teacher privately tutoring his favorite student, 'as opposed to when you're just feeling what you want to feel about them?'

'Well...' She sought an answer in vain and concluded it had to be a trick question. 'But you can't draw a line like that, can you, since I can't ever really know you, can I? Who you are to me will always, in a sense, be part of my imagination, of my way of perceiving the world. So maybe there isn't only one you.' She warmed to the concept. 'It could be there's as many of each of us as there are other people to perceive and experience us, so even though the unique seed of our being is mysteriously inviolate, there are still as many variations of us out there as there are minds in which our existence is planted... Wow.' She smiled, impressed with herself.

'What you're saying then is that an aspect of my being or personality is in fact the evil sorcerer Carol perceives?'

'Oh no, I didn't mean that...'

He smiled.

She was dismayed. 'Okay, it was a stupid theory,' she conceded.

'Nothing you say is stupid, Maia. In a sense, you're right.'

She fervently wished they would get where they were going so he would stop concentrating on the road and look at her. 'Drew, are you going to tell me more today about how you... how you saved me?' she finally dared to ask.

'I'll tell you anything you want to hear,' he answered in a sexy voice that flowed like liquid gold down the center of her body and made her feel infinitely precious. 'Just don't believe all of it,' he warned.

'Why not?' she asked, and decided he was teasing her. Then she was distracted from pressing him for an answer when she spotted a lovely sapphire-colored lake set in the rough emerald of the forest. And apparently, the lake was their destination because he turned off the road onto a dirt path. Although it also made her somewhat nervous, she was pleased to see there was not another soul in sight as he parked at the edge of the clearing and switched off the engine.

* * *

Shivering in the cold breeze despite the protection of her red sweater, Maia watched Drew pull everything they needed out of his small black car – a red blanket, a large white wicker basket (both of which he handed to her) and a silver wine cooler that made her think of an ancient urn. 'You certainly come prepared,' she observed, setting down the basket and helping him spread the blanket out at the edge of the trees, as far from the chilling breeze blowing off the water as possible. She anchored the edges down with some rocks she found lying conveniently nearby, and then cursed herself for wearing a short white dress as she seated herself on the crimson sheet. Wanting to look casual and sexy for him, she had not had a picnic in mind when she dressed that morning. She also hadn't realized it was so brisk outside when she slipped on red strap sandals. She bent her knees and wrapped her arms around her legs trying to ignore how chilled her bare feet were already.

Drew was much better dressed for the elements in his black vinyl jacket, black jeans and a pair of black boots that looked like they could do serious damage if he decided to kick someone. He seated himself comfortably cross-legged beside her and gave her a look she couldn't read since only the lake was reflected in his sunglasses. She was about to ask him to take them off when it fully dawned on her that she enjoyed how mysterious he looked in them. It wasn't until she began seeing Chris, then was introduced to Eric Wolfson and after that to Drew Landson, that she had fully realized what an aphrodisiac a man's clothes could be for her. She wondered if it made her superficial that what a man wore affected her so deeply, and decided she didn't give a damn if it did.

'I love your outfit, Drew,' she confessed. 'I wish all men dressed like that.'

'Let's make ourselves comfortable.' He unzipped his jacket, revealing the fine silver chain she had noticed resting against his chest last night. 'You might be in a lot of trouble,' he added quietly, and the old wicker emitted a high-pitched scream as he flung open the basket.

His sexy threat shifted her pulse into high gear and she shivered. Fortunately, there wasn't a cloud in the sky so the sun was able to rest a bracingly warm hand on her shoulders. 'It's cold,' she said, then coughed self-consciously. 'And I'm not just saying that so you'll feel obliged to keep me warm,' she elaborated, defending her virtue without much conviction. She was not surprised to find herself completely unable to resist when he placed one of his hands on the back of her head, and brought it gently down to rest against his chest, forcing her to shift her position on the blanket slightly. Her bent legs now rested against his as she awkwardly kept her hands clenched in her lap.

'Where should I begin, Maia?' he asked quietly. The wind was running curious fingers through her hair, and he smoothed it down gently across her back waiting for an answer.

'At the beginning,' she murmured, because already it was an effort for her to speak. Resting against his solid warmth made her feel so safe and relaxed it was almost like being drugged. Then she shivered again, but for a completely different reason, as she felt his hand slowly following the curve of her hip. 'No...' she whispered.

'It's all right,' he whispered back.

She watched the surface of the lake trembling as subtle waves of pleasure and contentment flowed through her beneath his light caress. Whatever he said now would feel as irrelevant as stones tossed into the water. All that mattered now was the power of his physical presence and the infinite promise of his touch. She couldn't tell whether the water was shallow or deep and she didn't care. She was curved like an embryo against him with her hands crossed at the wrists resting limply against her thighs.

'You know the story of Red Riding Hood, Maia?' he asked abruptly.

'Yes, of course I do.'

'Well, I'll tell you a secret.'

'Mm?'

'All fairytales are metaphysical lessons, equations summing up the magical relationship between energy and matter, soul and flesh. The wolf was actually a handsome man.'

'I'm sure he was.' She saw Carol's worried, wrinkled face in the rippling water lapping restlessly against the shore of the lake. 'I read somewhere that the story of Red Riding Hood is all about sex,' she added, staring down at her hands wondering when they would find the courage to move out of her lap and begin exploring him as gently and respectfully as his hand kept wandering up and down her back...

'Yes, but what is sex all about?'

'You tell me, Drew.'

'In sex, opposing metaphysical forces come together and create the dimension of experience. The wolf was wild and hungry, wasn't he? He thought only about himself and how he could get what he desired. In this context the beast is our own imagination, isn't it, Maia. We all know how powerful our fantasies can be, how swiftly and greedily they cross our minds without any consequences. We can sink our teeth into one pleasure after another in our heads.'

'Mm, yes...'

'Now, that poor old grandmother's life was very limited, she was bedridden and dependent on Red Riding Hood for her nourishment, hence she stands for the boundaries of mortal existence and the grave we'll all rest in one day. But don't worry because the wolf devours her, which means that our imaginative power can learn to use the limits of time and space in order to more fully appreciate and enjoy its mysterious nature.'

'If Carol heard you talking now she'd know she was right about you, Drew.'

'It's obvious Red Riding Hood's cloak is the blood-filled body,' he went on, clearly unperturbed by what Carol or anyone else might think of him, 'which her innocent energy slips on at the morning of every life, and the basket of fresh fruit she brings her grandmother every day represents all the pleasures of the physical senses.'

'But what does it mean that the wolf wants to eat her?'

He pulled gently on her hair to lift her face to his and looked silently down into her eyes, his own eyes still hidden behind the darkly reflective panes of his sunglasses.

'Tell me,' she whispered, but what she was really hoping for was the wordless explanation for everything that would be his lips moving against hers in a kiss.

'You tell me,' he said firmly.

'He wants to eat her because…' She felt she should be able to pluck the answer from somewhere inside her like a perfectly ripe apple juicy with meaning. 'He wants to eat her because if he eats her he won't be hungry anymore?'

'Why won't he be hungry anymore?'

'Because she's pure spirit, always skipping along and singing… to the wolf she's everything he could possibly desire, which is what fantasizing is all about… he wants to rip the flesh off her bones just as we long to wrest everything we desire from life's hard facts. What you said about her slipping on her red cloak like a body at the morning of every life, well, what the wolf, what our deepest self wants is this magical sensual power free of all responsibilities and consequences.'

'He's the devil, isn't he?'

'Yes, and he's so sexy…' She closed her eyes as his mouth finally opened over hers. His tongue was somehow both cool and warm, quenching her thirst and satisfying her hunger all at the same time, but the kiss did not last nearly long enough. She was too disappointed to protest when his lips abandoned hers as he leaned forward to reach for the wine. The dark bottle beaded with moisture from the melting ice in the cooler looked beautiful in his hand, as though it was sweating stars, and he suddenly seemed impossibly far away from her even though she was sitting pressed up against him. He removed his sunglasses, and without thinking she snatched them up curiously to slip them on. 'Wow,' she declared as the world was washed a brilliant violet color casting royal purple shadows.

'Careful.' He yanked the glasses off her and shoved them into an inside pocket of his jacket. Then he returned the wine to the cooler for a moment to slip out of the shining vinyl. 'You're just like a kitten,' he teased soberly.

'Why did you tell me all that about Red Riding Hood, Drew?'

'Why not?'

'Seriously.'

'What's the matter, didn't you find it seriously interesting?'

'Yes, but what does it mean, really... I mean to me, personally?'

'That's entirely up to you, Maia. Let's have some wine.'

She took this as a signal to reluctantly separate herself from him. But then she was glad she did because now she could look at him in the sleeveless black leather T-shirt he was wearing. She had to agree with him, she was like a kitten, because she wanted desperately to run her nails across his pale skin, which looked fine as silk stretched over the smooth rocks of his muscles. She had to resist the urge to curl over his lap, impatiently peel away the tough shell of his black jeans, and begin licking him clean of any thoughts that did not revolve around her. She was eager to continue honing her oral skills and what better way than to practice on two men at once? There was also Eric Wolfson's potentially gorgeous cock to consider, for she was sure she could learn a great deal sucking him down...

Suddenly, Maia could not believe what she was thinking. She had never had such slutty thoughts in all her life.

'You called me so early, I didn't have a chance to have breakfast,' Drew said, handing her a lovely crystal wine glass. 'So let's indulge in some food and conversation first.'

'First?' she echoed haughtily, turning her back on the water as she slid farther away from him on the blanket, but it was really so she could face him as they ate and drank.

'After all,' he tossed a hunk of soft white cheese between them, 'there's a lot to talk about.'

'I'm listening.'

CHAPTER SIXTEEN

D oes Chris know where you are?' Drew asked her as he filled
her glass with a beautifully clear white wine.
'No, he doesn't.' The stab of guilt she suffered somehow
only sharpened her appetite for this other man. 'Actually, he probably does, even though I didn't tell him. I think he can read my
mind.' She wasn't joking.

'Or maybe you're just not good at hiding what you feel.' He
peeled the shining plastic skin off the cheese.

She considered this. 'No, I get the feeling he's a touch psychic.'

'We all are. It's a muscle everyone possesses, but which most
people haven't learned to use, much less develop, yet.'

'He wasn't at all surprised when I told him about my parents
being modern Druids. In fact, he looked rather pleased.'

Drew pulled a pocketknife out of his jacket and cut into the tender white block of cheese.

'He told me he wasn't, but is he... is Chris one too?' She cast a
frightened glance at the interlaced branches of the trees above

them as she suddenly thought she glimpsed a sinister sensual web being spun around her.

'No, he's not.'

The world shifted out of the painfully sharp focus in which only her feelings had been a confused, vulnerable blur. 'I want to trust you, Drew,' she said earnestly, 'yet you told me yourself not to believe everything you said.'

'Maybe you shouldn't believe that either, Maia.'

'Oh that's a good one.' She laughed. 'Talking to you is like being lost in a maze.'

'And you have to find your own way out.'

'Not necessarily. Didn't I need your help just to get in touch with my body again when I was in that coma? Wasn't that what we were going to talk about? Instead you give me a lesson on the metaphysical meaning of the Red Riding Hood fairytale.'

'I suppose in your case it was more like Sleeping Beauty.'

She smiled despite herself. She had always wondered what sort of dreams the sleeping princess lived in for a hundred years. Maybe Aurora dreamed the birth of her savior in a far away land, her eyelashes flickering as she slept brushing him like invisible wings were he knelt in the shadowy chapel of his castle, candles glimmering around him like the whites of her eyes, which had been veiled by the snow-covered hills of her lids for over a century…

'Come back to me, Maia and have something to eat.' He gently insinuated a piece of cheese between her lips. 'Come on,' he insisted, 'digesting is as vital as dreaming.'

'No, thank you, I'm not hungry.' She set her wine carefully down in the grass, planting the stem in the earth like a glass flower so she could bend her legs into a pyramid against her chest and wrap her arms around herself.

'You're completely fulfilled by fantasies, are you?'

'What do you mean?' She was both annoyed and intrigued by the question and his superior, almost taunting, tone.

'Wouldn't you like the real thing?'

'Of course I would.' She relaxed into a cross-legged position, but once more her fingers embraced each other with a nervous restlessness in the hollow of her lap.

'Do you want me?'

She quickly picked her glass up again to avoid his eyes, unsettled by his straightforward, almost brutal, honesty.

'Has it occurred to you, Maia, that what you think is the past might really be the present in which you're imagining all this? You asked me how I brought you back into your body...' Their glasses chimed a pristine musical note in the beautiful morning as he touched his to hers in a toast, the atmosphere clear and taut as a string played on by the breeze. 'Maybe that's what I'm doing right now.'

In a burning flash of indignation she emptied her glass of wine across his chest like someone instinctively trying to put out a fire. 'You have no right to play with me like this, Drew!' she cried, then was immediately ashamed of her unbelievably rude gesture, yet she had had no control over herself for a blinding instant. 'Oh God, I'm sorry!' she said miserably. 'I don't... I don't know why I did that...' Her lack of self-control seriously worried her.

His only reaction was to glance down at his chest, glistening with wine like a divine perspiration. 'You'd better tell me how sorry you are for wasting perfectly good wine, Maia.'

For some reason his placid attitude roused a defiant response in her again. 'It's only fitting, isn't it? I mean, I wasted a perfectly good month of my life when I was asleep in the hospital, didn't I? What's a little wine compared to a whole month of my life?'

'There were years stored in that particular bottle, which was quite expensive, by the way. It contained months of ideal weather and soil conditions it was foolish to waste.'

'I'm sorry,' she declared, but she wasn't; she was angry with him for remaining so calm while managing to disturb her so profoundly.

'Too late,' he said coldly.

She lay her empty glass down on the blanket like a dead queen in Chess and searched the wicker basket for a napkin to dry him off with. She found one made of fine white linen, and kneeling beside him she quickly applied it to his chest trying not to let herself become distracted by the muscular firmness of his pecs almost completely exposed by his loose black T-shirt.

'That's enough.' He drained his glass, planted it upright in the grass, and stood up abruptly.

'Oh please don't be mad at me, Drew,' she pleaded in despair. Forgetting her pride, she wrapped her arms around his thighs and pressed her cheek shamelessly against his crotch. The fact that his hands came to rest gently on her head reassured her, and the hard-on buried in his jeans she could feel pressing against her soft cheek filled her with hope. 'I'm so sorry,' she murmured, 'but… but you scared me saying that. I won't do anything like that again though, I promise. I want to keep talking to you. I need to talk to you, Drew, please don't leave me.'

'I wasn't planning to leave you, Maia. I just thought you might enjoy a little dip in the lake.

She looked up at him in astonishment. 'But the water must be freezing!'

He peeled her arms from around him. 'Yes, it probably is,' he agreed, grasping her hands and pulling her to her feet. Then he turned her around and yanked her sweater off before she could even protest. She felt him grip the hem of her dress and still she didn't say anything. He paused a moment as if waiting for her to resist him somehow, but her body language must have told him he could go as far and as fast with her as he wanted to. She willingly raised her arms as he lifted her plain white dress up over her head, and then closed her eyes in anticipation as she felt him hook his thumbs into the elastic of her white cotton panties. She could scarcely believe she was letting a man she had only met last night take off all her clothes in the middle of the woods, and she shivered in the throes of an excitement that felt like the cold edge of a knife's blade licking up her spine and terrifying her even as it gave her the thrill of her life. Because of course he wasn't a total stranger, both her mother and father had known him, her parents had been his friends, and it was because she sensed beyond a shadow of a doubt that she was perfectly safe with him that it turned her on so much to pretend she was letting a dangerous stranger have his way with her. The truth was he was only doing what she wanted him to as he slowly slipped her panties down her legs while deliberately letting only the backs of his thumbs teasingly caress her skin.

She stepped gracefully out of her delicate undergarment. She was getting good at stripping outdoors, balancing on the uneven ground in her high-heels. She was also growing increasingly proud and fond of her body, which seemed to possess much more of a mysterious personality naked than it did clothed. The pert white mounds of her breasts looked so pretty crowned with pink nipples that relished the kiss of cold air so much they became almost obscenely long, and her labial lips also enjoyed being made even more acutely aware of her inviting, innermost warmth. She had been shaving her pussy for a long time, initially for aesthetic reasons, but now also because she knew Chris preferred her sex smooth and naked. As an artist, she had wanted her body to possess the sensual flawlessness of a statue's and she had shaved between her legs in order to better appreciate the sight of her full little pudenda in the mirror. She had even sat in front of the glass once with her legs spread wide open so she could gaze in wonder at the gently gaping mouth of her sex, the mysterious cleft in her flesh where so many aspects of the natural world metaphorically converged as the sight of her rosy vulva made her think of a seashell haunted by the ocean's wet and salty depths... yet it was also like the heart of an exotic orchid... or like the entrance to an enchanted cave glistening with bio-luminescent bacteria...

'You're so beautiful,' Drew whispered in her ear, 'and I mean that in every sense, Maia.' He was still standing behind her, still teasing her, this time with his lack of urgency to see all the most delectable parts of her body she had willingly let him expose. His warm heavy caress passed slowly down her arms. 'I want you,' he admitted, his fingers thrusting between hers, and she whimpered as he grasped her hands with all his strength. 'I want you all for myself, Maia.'

She longed to turn around and embrace him, but she was pinned helplessly back against him, increasingly tormented by the warm feel of his breath on her cheek and the knowledge that he was tall enough to be able to look down and see her breasts aching for his touch. She desperately wished he would stop talking, which kept forcing her to think, and she didn't want to think right now, not about Chris or about Eric or about anything. Yet she couldn't just beg him to fuck her like she begged Chris to fuck her. What she felt for this modern Druid priest was already too deep. It didn't matter that she was living with another man. All that had seemed to matter to her since she met him last night was what Drew wanted, what Drew thought about everything, what Drew thought about her and what Drew wanted from her...

'But before we can be together, Maia, there's something you have to do for me first.'

She looked over at the lake. The water did indeed look cold, much too cold for a casual dip, and certainly much too frigid to play in for long. He abruptly let go of her hands and she dared to hope he would turn her around and do something to her, anything he wanted. She was not expecting him to literally sweep her off her feet into his arms. The way he snatched her up was not romantic, it was sudden and urgent, as though he was pulling her body out of some imminent danger.

She gasped, 'What are you doing?' and then cried, 'No, put me down!' as he strode towards the water with her and she suddenly knew what a cat felt like when faced with a bath. Her skin was already covered with goose bumps in a useless evolutionary throwback to fish scales as it tried to prepare itself for the water's icy embrace. 'Drew, please, what are you doing?' she repeated, her arms wrapped around his neck, and it felt so good to be so close to him, to be holding onto him for all she was worth, that her body languidly surrendered to his superior strength without caring that her brain was seriously worried about what he was planning to do with her. Her ability to think was further undermined by a wonderful sensory overload... the soft caress of his hair falling over her fingers clinging to his firm neck... the sharp buckle of his belt giving her naked belly stimulating little nips... the warm tenderness of his flesh beneath the cool reptile skin of his black leather T-shirt... and best of all, the hard gravity of his arms surrounding her... 'You're not really going to throw me in, are you, Drew? I could catch my death in there.'

Her choice of words seemed to affect him because a faint web of frown lines formed between his dark eyebrows that captured all her attention as he paused just a few feet from the water. 'You'll catch your death,' he repeated, looking intently down into her eyes. 'That's not what you want is it, Maia?'

'Of course not, but that's what will happen if you let go of me, Drew.'

His smile was strange, a brief flash of upturned lips that did not send the slightest spark of amusement up into his eyes.

'What are you thinking?' she asked, abruptly wondering why she trusted this man so implicitly. Carol had warned her about falling under his spell the way her mother had, and yet here she was, naked in his arms in the middle of nowhere with absolutely no one around to help her should he desire to hurt her. She was lying to her lover, who believed she was innocently visiting her little old aunt today, and yet she was foolish enough to trust everything a stranger said to her even when he himself had warned her not to. Carol had verified the story of how Drew exercised inexplicable supernatural skills to rescue her from a coma, and naturally she was grateful to him for that and intensely curious about how he had managed to meet her in another dimension, but his otherworldly sensibilities didn't necessarily make him a nice person in reality...

His whisper was barely audible over the rustling of the leaves, 'Are you frightened, Maia?'

'Yes, a little...' And yet she realized she was letting herself be scared only because she took a perverse pleasure in this fear, and this strange excitement was made possible by the fact that deep down she knew he would never hurt her, on the contrary.

'You should be afraid, Maia.'

'Why?' she asked, but her blood was purring through her body in a way that made it hard to think at all.

'Do you trust me?'

'Yes, Drew, I trust you.' Her eyes narrowed gazing up into his. Part of her felt languorous as a cat keeping the annoying nervous dog of her reason at bay, how profoundly peaceful she felt resting in his arms making it easy to ignore the protective barking of doubts and fears in the back of her mind.

'Will you do anything I ask you to do, Maia?'

'I... I don't know...'

He shifted her in his arms to bring her face even closer to his. 'Will you do anything I ask you to do, Maia?' he repeated urgently.

'Yes,' she answered fervently, and tried to kiss him.

He set her down abruptly. 'Then get your clothes back on.'

She swayed a little on her feet. 'What?' She was stunned. 'You're not still angry with me for-?'

'No, I'm not angry with you. I care about you, Maia.' He cupped her face passionately and possessively in his hands. 'Don't just give yourself away. You're worth a fight.'

'What do you mean?'

He pressed his mouth fiercely against hers and subjected her to a long, deep kiss that was exquisitely giving as well as demandingly forceful. Then leaving her breathless, he walked back towards the blanket and picked her white dress up off the ground. 'If we stay here any longer,' he said, also snatching up her discarded panties, 'I'll do something we'll both regret.'

'I wouldn't regret it,' she said weakly as he approached her again.

'Yes, you would,' he insisted shortly, handing her back her clothes. 'You're not ready for me.'

She looked shyly down at her feet. 'Yes I am...'

He smiled as he gripped her chin and forced her to look up at him. 'Stop pouting and get dressed.' He ran the tip of his thumb teasingly between her lips. 'We'll talk again soon, I promise.'

CHAPTER SEVENTEEN

Maia was sitting before one of Chris' wall-to-ceiling bookshelves, her thoughts flitting in rhythm with her pulse from one man to another making her feel light-headed as a butterfly wandering from stamen to stamen. But it was impossible to remain unaware of the danger lurking behind this uncontrolled blossoming of desire happening inside her, and of the evanescent nature of the stimulating situation, because eventually she would be forced to choose one man, and if she didn't choose soon, she might lose all of them.

She stared fixedly at the dark-green binding of a large volume without really seeing the title, only vaguely aware that it was a book about the Celts.

She didn't want to be forced to choose, not so soon. She was hurt and disappointed at the time, but now she was relieved that Drew had not immediately indulged her willingness to be unfaithful to Chris. He dropped her back off at Carol's house, and after she paid her aunt another brief courtesy visit, she returned home early in the afternoon in order to fix her hardworking carpenter a delicious supper. They ate in silence. She could barely swallow the sinfully rich cauliflower-and-cheese with her guilt like a poison concealed in the savory dish mysteriously killing conversation between them. Chris had smiled at her while he chewed as though nothing was wrong, but he had not said a word, and she was sure she could see in his eyes that he somehow knew everything about her day.

He was reclining naked in bed now reading a book that hid his face from her, but she did not doubt he was much more intent on her concealed thoughts than on the printed text and only biding his time before he confronted her about her day.

'What are you daydreaming about, Maia?' He finally deigned to address her. 'You've been awfully quiet this evening.' He looked down at her from over the black rim of his book. 'What's wrong, sweetheart, did you have a hard day?'

Lying felt like a piece of glass resting on her tongue she had to get the words around. 'It was all right,' she replied.

'Well,' he rested the book on his lap, 'judging by the wonderful supper you fixed me, you got what you wanted, and yet on the other hand the despondent way you're sitting there staring at nothing would seem to indicate that perhaps you didn't.'

'I spent the morning with Drew because I wanted to ask him about my parents.' It was an intense relief to confess at least part of the truth.

'I imagined that's what you were up to.' He didn't appear in the least bit jealous. 'Did you find out anything else?'

'Not really.' This fact had begun to bother her. She should have questioned Drew more thoroughly and demanded clearer answers from him, instead she had just let him go on and on about Red Riding Hood...

'I'm not surprised.'

'And why is that?' Anger at his condescending tone prompted her to pull out the book she had been staring at blindly. It was so heavy she could barely lift it, so she let it fall open in her lap.

'Why am I not surprised he didn't tell you more? Because I'm sure he had other plans for his tongue.'

'You have a filthy mind, Christopher Thorn.' She couldn't look at him.

'And you love it, so stop sounding like your dear old aunt.'

'Leave Carol out of this, please.'

'Gladly.'

'I asked Drew if you were a member of this cult,' she confessed. 'I asked him if you were a Druid, too.' She found herself wondering about how closely the word 'cult' resembled the word 'cunt', a harsh, cynical sound that seemed to deny a woman's inner self any sacred dimension.

'And what did he tell you?'

'He told me the truth,' she replied casually, hoping to trick him into revealing it, but all he said was, 'I see' and she felt a cold wave of dread wash through her. Desperately, as though it might offer her a life-line out of the terrible sinking feeling inside her, she focused down on a sentence in the book spread open across her lap.

It seems clear that this ritual involved a young woman passing from her husband to a lover and back again, just as nature passes from summer to winter and back to summer again, from a young man to an older rival.

'My God,' she whispered.

'Don't be so shocked, Maia. What's that Spanish expression… if it was a dog it would have bitten you. You gave this dog enough time to devour you.'

'Chris,' she looked over at him finally, 'Drew told me you weren't a Druid.'

'Then I'm afraid he didn't tell you the truth. You're mother was absolutely beautiful. She was a great loss to us.'

Maia slowly closed the book and occupied herself with the effort of slipping it back into its place on the shelf as her mind raced with the urgent efficiency of someone trying to dismantle a ticking time-bomb. She had made a mistake moving in with a man she didn't really know just because he was handsome and intelligent and sensitive to all her feelings and knew how to make love to her as no other man ever had... because he knew how to fuck her. Yet how could everything she felt be a mistake? And what did it matter that he considered himself a modern Druid if her parents had been involved in this cult, too? And calling it a 'cult' made it sound so negative and unhealthy. Why couldn't she think of it as a group, as a club, as something perfectly innocent? It was not innocent, however, that all she could think about was Drew and the way he had held her naked body against his... that all she could think about was the way she had felt with her head resting against his chest... that all she could think about was the way he had kissed her...

'Maia, I want you beside me, please. Why are you so far away?'

She got slowly to her feet, but then found she could not look at him again. He was so beautiful that resisting him was like trying to dance ballet on ice. It was possible to think clearly for herself only when she wasn't looking at him, when his penetrating stare wasn't weakening her own much too malleable willpower. She had to assert herself with him, so she stared courageously at the menacing silhouette of the tree in the wall. 'Why didn't you tell me before, Chris?'

'But I was telling you, Maia, in stages, in small, easy to swallow doses. I almost confessed when you told me Carol had revealed the secret about your parents, but I thought better of it. I didn't want to hit you with too much too fast. You seemed shocked, so I didn't dare add to your distress by saying "Oh by the way, I'm a Druid too". I thought it best to assuage your fears by telling you the truth, that these groups are really quite harmless. And contrary to what you might believe now, I hadn't planned on running into our amazingly talented high priest the other night at the restaurant.'

'But then why did he tell me you weren't…?' Maia realized she was more distressed by the fact that Drew had lied to her than by anything else. Exciting revelations and events were springing up around her lately as casually as dandelions, teaching her that the normal surface of life was actually sustained by deep, sensual roots that seemed to thrive in a secret darkness. The possibility that Drew might be lying to her threw dirt on all her most profound feelings and instincts and made her want to die. In twenty-four hours this enigmatic stranger had become the most important thing in her life. He was more important even than her ideal new lover, and she wasn't sure she could handle this turn of events. She had been so convinced she could be happy with Chris forever, but then this Druid high priest had come along with an unbelievable story about saving her in the past, and paradoxically killed her happiness and peace of mind in the present.

'Maia, didn't you hear me? I said I want you beside me. Come to bed, please.'

She turned slowly around to face him, but she kept her eyes downcast as she slipped out of one of his shirts. She let it fall to the floor at her feet and presented her naked, potentially unfaithful body up to his scrutiny as a form of penance, because it forced her to struggle against her natural shyness.

'Did you let him fuck you, Maia?' he asked quietly.

'No,' she replied firmly. There was no need to mention she had wanted Drew to make love to her. 'All we did was talk.'

'I don't believe that.'

She finally found the courage to meet his eyes. 'All he did was kiss me and that's the truth, Chris, I swear it.'

He smiled. 'What are you willing to swear by, Maia? Certainly not by the moon, "the inconstant moon that monthly changes in its circled orb, lest that thy love prove likewise variable".'

'"What should I swear by"?' She was proud to be able to quote Shakespeare right back at him, her head held high as she stood naked before him, the way his eyes caressed her making her thrillingly conscious of how desirable she was.

'"Do not swear at all",' his smiled deepened as he set the book he had been reading on the night table, '"or swear by thy gracious self…"'

'And you will believe me?'

'Probably not, but there's no need to torment yourself, my love. What we have together can last forever if you want it to. I'm not asking you to deny your desires, only to understand that love transcends them all. Love is not threatened by lust. Love is made even stronger by desire if you handle your thoughts and feelings properly.'

She went and crouched on the edge of the bed at his feet, unconsciously assuming a cat-like pose with her knees bent beneath her and her arms held straight in front of her supporting her while at the same time modestly concealing her nakedness. 'Chris, what do you mean by that?' She stared earnestly into his eyes in an effort to avoid the silent but indelible statement of his erection, which she couldn't quite bring herself to understand yet. As they spoke she had watched his cock swelling to life between his thighs, rearing its blind head and transforming the tender seed of his resting penis into a magnificent hard-on that told her more clearly than words how much their conversation excited him. She had not wanted to face it, but it was staring her so blatantly in the face now she had no choice. Her lover was aroused by the fact that other men wanted her and by her own guilty tormented longing to surrender her body to their lust.

He wasn't smiling anymore, but a spark of sinister amusement flashed in his eyes as he said, 'You'll come to understand it all in time, Maia.'

'But-'

'Stop thinking about it so much.' He grabbed one of her wrists and pulled her down into his arms. 'Just ride my cock like a good girl.'

'But-'

He gave her a quick, hard spank, but that was all it took to make her accept how wet and ready her pussy was for him. Her slick sex didn't care why she was so aroused. Her body didn't care whether it was thoughts of Drew or of Eric or of Chris that made her hole feel so achingly deep. All she wanted for the moment was relief from the emptiness this big, thick cock gave her as she grasped it by the base and guided it up inside her. Then she braced herself on his more yielding chest as she sank all the way down over his irresistible hardness.

'Ride me,' he commanded.

She sat up and flung her head back as she fully impaled herself on his erection challenging her deepest natural boundaries.

'Go on, baby, ride me,' he urged. 'Make yourself come…'

She wasn't at all sure she could bring herself to orgasm in this position, but she found herself more than willing to try as he supported her efforts to slide her pussy up and down his hard-on. She loved the feel of the thickest part of his rigid cock forcing her open around it, stretching the lips of her sex so her clitoris was forced to come out from hiding beneath its protective hood. Then she was surprised by how much her pleasure intensified when he reached up and trapped both her stiff nipples between his thumb and forefinger. He rubbed them slowly but firmly, giving them a hard squeeze occasionally, and it felt so painfully good she began stroking her clitoris with one hand while caressing his firm belly with the other. Her nipples felt like charged knobs directly connected to her cunt by a mysterious sensual electricity because the instant he began turning them between his fingers, she felt a climax spark to life between her thighs she eagerly stoked into a blinding ecstasy with her fingertips.

'Mm,' he said when she finally grew quiet. 'Now it's my turn.' He eased her up off his erection and she rolled weakly onto her back beside him. 'Turn around,' he instructed, and she obeyed him languidly. 'That' it, just relax and spread your legs for me.'

She rested her cheek against the mattress and bent her arms around her head as she obeyed him. She moaned in trepidation when she felt his hard length brush the tender cheeks of her bottom, but thankfully it was the wet and welcoming mouth of her pussy he was after, and this time her moan was one of pure fulfillment as he thrust his cock into her from behind. The quality of the pleasure was different from every angle, and in this position she was able to fully experience and enjoy the feel of his erection pushing between her thighs and through the clinging folds of her labia to rend its way deep inside her.

'Oh yes,' she whispered, 'oh yes, yes…' She clutched the sheet to keep from sliding up the bed beneath the violent pounding of his hard hips against her soft ass as he climaxed, and she helped him milk every last drop of cum from his pulsing penis by squeezing him with her vaginal muscles. He spread his body breathlessly on top of hers, and she relished the feel of his heart beating against her skin. For a few timeless moments she was content, until thoughts began worming their way back into her brain and she found herself right where she had started – lying in bed with one man while thinking only of another.

CHAPTER EIGHTEEN

I t might strike you as funny now, but it wasn't very amusing then, I can assure you.' Carol pulled her chin down against her chest in a stubborn gesture that always reminded Maia of Peter. 'Your father found that Landson fellow sitting on a red blanket spread out in the middle of your bedroom drinking a bottle of white wine with your favorite doll sitting across from him as though he was playing some sort of childish game. He had moved most of the furniture around in your room (without even asking your parents' permission I might add) yet Stella very calmly explained, as if it was the most natural thing in the world, that he had needed to reflect your entire bed in the mirror in order to use your blue-and-white comforter to evoke clouds reflected in a lake. You should have heard how matter-of-fact she sounded when she explained his actions. I loved your mother dearly, but she-'

'But she enjoyed her pagan games a little too much for your comfort,' Chris concluded for her.

Carol, Maia and Chris were all formally seated in the old woman's parlor. Maia and her aunt occupied the comfortable old couch, while Chris effortlessly dominated the small room from his position in a big old armchair facing them, almost like a witness on the stand.

'So, you were sixteen when you joined,' Maia addressed him, continuing the polite interrogation concerning his membership in a modern group of Druids as she tried very hard not to worry about Carol had just said... Drew must have deliberately driven her out to that lake yesterday so they could actually live what they had shared only as some kind of astral dream in the past... because obviously she was not lying unconscious on some hospital bed now dreaming, everything around her felt quite real and solid...

'Yes, I was sixteen when I joined,' Chris replied patiently, 'only a year before your mother left us, sadly enough.'

'When she was on her way to one of those...' Carol promptly brought up a fact she considered damning, but managed to stop herself from elaborating since she could offer no proof whatsoever to back up her suspicion.

'As I've tried to explain to you, Maia,' Chris went on serenely, 'your painful perspective of your parents' accident isn't the only one available to you. Dying together was a blessing for them. The pure force of their love ascended through the flames and left nothing behind for the worms. They were spared the slow decay of old age and the pain of separation.'

'I don't have to sit here and listen to this.' Carol attempted to rise, but her knee was bothering her more than usual today and Maia was easily able to hold her down by gently touching her hand.

'I apologize.' Chris bowed his head. 'It was not my intention to insult or upset you, Ms. Wilson, I was merely suggesting a more positive angle from which to view the painful matter of deceased loved ones.'

'My word, at least Peter still talked like a normal human being with real feelings! I ask you, young man, are you allowed to feel grief and remorse or can you always spin the cosmic wheel of fortune and come up with some winning formula to do away with such poor mortal reactions?'

Chris laughed, apparently genuinely amused, and the sunlight pouring in through a window formed a luminous aura around his blonde head that uncannily resembled a halo belying his devil-may-care attitude.

'If you two don't stop arguing,' Maia said impatiently, 'I'm never going to find out anything. I'm not interested in listening to a debate on Christianity vs. Paganism. That isn't the point here.'

'Well, if you manage to find a point,' Chris said, 'I'll sharpen it for you as best I can.'

Not permitting herself to be annoyed by his irreverent attitude, Maia tried to keep all the feeling out of her voice as she asked, 'What exactly are the duties of the high priestess in your… religion?'

'I'm afraid the term "exactly" doesn't apply as there is no exact division between the worlds and as high priestess Stella acted as a bridge between them.'

'And how did she become this… bridge between the worlds?'

'Be and come.' His smile deepened. 'Language often reflects metaphysical truths, doesn't it? To study the roots of words can be a very enlightening activity. To come is to be in the sense that at least one person had to come in order for you to be.' He stared coolly at Carol, who squirmed indignantly but could hardly deny the statement.

Maia felt as though she calmly pulled a trigger when she mused out loud, 'And Drew was the high priest.' Then all the implications of this fact hit her and nearly blew her mind.

'Drew is the high priest,' Chris corrected her.

'Do you mean to say that he and my mother…?' She couldn't

possibly finish formulating the question in her head much less utter it out loud.

'No!' Carol gasped. 'Peter would never have-'

'Of course not.' Chris remained unperturbed by all the emotions he was stirring up, but he must have enjoyed shocking them with the assumption that the high priest and priestess formed a bridge between the worlds by way of sexual intercourse with each other. 'Our ancestors may have been so crudely literal, but the rituals of the group I belong to are all purely symbolic, purely being the operative word here.' He didn't sound entirely pleased about this himself.

I'm very fond of your mother... Drew's voice rang in Maia's head. I'm very fond of your mother... And what if Stella's daughter were to follow in her footsteps as high priestess? She realized the idea had been fermenting in her subconscious ever since she met Drew and discovered who he was, but it had only just now broken through her tense moral resistance.

Carol demanded to know in a tightly outraged voice, 'What exactly did Stella and that man do together while her husband watched?'

Chris sighed. 'There's that word again.'

'If their actions were symbolic, which they obviously were or daddy would never have been involved,' Maia heard herself speak with authority, 'there's really no need for us to pry, Carol.'

Chris rewarded her for taking his side with a smile that slipped straight between her legs and promised her whatever she desired when they were alone again.

'But Maia,' Carol gave her a betrayed look, 'I thought you wanted...'

'I got what I wanted. I think I know what's going on now.'

'Then would you mind terribly explaining it to me, dear?'

'Yes... I mean yes, I'll tell you, but first I want to know why

Drew lied to me about your being a Druid, Chris.'

'It's very simple, my love, he respected my right to tell you in my own way and in my own good time. It was obvious I hadn't mentioned it to you yet, so he assumed I had my reasons and, very wisely, respected my deeper knowledge of your feelings. In other words, he left you in my hands.'

'I see.' Maia's outward smile was an intense inner frown as she reflected on this disappointing fact. 'Will you please assure my aunt, Chris, that Drew doesn't possess the ability to command lightning or anything fantastic like that.'

'I can only tell you that he would never deliberately hurt any-one, especially not the daughter and sister-in-law of his high priestess.'

Maia glanced at Carol and wasn't surprised to see the old woman's mouth hanging open in disbelief.

Chris crossed his long legs and gazed nonchalantly out the window.

'This is very strange,' Maia said carefully, making an effort to sound detached, but she knew her lover was contentedly picking up on her growing excitement. Drew's black vinyl jacket seemed to fill her mind glimmering with silver highlights like dark water reflecting flashes of lightning, his living chest beneath it the earth's atmosphere surrounded by the cold universe…

'Maia, dear…' It was Carol's turn to gently touch her hand. 'Don't fall into this like your mother did, please. I can't help but feel that these are evil games.'

'Miss Wilson,' Chris' voice rang clear as a bell, 'your irrational fears are the only evil in this room.'

'Dear, are you all right?' Carol deliberately ignored him as she focused on her niece. 'What are you thinking? I'd like to speak with you alone for a moment, if I may.'

'It's all right, auntie.' She relaxed against the soft old cushion, stretching her legs out before her as she met Chris' steady, challenging gaze. She was helplessly hooked by the erotic quality of his smile rather like a mermaid being dragged into a whole new world unable to distinguish between its pleasures and its dangers so soon.

'No, it is not all right,' Carol declared in her most authoritative voice, which means she only sounded desperate.

Chris rose. 'I'll wait out in the car, Maia. Good day to you, Ms. Wilson.'

'You may wait a long time, young man.'

'I don't think so. Try not to worry so much,' he advised. 'Your niece is in excellent hands.'

'Why is it so impossible for you to consider other people's beliefs?' Maia demanded once she and Carol were alone. 'How can you be so ready to think that you're own brother, who you loved so much was, involved in something even remotely wicked? You know daddy wouldn't have had anything to do with evil people.'

'Maia, what you don't know is that for the last few years of his life Peter did everything in his power to convince Stella to leave that cult.'

'Is that what they argued about in the library sometimes?' She was distressed by this bit of news. For some reason, proof of disharmony between her parents made her feel less sure of herself and of her ability to judge right from wrong. 'But they still loved each other, didn't they?'

'Yes, of course, dear, you know perfectly well they did. Peter positively worshipped Stella.'

'And I'll never believe she was unfaithful to him. Drew would never have-'

'Maia, you suffer from the same inexplicable faith in him your mother did. It's no use talking to you about it.' She sighed and rested her forehead in her hand for a resigned moment.

'Drew is a good person, Carol, I can feel it.' Stella's approval was more than sufficient evidence to back-up her own intuition concerning Drew's nature. 'Everyone dances to a different tune, so it's silly to imagine God only plays the organ in church.' She paused to let the metaphor sink into the old woman's resisting mind. 'The beat of their beliefs may be a little wilder than yours, the melody somewhat darker and the harmonies a bit more haunting, but the Spirit is like music, it's the same no matter how many songs or religions are composed from it.'

'But there are two Conductors, Maia,' Carol reminded her gravely, lifting her head out of her hand.

'You mean God and the devil? I don't believe in the devil, or even in God as a person.'

Carol automatically crossed herself. 'We're talking about good and evil, dear. You're very naive if you still believe there's no such thing as evil in the world, and everyone knows it always takes a seductive form. You know what they say, "the devil is a charming man". Please don't think I'm implying that your parents, God rest their souls-'

'Oh I hate that expression! Who wants to rest forever? I certainly don't.'

'Please, hear me out. I'm not implying that your parents were members of a Satanic cult, far from it, but there are different degrees of evil and it seems to me, as someone who has observed its effects, that this particular group did them more harm than good. Our souls are nourished by humility, by giving thanks for our blessings and enduring our sorrows with the knowledge that it is all for a higher purpose. These Druids feel they can ultimately control things through personal power. They're not humble, Maia, they imagine they can shape and influence events and nature, yet this is rightfully the domain of angels not of self-centered mortals who glorify their own basest instincts.'

'Carol!' Maia laughed despite herself. 'You certainly can raise hell when you want to.'

'I'd rather lower heaven and make it more a part of this world where there are too many other people raising hell.'

'You should have been a Minister, auntie.'

'That's what Peter always said,' Carol admitted, absently caressing her bad knee again.

'Believe me,' Maia said earnestly, needing to bring an end to a conversation that wasn't getting her anywhere, 'I intend to get to the bottom of this group of Druids. I don't want to call them a cult; it's too judgmental and I don't know enough about them yet. All I know is that I need to know why mummy was so into them and why daddy lost his faith in his involvement. I have to know, Carol or it'll obsess me for the rest of my life.'

'I understand, dear,' she agreed reluctantly. 'Just promise me you won't actually become a member yourself. Don't lose your objectivity. Stay detached. Chris is charming, I can't deny that, but he's also extremely arrogant. I suppose that's natural in a young man, and if you're happy with him, if he treats you well, then I'm happy too, but Drew Landson is over forty-years-old by my count, just a little too old to still be playing games.'

'It's not a game to him.'

'Some persons never tire of playing with other people's heads. You just keep that in mind, young lady and promise me you'll visit me regularly. I can't bear not having any way to reach you. Why can't he buy a telephone, for Christ's sake?'

'I promise I'll come by often.' She got up to go, but the only conclusion this lengthy conversation had given her was what she already knew – she wanted Drew. And then there was Eric Wolfson. The sexy musician was easy to forget when he wasn't around, but she already knew from experience that he was irresistible in the flesh. He had gone so far in his efforts to flatter her that he had bought one of her paintings sight unseen, and commissioned Chris to build a frame for it so she could have the pleasure of seeing her work displayed in public for the first time at his party.

CHAPTER NINETEEN

Maia had never seen so many beautiful people in all her life. Try as she might, she could not find one unattractive person amidst all of Sir Wolfson's guests. When she and Chris arrived at the party, she had to force herself to cross the threshold, totally unprepared for the roaring crowd that greeted them in the vast entrance Hall. If Eric described this as an intimate affair, she could not imagine what one of his big bashes was like. Obviously, he had been teasing when he said only a few of his best friends were invited, and he had been especially sarcastic when he assured Maia she would be the most beautiful woman present. Her opinion of the sexy musician plummeted along with her stomach as Chris literally dragged her in into the Hall, into a sea of glittering eyes, flashing white teeth and shining lips sipping expensively aged spirits on the rocks. She was so unsure of herself in the sophisticated cosmopolitan crowd that if Chris had not kept a firm grip on her arm, she would have walked right back out into the comfortably spacious darkness alive only with gently singing crickets.

Dressed entirely in black, her strikingly handsome carpenter fit right in with Eric's guests as he led her past smiling groups of breathtakingly attractive people towards the heart of the Hall – a large open bar. She felt painfully shy and out of place, but at least she had one good reason for being there. As she followed a few steps behind Chris, her hand imprisoned in his, she searched the crowd for Drew. Earlier that day, Eric had called Chris at his workshop to remind him that he was expecting them at his party. He had also mentioned they could bring whomever they like, and to Maia's astonishment and carefully concealed joy, Chris had chosen to invite Drew. She had believed his reason for asking Drew to the party had been to tease and torment her, until he explained that it was so he and the Druid high priest could have a little conference with Eric concerning his music video. She still didn't quite know how to handle Chris' lack of jealousy and so determined not to worry about it for the time being. The truth was she was thrilled that Drew would be here tonight. She had casually asked Chris what the older man did for a living (the fact that Drew had been asleep when she rang him at ten o'clock in the morning seemed to indicate he didn't have to get up to go to work) but Chris only laughed in response and she knew him well enough by now not to press him for an answer. She simply added the question of Drew's financial livelihood to the list she was determined to fire at her parents' old friend when she saw him again.

The moment she stepped into the musician's mansion, she almost literally felt her elegant black silk dress turn to rags in a nightmarish reversal of the Cinderella story in the face of so many expensive designer creations. The idea of spending hundreds of pounds on a single outfit filled her with an almost existential terror, and she observed at once that almost all of Lord Wolfson's lady friends clearly starved themselves in order to maintain their runway figures. The ribs of one tall blonde were actually visible through her dress like the bars of a bird cage covered with a silk cloth.

By the time Chris found the modern open bar Eric had set up in the back of his Medieval Hall, she was already desperate to go home, and only the knowledge that Drew was also coming to this party in any way motivated her to stay. Electric light's cruel honesty had been banned for the affair. Black and violet candles had been set into ornate candelabrums placed on small antique tables along the walls. There seemed to be a flame burning for every person present, some of them pulsing gently beneath the arctic breeze of the central air-conditioning.

Drew was nowhere to be seen yet and neither was Eric.

She concentrated on sipping the red wine Chris procured for her as she wondered what on earth she was doing there. She especially wondered why, when he could obviously have any woman he wanted, Eric had chosen her to be in his music video. Perhaps she underestimated the sexy rock star; perhaps he enjoyed surrounding himself with model-types, but he actually had an eye for real beauty, the kind that shone from within. Maia was profoundly self-confident enough these days to believe that when her soul became visible in her eyes and radiated through her flesh she could easily be considered the most beautiful woman in any room, even if she would not qualify for that title with a measuring tape and a scale.

'Let's mingle,' Chris said cheerfully, and took off purposefully into the crowd without her.

She followed him desperately for a minute, but so many laughing and talking people came between them she finally gave up the pursuit, vowing never to forgive him for abandoning her like this. She was standing perfectly still listening to the roaring waves of conversation breaking all around her, pondering what to do with herself, when suddenly an idle comment hit her like a cold spray...

'I heard he wants a complete nobody to star in his next video, some local twit he seems to fancy.'

She forced her body to move even though she had no idea where she was going. Her nerves had already soaked up most of the wine in her glass and she dreaded the loss of this self-contained activity, so she turned back towards the bar.

Her slow progress towards the island of bottles and male bartenders in white jackets as immaculately pressed as idyllic Caribbean beaches obeyed the room's main current, and small eddies of people drifted along with her as she wished herself invisible while continuing to curse Chris for abandoning her. She was half hoping Drew wouldn't show up after all because she had no desire to fight the army of contemporary sirens Eric had assembled for the high priest's admiration. Her own unique charms felt powerless against the combined force of so much alluring female flesh, a veritable explosion of glossy hair and lips, deep cleavage and long legs in which her own body parts were nice but essentially insignificant fragments. She might be able to lodge herself in Drew's attention for a moment like a piece of shrapnel clinging to his suit on this sensual battlefield, but there was no chance in hell she could keep him focused entirely on her all night long. In this sea of femininity, she was just one deep little wave of sensuality.

Maia managed a refill for her empty wine glass and decided to remain close to the bar for regular infusions of courage. The more fruit-of-the-vine she poured into her veins and mixed with her blood, the easier it was to objectively pluck herself from the scene and observe it with an invulnerable bird's eye interest. She chose to ignore the fact that below the frosty layer of her anxiety her warm body was growing hungrier by the second.

A handsome young man with short black hair smiled at her in passing, then one of the attractive bartenders took it upon himself to refill her glass again before she even asked, and suddenly she realized there were just as many good looking men milling around her as there were lovely women, which helped balance the scales a little and gave a bit more weight to her self-esteem.

Tentatively, she began walking down another distinct current in the crowd, reasonably assuming that if she followed other people who looked as if they knew where they were going she would eventually run into food.

The buffet tables in the dining room had been thoroughly attacked, but there were still so many gourmet finger foods left she didn't know where to start as she wandered alongside antique tables protected by golden cloths. The loudly muffled beat of rock music emanating from an adjoining room made her feel at once small and intensely alive like a single blood cell flowing inside the heart of a massive body as it expanded and contracted with people moving to and fro.

'There you are.' Chris abruptly materialized beside her and handed her an empty plate. 'By the way, Drew's here.'

'That's nice.' A slave to her appetite at the moment, she shamelessly stacked her plate with culinary treasures determined not to show how much this announcement affected her.

'He's upstairs examining the torture room.'

She barely heard him over the music pounding through the walls. 'That's nice,' she repeated with her mouth full, refusing to give him the satisfaction of reacting one way or the other.

'I'm surprised that particular room isn't the center of attraction.' Chris followed her along the table filling his own plate with delectable confections. 'But in fact, there's no one else up there at all.'

She was annoyed by how obviously he was baiting her, yet her pulse inevitably quickened at the thought of encountering Drew all alone upstairs. Resisting the urge to abandon her food, she bee-lined it towards some empty chairs, and he continued following her. It didn't take her long to devour the sumptuous repast she had assembled, and since she had somehow lost her wineglass along the way, it was time to procure another one. She was suddenly filled with a comfortable sense of purpose and direction inde-pendent of her lover's. She set her empty china plate on a side table, echoed his earlier words to her, 'Time to mingle' and took off for the bar alone.

Maia had grown quite fond of the young man who offered her a fresh glass of excellent Merlot, and her lips curved unconscious-ly upwards as she headed for the central staircase located in the center of the Hall. Maybe she would run into Drew on his way down or maybe Eric would finally appear on the landing…

The staircase wound up at forty-five degree angles so there was always a section of floor visible below her as she ascended. Yet oddly enough, every time she looked down during her careful climb (she was fearful of tripping in her high-heels) no one walked across the floor below her. When she was nearly at the top, she leaned over the inner railing to try and catch sight of at least one body moving about in the subterranean roar, but all that happened was she suffered a strange vertigo. Her mind remained perfectly clear and she didn't feel in the least bit dizzy, yet she suddenly per-ceived the rectangular section of polished wood floor far below her as a coffin that had just been lowered into the ground. Her glass of wine tipped slightly in her curiously nerveless fingers as she suf-fered this disturbing impression and a dark red stream descended in haunting slow motion to baptize the coffin with blood…

'There you go again,' Drew steadied her against him, 'wasting perfectly good wine.'

'I didn't mean to…' Her voice died in her throat. Her memory had seriously underestimated the effect his physical presence had on her. Apparently her brain was capable of registering only certain amounts of sensual voltage, but now her body absorbed the real amount with a shiver as his touch burned all her thoughts away.

'How are you, Maia?' He kissed her cheek, leaving a cool wet spot on her skin into which her awareness dove for a debilitating instant. 'Cat got your tongue?' he teased soberly.

'Yes,' she eyed his all-black attire, 'a big black panther.'

'Unfortunately they don't make very good pets. They're not content to sleep at the foot of the bed.'

'I would let him sleep right beside me.'

'That might not be wise. One night he might have a bad dream and scratch you up pretty badly.'

'He would never do that to me,' she said faintly, confused by how much it excited her to both trust and fear this man. 'Besides, I could always have him de-clawed.'

'If you do that you might as well kill him.'

'Well, they don't make flea collars that big anyway, so it's a mute point.'

'Are you enjoying yourself, Maia?'

'Not really. I've never liked parties much.'

'What would you like, princess?'

'More wine.' She drained what remained in her glass.

His mouth hardened as he looked at her in a way that mysteriously whipped her straight between the legs. 'Then shall we descend together?'

'Drew, Chris tried to explain to me why you lied about his involvement in your... whatever it is, and since you told me yourself not to believe everything you said, I don't have the right to be mad at you, but...'

'That's not why you're angry with me.'

Pride made her turn away from him so abruptly one of her high-heels snagged on the carpet. If he hadn't caught hold of her arm she would have tumbled down a dozen steps to the next landing. 'These damned heels!' she gasped, tears of frustration and embarrassment burning in her eyes.

'Death opens its arms for you when you run from what you really want,' he murmured.

She allowed her arms to slip around his chest as she enjoyed the soft material of his black shirt against her cheek. 'Why do you do this to me?' she was talking to herself as much as to him. 'There's so much I need to ask you, and yet when I'm with you I feel there's really nothing else that matters… when I'm with you there's only one thing I want… and yet I'm not sure what part of me wants it, because if it's only my body, I just can't…'

'You can't?' His hands rested heavily over each other against the small of her back.

'I can't give into it.'

'Why not?'

His whisper blew her mind as if it was only a candle flame burning from the wick of her spine. 'Because, I just can't,' she repeated desperately.

'Why not?' he asked again remorselessly.

'Because I don't want to ruin my chance of a long-term meaningful relationship with Chris…'

He brought one of his hands forward to finger one of her silver star-shaped earrings appreciatively. 'These are nice… I want you to live your life, Maia, in whatever way feels right to you.' His eyes reflected two candle flames as they gazed down into hers. 'Let's be friends.'

The universe could not have been vaster than her disappointment. 'If that's what you want.' She dropped her eyes.

Without warning he slipped both his hands into her low-cut dress. 'Is that what you feel I want?' he whispered.

'Oh Drew…' At once she loved the feel of her breasts resting in his palms as though her sensitivity was perfectly equal to his ability to grasp and stimulate it. She had chosen not to wear the armor of a bra tonight so she was defenseless against his caress. 'I want to be your priestess!' she breathed, her heart beating the truth out of her even as her mind cringed with shame at the way she was throwing herself at him. Then she was glad to have confessed her deepest longing because the way he stared down into her eyes felt better than a sexual penetration. She could sense the power of his will and how firm it was without being at all cold or inflexible, and it aroused her as nothing else ever had.

'Tell me that again,' he said quietly.

His face was so close her breath grappled with his as she whispered, 'I want to be your priestess, Drew.' The proximity of his mouth was torture, the teasing sight of it so close to hers like a whip lashing her soul.

'You want to be my priestess,' he repeated slowly, as though savoring her confession. 'Like your mother?'

'No.' She was thinking that with them the rites joining heaven and earth could cease to be merely symbolic. 'Better…'

His eyes narrowed. 'I've been waiting for you, Maia.'

Her sense of triumph was so sharp she had to close her eyes to endure the stab of desire she experienced as he squeezed her breasts possessively. It felt like her own life-force draining out of her when he slipped his hands out of her dress. She had to remind herself there were hundreds of people milling below them because the corridor behind him looked long and dark as a tunnel leading into another dimension not just to the other side of an old house.

'Has the position of your high priestess remained vacant all these years?' she asked with ill concealed jealousy.

'Yes, officially it has.' He reached for his heart.

'I see.'

He lowered his head to light a cigarette. 'Do you?' He glanced up at her over the small flame, and in her opinion the fire reflected in his eyes was hotter than the real thing.

'I think I'm beginning to.'

'Perhaps, but you still have a long way to go, Maia.'

'I know that.' As usual his cool patronizing made her a bit cross. 'But I learn very quickly and I'm sure you're an excellent teacher, Drew.'

'Have you seen all the goddesses down there?' he asked abruptly, leaning casually against the wooden railing as he smoked.

Immediately, Maia wondered if her eyeliner was smeared and realized she must have lost most of her lipstick to the unfeeling rim of two wine glasses, not to mention the fact that she hadn't bothered to comb her hair after the windy drive from Chris' house to Eric's mansion.

Drew chuckled to himself as he sent ashes down to the hall below as though hearing her thoughts.

'All those women down there look like they've been stretched out on the rack,' she declared cattily, self-consciously smoothing down her unruly hair.

'If you're going to be high priestess, Maia, your self-esteem has to be as big as the world.'

'Oh it is, believe me, I'm not in the least jealous of any of those glamorous birds down there. I'm sure not one of them can fly as high inside as I do, so high you can't even imagine it!' The way he looked at her encouraged her to go on in this vein without holding anything back, so she did. 'I'm hungry, Drew, I'm so hungry for something! I don't know what it is only what it isn't, and it isn't just sex or money or fame as an artist. What I long for is to merge all these hungers somehow, all these separate passions into one glorious... something!' She sighed in frustration because there was no way to express how she felt in her soul. 'It's the sense I have when I'm painting that I'm revealing the world as it truly is, the way I know it to be deep down inside me where my desires are its only laws and where love is the atmosphere itself. I've never cared about money,' she shrugged, 'but it seems that if you don't have a lot of it then you also don't have the time or the energy to truly explore yourself. What do you do for a living, by the way?'

He studied his cigarette. 'Amazing.'

'What's amazing? I think it was a natural progression from those women downstairs to the topic of lots of money.' She couldn't prevent another catty remark from escaping her. 'You have the look of a man who doesn't need to get up at a certain time every morning. You're rich, aren't you?'

'Very.'

'Did you inherit your wealth?'

'No, I wrote myself into paradise and now I live like an ancient king on royalties.'

'You're a writer?' She was enthralled. 'What genre? Fiction? Non-fiction?'

'All of the above. Pornography. When I first started whatever poetry I tried to slip between the sheets invariably got cut, so I divided myself in half and now I write under two different names. One of me makes ungodly amounts of money banging out smut, and the other me is spiritually fulfilled.' He killed his cigarette on the sole of his boot and tossed it away without any consideration for their host's domestic staff. 'Wouldn't you like to inspire both sides of me, Maia?'

'Stop teasing me, Drew, please.' She had no desire to leave their shadowy privacy at the top of the steps, but there seemed no avoiding it as he offered her his arm. At least she would have the pleasure of making an entrance with him, before a group of models clad in colorful designer dresses surrounded his hot coal-black figure like hungry sparks. She fanned this depressing scenario with a hopeless sigh as they started walking down the stairs together.

'Why such a melancholy air?' he murmured against her temple. 'Careful with those heels.'

'When are we going to have a real uninterrupted talk, Drew?'

'Later tonight, I promise, after I've spoken with our host about this video he's filming. There's no reason why we shouldn't make it truly interesting.'

The roaring river of souls was drawing closer. 'But how can you pretend to use authentic details in this video when the Druids left absolutely no physical evidence behind as to the actual nature of their rites?'

'There are ways of knowing things that have nothing to do with shovels and carbon dating, but we'll discuss that later. Right now there's something you have to do to prove you can handle the position you desire as my priestess.'

'What do I have to do?' she asked eagerly.

'I want you to be unfaithful to Chris tonight.'

Her heart began racing for its life as she gazed incredulously up at his profile. 'What did you just say?'

'I want you,' he kept his eyes on the stairs, 'to fuck Eric tonight.'

'You… you want me to have sex with Eric Wolfson?' She couldn't believe what she was hearing. 'Why?' she asked desperately, forced by his uncompromising silence to accept the fact that he was serious. When he had said he wanted her to be unfaithful to Chris tonight she had dared hope he meant with him. 'Why

Eric and not you?' They had reached the Hall and already she noticed several female gazes fluttering covetously his way.

'No more questions, Maia.' He still refused her even the small consolation of meeting her eyes. 'Just do as I say.'

She slipped her arm out of his, but it was like letting go of a life raft in the middle of an ocean rocked by the storm of her emotions. The music had been turned up to a deafening volume and she was glad she almost had to scream to make herself heard. 'Why are you hurting me like this?'

Turning towards her, he idly played with one of her star-shaped earrings again. 'I'm challenging you, not hurting you, Maia. You said you would do anything I told you to.'

She could only look beseechingly up into his eyes attempting to brace herself for his departure feeling like someone lost in deep space storing up enough oxygen to survive until she could safely dock with her ship again.

'Slip that tight moral leash off your inner wolf, Maia, and spend some time with it,' he commanded quietly. 'Throw your wolf some raw flesh that hasn't been properly prepared for you over a romantic flame. Don't be afraid to surrender to lust and to just enjoy what your body has to offer without worrying about the consequences and your so-called meaningful long-term relationship with Chris. If you can't do this for me, then you can't be my priestess.'

'If discarding my moral sense is part of preparing myself to be the priestess of your so-called religion, then it's the devil you worship,' she accused him listlessly. 'I can't separate sex from love. I have no desire to.'

'Don't be a fool,' he said shortly, and she became aware of several people watching them as he slipped an arm around her waist while his other hand cradled the back of her head. 'You'll do as I say, Maia. Understand me?'

She closed her eyes. 'Yes, Drew.'

'Trust me this is for your own good.'

'I do trust you, Drew, I don't know why, but I do.' She felt irrationally humiliated by a sudden burst of laughter nearby just as she opened her eyes again and let her soul dive up into his unfathomable blue irises. 'Please tell me you're real and not like all these other people here, Drew, I mean truly real.'

'I'm real, Maia,' he caressed the back of her head gently, 'and I know that one of the hardest things in life is not belonging to a tradition and longing to fit into one. It took me a long time, but I finally realized the answer was not trying to belong anywhere anymore but just being myself. The only problem is new ideas and ways of being don't come with maps and safe comfortable little arrows pointing you in absolutely the right direction, it's the price you pay when you're forging your own way through life. You find yourself trying to unite paths that have been unnaturally split, forks in the road that lead to dead ends if you choose one over the other, which is why the devil carries a pitchfork, because evil lies precisely in this unnatural division. The truth is that your spirituality and your sensuality work together like your lovely legs, Maia, and tonight I want you to spread them wide for me. I want you to think about me while Eric is fucking you, and I want you to climax, I want you to come fully into your body for me. Will you do that for me?'

'Yes, Drew.'

'Good.' He let go of her. 'Now go find him. He's out by the pool.'

CHAPTER TWENTY

Maia suspected she had been elaborately set up, but there was nothing she could do, or even wanted to do, about it. She was so profoundly excited it was impossible for her to pull out of the game now – a sinisterly seductive game in which her heart was the ball being tossed around by three men, and just how far she would spread her legs for all of them determined the boundary lines. The web spun around her had its dark heart on the evening she drove into the cemetery, yet she realized it had to stretch even farther back in time than that. If Drew was behind it all, which she was sure he was somehow, he must have known where she would be that night, which meant he had been secretly observing her. It would then have been a relatively simple matter to tamper with her car, although she could not help but be curious about how they had managed to rig it so it would stall exactly when it did. As she parted from Drew at the foot of the stairs, her frightened indignation was like a hand angrily sweeping away a spider's intricate work because of course she couldn't possibly be unfaithful to Chris merely because some arrogant so-called high priest had told her to. She had no proof whatsoever the three of them were acting together in a bizarre erotic play, but the instant the suspicion sparked in her mind it fanned into a blazing certainty as she thought about everything that had happened to her lately.

She had left her empty wine glass on the railing at the top of the stairs, and blind to the crowd now, she thought about making her way back to the bar and remaining there until Chris was ready to drive them home. But even as she considered this course of action, Maia found herself walking towards the back of the Hall. Naturally she had no intention of obeying Drew's immoral command, yet her body was making its way to the French doors reason told her led out to the pool he had mentioned, the host of contradictory emotions raging inside her buffeting her in this incriminating direction.

Part of her wondered furiously how these men dared play with her like this even as another part of her was so turned on by their intense, concentrated interest in her that she literally felt weak in the knees. Nevertheless, it was humiliating how easy it had been for them to trap her in their sensual web. Whatever it was they were up to, she must have been chosen because her mother had once been high priestess of their religion. It seemed obvious now that Eric was a Druid too, hence the theme of his music video. She reminded herself this was all a fantastic speculation on her part, but her intuition told her she was right to believe nothing that had happened to her since she drove into the graveyard on the evening of May 1st was a coincidence. From the moment her engine stalled, her life had been mysteriously choreographed.

As she made her way out of the Hall, Maia was deaf to the noise around her wrapped in a cocoon of fantasies her suspicious brain warned her were too good to be true, fantasies about Drew waiting for her all these years. She had always believed she was special, that she somehow rose above all the other young women in Stoneshire with her unusually deep thoughts and feelings and the intensely passionate nature she expressed in her paintings. Most of her school friends had dreamed only of becoming wives and mothers, and her co-workers at the solicitor's office were equally listless in their ambitions. She could easily believe Drew had been waiting for her all these years to succeed Stella as his high priestess. Or perhaps she had been chosen for this wicked sexual triptych because she was no naïve and easy to manipulate, because she was swiftly seduced and slow to become suspicious…

This disturbing possibility stopped her in her tracks, and once more she thought of turning around and heading for the bar. She could stick close to her handsome young wine-bearer and his reassuringly candid smile. She even toyed with the thought of leaving the party with him later and forgetting all about the self-centered Druids she had inadvertently become involved with. Yet of course she knew there wasn't a chance in hell of that happening because her misgivings were not as strong as how intrigued and aroused she was. And naturally she was flattered to be the center of three handsome men's attentions, how could she not be? Whether Eric was a Druid as well was the question it was seriously entertaining her to toy with at the moment like a cat tossing a tasty mouse around. Whatever the answer, the musician was definitely a savory dish and the truth was it would not be at all distasteful to her to obey Drew's command. Inexplicably, she still desired and trusted her parents' controversial old friend even though he had just told her to sleep with another man. She trusted him in the same way she knew the wine she had drunk was not poisoned but rather complex, delicious and intoxicating, just like this powerfully sexy high priest. She couldn't bring herself to believe he was intent on hurting her somehow, but she could easily bring herself to believe he was challenging her, testing her boundaries…

'There you are, my love.' Chris suddenly materialized beside her again.

'Where did you meet Drew?' she fired the question at him, but then found her body leaning comfortably against his.

'Mm, you're tipsy,' he observed approvingly. He himself did not appear to be drinking.

'I know he writes dirty books for a living,' she went on languidly. 'Is Eric a Druid too?'

He looked around them. 'Keep your voice down, Maia.'

'Stop squeezing my arm, please,' she demanded mildly. 'You know, Chris, I don't believe you love me.' She gazed regretfully up at his flawless features. 'I think I know what's going on now. I'm just a fly caught in a web, aren't I?'

'If you are, you're the most beautiful fly I've ever seen. But don't forget, pretty butterflies get caught in spider's webs too.' He essentially confirmed her ambiguous statement by not asking her what she meant by it. 'What did Drew say to you, Maia?'

She had never seen such a vulnerable expression in his eyes before and she savored it for a moment before replying. 'Everything that's happened to me since I met you is part of some mysterious rite, isn't it? It's all been planned somehow. Our relationship isn't real, it's just part of a play directed from day one, or more appropriately from night one, by Drew Landson. Someone tampered with my car so the engine would appear to die just a few minutes after I drove into the cemetery so you could pull in after me and pretend to rescue me. Am I right?' She knew she had every conceivable reason to be angry, and she was trying her best to be, but all she could still manage to feel was excited. Her response probably had something to do with the wine seducing her blood and dissolving all negative jagged emotions such as fear and resentment.

Chris smiled at her indulgently. 'You're definitely toasted, sweetheart.'

'Don't treat me like a fool, please.' She walked away from him confident he would follow her. 'I'll admit,' she went on almost contentedly, 'I've been naively blind to the obvious, but I think that's only because I've been having such a good time and I didn't want to see the fact that it couldn't all possibly be really happening. I mean, this is Stoneshire!' She laughed incredulously. 'What are the odds of meeting three sexy men right after the other and then have it turn out that they're all passionately interested in me as well?'

'Maia,' Chris turned her towards him and pressed her body against his, 'I love you. Never doubt that.'

She gazed up at his face almost indifferently, suddenly tired of his blonde buttery beauty which she now sensed was full of lies like empty calories. She slipped out of his grasp and began walking purposefully towards the French doors, eager to get out of the stuffy noisy Hall and out into the fresh night air.

She saw that torches in sconces had been set up along the veranda on which she stood and around the pool, where no one was swimming at the moment because they were all too engrossed in their host's unusual performance. Wearing a light-brown suit decorated with vertical ivory stripes, and a half unbuttoned white shirt exposing a vulnerable slice of his chest, Eric Wolfson was dancing with two flames. Relieved that Chris chose not to follow her outside, she nearly tripped down the porch steps she was so immediately enthralled by the musician's hypnotic hybrid of sophistication and savagery. He held two torches in his hands like SOS flags, and they even made a flapping sound in the strong breeze as he crossed his arms against his chest and let the hot tongues of fire lick up around him, his long brown hair whipping his neck as he flung his head back passionately, surrendering himself to this dangerously hot embrace for a breathtakingly long moment. Then he opened his arms wide and leapt over a plastic chair in which a coolly beautiful woman was reclining watching his performance. She screamed in fear and surprise, and then laughed self-consciously as he sprinted away from her around the pool, the torches in his hands sending luminous streamers behind him like the long red hair of Viking warriors. He ended up in his original spot, the skin of his face and chest gleaming with what struck Maia as a much purer, smoother energy than that of the raw, restless blazes he was commanding. When he suddenly looked her way, as if he had been aware of her presence for some time, every vein in her body ignited like fuses all coming to one explosive conclusion – she was going to obey Drew.

Bending lithely to one side, Eric swung a torch over his head in a fiery arch as he pointed the other flame at Maia as though symbolically offering it to her. He repeated this powerfully graceful gesture three times, surrounding himself with a burning halo as the other rigidly erect torch pinned her raptly to the spot watching him. He was basted in salty sweat and he looked so hot to her in every sense it was torture not being able to lick him and bite him right there and then.

The woman in the chair he had leapt over laughed again and applauded slowly, an oddly contemptuous sound that echoed over the pool like a dripping faucet.

Eric let his arms fall to his sides, pointing the dying flames towards the ground. He held them far enough away from his legs to keep them from charring his pants and yet close enough that he looked superbly cool and collected in the suit's expensive lines. He stared over at Maia, and her brown eyes absorbed the vision of him in their earthy depths as she sincerely hoped he would indeed make it possible for her to obey the high priest's command.

'That was fucking great, Eric!' someone declared as the lady in the plastic chair glanced over her shoulder to see who Eric was looking at so intently. Her expression when she noticed Maia standing there became an exquisitely made-up shield over her fierce jealousy.

'Who's that?' someone else wondered out loud.

Eric set the torches back in their sconces, smoothed sweat-soaked strands of hair away from his face with one hand, and extended the other hand towards Maia. She noticed he had gotten some sun lately. Wet with perspiration, his skin gleamed like molten gold flowing over his ideal cheekbones.

'I'd like you all to meet the lovely star of my next video,' he announced in a deep relaxed voice that carried effortlessly.

Maia walked towards him, shyly ignoring all the speculative eyes on her, and tentatively accepted his proffered hand. His grip was so hot and hard it immediately melted all her thoughts into an incoherent jumble like candles left too long in the sun. Suddenly, all she could think about was his touch and the way her flesh fused with his as she distinctly felt him promise her the pleasures of his cock through his hard fingers. She ceased caring about anything except the lean strength of his body so close to hers and of how much she wanted to feel it against her skin.

'Excuse us, please,' Eric said to his other guests as he led her off the concrete halo surrounding the pool and onto the grass.

Maia couldn't resist casting a triumphant glance back at the gorgeous model he was casually abandoning, but then she forgot about everyone else as he led her away from the house across a closely cropped lawn in the direction of the woods surrounding his estate, the ancient forest where he planned to film his video.

'Ready?' he whispered, and keeping her hand firmly in his, he began running.

Taken completely by surprise, she surrendered to the strenuous exercise of sprinting in high-heels across uneven ground in nearly complete darkness, the blood surging through her heart thankfully drowning her brain's need to understand what exactly was happening as they careened between the trees. Her eyes gradually adjusting to the gloom, she miraculously avoided tripping over roots, but branches caught at her dress and she was afraid of ripping it beyond all hope of repair. Yet he completely ignored her breathless protests as he tugged her remorselessly along behind him.

When they at last burst into a clearing, it wasn't a moment too soon for Maia. Her lungs felt as though they were about to burst and the muscles in her calves had tightened almost beyond her control. The nocturnal woodland peace was broken by the sound of her labored breathing, and by the quietly urgent crackling of flames hungrily consuming their wooden hosts. Two torches burning on tall sconces thrust deep into the earth sent shimmering golden paths across a black body of water whose boundaries she could not make out, and the strangely eloquent sound they made seem to mysteriously communicate with the whispering of the leaves around them. The sconces rose straight out of the ground a few feet apart, forming a gateway between water and earth.

Eric stepped behind her.

'What are you doing?' she asked him even as she bent over to slip off her tortuous high-heels.

'What do you think I'm doing?' He drew the tiny car of her zipper slowly down its track.

With Drew's black-clad figure a haunting shadow across her mind she concentrated on the feather-light caress of the musician's fingertips. Because she was doing what he wanted her to do, she felt as though Drew was there with her... his will had penetrated deep into her heart and soul and he was there with her now even as she prepared to let another man enter her body...

Her silky black dress slipped easily down her legs and she stepped out of it gracefully in her bare feet. The lake looked as dark and menacing as a primordial pool before life came into being, and still wearing her black silk panties, she found herself walking bravely through the torches' burning portal towards the water's cold and unfathomable darkness. But then she paused, crossing her arms over chest as she stared at the forbidding black stillness. For some reason she felt that Drew would want her to enter it and she was trying to summon the courage to do so. Then added to the secret whispers of the trees behind her was the subtler yet even more significant sound of Eric slipping out of his suit, and suddenly she wanted to postpone the inevitable. She deliberately didn't look back at him, but it wasn't long before she felt him step up tightly behind her again. The tender head of his erection kissed the base of her spine and sent an invigorating shock through her whole body that propelled her away from him towards the lake.

The water was so cold she shuddered uncontrollably as it licked up around her ankles, then her knees, then her thighs, at which point she couldn't stand it anymore and forced herself to dive into one of the golden paths forged by the torches. She surfaced with every muscle in her body silently screaming in outrage, and felt literally impaled on the glimmering blade of light as she desperately hugged herself. Then she cried out when something gripped both her ankles and pulled her under again.

Eric's limbs entwined with hers beneath the surface, forming one writhing organism that might have been eons old, and during this silent struggle he managed to pull off her panties. They rocketed back out into the air together gasping for breath. Maia clutched herself for warmth, shivering to the core of her flesh as he swam elegantly over to stand in his own gilded path. The cool mud bottom sucked on her toes as she watched him dunk himself slowly over and over again, peacefully smoothing his dark hair back away from his face as he relished the water's cold embrace after his hot dance with flames. He was ostensibly ignoring her for the moment, so she sank back down below the surface again herself... down into a black space free of gravity... into an unrelentingly icy embrace in which she grew eerily languid...

When she shot back out into the air again, Eric was gone. She waited for what felt like a small eternity, and then nearly choked on a laugh as her mouth filled with water when he pulled her down into his arms again. This time when they emerged he was still holding onto her, and he answered her gasps for air with a violent kiss that doubled as mouth-to-mouth resuscitation. When he finally let her catch her own breath, she felt all her ability to resist him drown in the deep shadows masking his features. He kissed her again, boldly exploring her mouth as he pressed her body even more firmly against his. Then he thrust one of his hands between her thighs and clutched her pussy while his other hand cradled her from behind and she felt caught on an open shell in which her clitoris was the precious pearl. He gently rubbed her labia as his tongue kept playing between the lips on her face, and the pleasure was so delicate it felt like feathers brushing her veins as she mysteriously evolved into a higher form of life caught in the net of his fingers.

She was vaguely aware that the wind had dropped; the two

torches were burning with concentrated control as he took her hand and led her back towards dry land. As he rose out of the water's dark mirror before her his naked body glistened beneath the flames, and his long narrow back made her think of a wild cat's spine magically learning to walk on two legs in the blink of an eye. His leanness was all muscle and his dark wet hair clung to his skull sleek as a panther's skin. He turned to face her beneath one of the torches, where they could absorb its warmth. His high cheekbones stood out dramatically, heightening the sensuality of his curving mouth, and the dark trees behind him were almost reverently silent as she slipped her arms around his neck.

The cold water had temporarily dissolved his desire, but she felt it quickly resurrecting against her belly. Yet she didn't want to make it too easy for him, so she pulled away and caressed his chest with her fingernails.

'Mm…' he said. 'Harder.'

She allowed her nails to rake down his body with a ferocious delight as she glanced up at his face to make sure she wasn't scratching him too deeply, but his gray eyes were a polished silver in the torchlight giving nothing away even as they let her catch an exciting glimpse of her true nature. Very carefully, she grazed the sides of his stiffening cock with two claw-like hands. It reared up stiffly in response and she let her nails stroke it a little more cruelly relishing the sight of its quivering response. His penis was not so very different from Chris' in appearance. They were both unusually fine examples of the circumcised male organ, the thick, straight shaft crowned by a head shaped like a mushroom cap, and the mere sight of it growing straight out from between the muscular trunks of his thighs was intoxicating to her. Curiously cradling the hard-on she was responsible for, Maia found herself giddily wondering if a great cock was a requirement for membership in this modern Druid cult, which naturally led her to try and picture what Drew's erection would be like… which proved a mistake since he was the man she really wanted inside her.

Eric sensed her hesitation and promptly dealt with it. He turned her around so she was facing the water and put a gentle but determined pressure to bear on both her shoulders.

She was at once stunned and thrilled by his absolute indifference to her thoughts. He didn't care about any moral battles she might be fighting inside herself anymore than a cat pays attention to the desperate beating of wings from a bird caught in its jaws. He did not actually force her down; she ended up on her hands and knees on the ground because she wanted to. It turned her on that he said not a word and wasn't even bothering to tell her what to do. She knew how he wanted her because it was what her body wanted too. It was intensely relaxing how right and natural it felt to be on all fours in the grass as he positioned himself behind her. She imagined Drew watching her submissiveness to a man's will. For all she knew the high priest was standing in the darkness between the trees observing her obedience to a man's desires, and it was an intensely stimulating thought as Eric filled the entrance to her pussy, then paused to give her time to savor the anticipation of a cock she had never felt inside her before preparing to penetrate her. She moaned to tell him she was ready for the incomparable sensation as in her mind his erection transformed into much more. She felt herself opening up to the unknown as he sank leisurely into her pussy, forcing her to dwell on the violation of her moral and romantic being as she let herself be filled with a complete stranger's hard-on. She felt herself opening up to her deepest feelings for Drew, letting go of her resistance to them and blissfully accepting them… the sharp pleasure she suffered amazed her as she allowed her willingness to do whatever Drew wanted her to do completely sink into her soul through another man's cock stabbing her body... a cock the Druid high priest commanded like a scepter with which he ruled her mind and heart as no other man ever had before or ever would again... she fully opened up to the mysteriously beautiful certainty that Drew Landson was her destiny as she let another man penetrate her in his name, as she let another man fuck her so he could know he truly possessed her... she was ecstatically filled with images of the high priest as Eric thrust himself all the way into her pussy, and it was the excitement she experienced in fulfilling Drew's desire that made this other man's vigorous strokes feel so impossibly good...

She was on her hands and knees for a long time as Sir Wolfson enjoyed indulging himself in her slick hole, and the whole time he said not a word. She kept her eyes open as he fucked her long and hard, until there seemed no end in sight to his driving energy and she almost couldn't stand how much she loved it. She was strangely proud of how wet and deep her pussy felt in response to her fantasy that Drew was watching her body being taken on his command. Every beat of her heart and of Eric's cock said I love you, Drew, I love you, I'm doing this for you, I love you! as she sustained the submissive position enabling another man to plunge into her body with nearly vicious strength. She loved having a big hard dick inside her. Her innermost flesh felt achingly, meaninglessly empty when a man wasn't packing his rampant cock into her tight cunt and taking her feelings farther than they could ever go alone, and the thought of Drew was deliciously confused in her clitoris with the force pulsing between her thighs, the crackling torches perfectly reflecting the hot sensual rhythm of their coupling bodies...

'Oh yes, yes!' she pleaded softly, clutching the grass and concentrating on the exquisite quivering of her clit as Eric banged her with a casual fierceness that made how gloriously cheap she felt border on the mystical. Somehow managing to hold herself up on one arm trembling with the effort, she reached down to caress herself, and the sensation of his erection swelling to critical mass between her thighs easily pushed her over the edge into her own soaring climax.

CHAPTER TWENTY-ONE

Maia felt strangely like a ghost re-entering the festivities in the mansion after being magnificently stabbed to death in the woods. Only a quarter of an hour ago she had been a body crouched facedown in the ground, the dark hole between her legs the entrance to paradise even as her hair mingled with the dirt. Now she was wandering through a candle-lit manor house scarcely able to recall what had happened before her wonderfully rough encounter with Sir Wolfson in the forest. The walk back from the torch-lit lake to the French doors had felt curiously unreal to her as the tall trunks of trees all struck her as god-like shadows of a man's erect penis. Her pussy's longing to be filled by a big hard cock transcended the slight discomfort she was experiencing between her thighs as a result of how long and selfishly Eric had used her. He had relentlessly subjected her to his pounding rhythm, the shocks of his lightning-swift penetrations blinding her to everything but the searing pleasure they suffused her with.

He carried her shoes for her during their leisurely walk back to his palatial abode looking refreshed and devastatingly elegant dressed in his striped suit again. She had no idea how much time had passed since she parted from Drew at the bottom of the staircase. Every now and then the musician paused to kiss her gently, almost reverently, cradling her face in his free hand, and even in the nearly total darkness beneath the trees she could make out his gratified smile when she turned her head to suck hungrily on his thumb.

When they stepped out onto the open lawn leading up to the pool and the veranda, he gave her back her sandals and walked on ahead of her as she paused to slip them back on. She thought he was abandoning her until he turned around and held his hand out to her. She took it gratefully, but when they reached the French doors he let go of her again and gave her a chaste kiss on the cheek. 'I'll catch you later,' he said. 'You're not leaving here tonight.'

'I'm not?' She was surprised, and then quickly decided this was merely a polite line he was throwing her before diving back into his sea of guests, at least half of whom were beautiful women.

'Don't even try,' he warned.

'Well, I may not even have a ride back if Chris suspects...' She wondered if Drew would drive her home, and yet she had no idea where home was anymore. She had just been unfaithful to her lover, the man she also lived with, in order to obey the desire of another man she barely even knew. It made no sense at all.

'I wouldn't worry about Chris,' he said lightly, turning away.

She caught him by his expensive sleeve and asked him quietly, 'You're one of them too, aren't you?'

He gazed soberly into her eyes, but a group of women had already spotted his return. They descended upon him, all laughing and talking at once, and Maia couldn't prevent him from being swallowed up by the carnivorous silk petals of their evening gowns. She found herself politely but determinedly elbowed away by the group of skeletal birds, and suddenly she was right back where she had started wandering alone through the party. However, she now desperately needed to use the bathroom, and the idea of finding an isolated space on the second floor – a little marble sanctuary cool and quiet and private as a tomb – appealed to her immensely at the moment. Safe inside there she would be able to relax and soothe her sore muscles, particularly the ones in her calves and thighs that ached like smoldering flames burning along the haunting sconces of her bones. She prayed she could find a bathroom all to herself; she desperately needed a haven in which to try and sort out the passionate mess of her thoughts and emotions.

This time she ascended the grand staircase in her bare feet, not giving a damn what anyone thought as she dangled her sandals by the straps in one hand while holding carefully onto the railing with the other. She scanned the Hall below her for Drew's dark figure, but to no avail. Now that she had actually gone and done what he had told her to do, she began to fear he had simply been testing her moral fortitude. If so, she had failed miserably. Yet perhaps all would not be lost if she could somehow manage to keep Chris from finding out about her infidelity.

At the shadowy summit of the staircase on the second floor of the mansion where Drew's aura still lingered to haunt her, she knew it would be impossible to lie to him about what she had just done for his sake, and if he knew, then so would Chris in the end. And if Eric was indeed a Druid, the pussy was already out of the bag.

Maia thanked whatever unseen forces watched over her that the upper floor remained deserted and she found what she was looking for just down the corridor. She locked the heavy door behind her and prepared to remain in the luxurious bathroom a good long time as she attempted to pull herself together. The shining metal fixtures were contrasted by large potted plants, and her bare feet (still aching a little from sprinting across uneven ground in high-heels) were grateful for the cool black marble tiles. She had lost her black silk panties in the lake, so all she had to do was lift her dress as she perched on the polished black toilet seat.

She still couldn't quite believe she had met Chris in a graveyard on the first day of May. 'On May Day,' she said out loud, and her quiet voice reverberated sinisterly in the pristine space. 'Jesus, I met him on May Day!' She laughed even though she was anything but amused. In fact, she was just a bit frightened, for one of the Druids' sacrificial victims had supposedly been the May Queen...

'I'm a loose woman,' she murmured, trying the old-fashioned label on for size, but it was too broad for her rather slender sin. After all, she and Chris were not engaged; they had only just met and she more than half suspected he and his friends were using her for their own bizarre purposes anyway. 'Oh mummy, I wish I could talk to you,' she sighed, and buried her face in her hands.

Drew's priestess... would she truly inherit this highly enviable position from Stella? Had her parents ever planned to tell her about their secret life as pagans? Neither one of them had died a natural, peaceful death; they had been killed together in a violent accident. They were killed... was it really a coincidence that a truck had swerved directly into their path on the icy road or had their hand-in-hand entrance into the next world been... arranged? They had burned like sacrificial victims in a cage, a modern cage made of metal and leather rather than the traditional wicker...

She raised her face from her hands and stared fixedly at the gleaming white oval bathtub surrounded by a small forest of pot-ted plants. She stared at it without blinking until it began to resemble a magically gleaming dragon's egg...

'Stop right now,' she told herself firmly, at once unnerved and reassured by the sound of her own voice. 'These are crazy thoughts you're having, Maia. None of them can possibly be true!' If she took this train of thought any farther, she would plunge into a void from which she would not be able to save herself, because if she even remotely allowed herself to entertain the thought that Drew was evil, she would not wish to go on living.

She pulled out a long white carpet of sanitary paper and wiped herself clean with it. She stood up, her dress falling soothingly around her legs as she flushed the toilet and then turned to cling to the sink's comfortingly solid edge. Her reflection in the mirror above it shocked her. She had not expected her disheveled condition to outdo any professional hairdresser or make-up artist. Her hair was a tangled mass of dark coils with fiery highlights, the color of burned wood in which the sap is still smoldering. Her lips had lost their artificial gloss, but the wine and her recent exertions had kept them naturally rosy and they had been kissed into an even sweeter fullness. But it was her eyes that held her, their intensity the visibly smoldering core of this lovely package of flesh the immortal force inside her had sent to itself for its own mysterious pleasure, postmarked with her birth date. As she stared at her reflection, she saw both the divine shipper and the mortal receiver of the skin wrapped around her bones containing the gift of her life, and both were absolutely beautiful. It was no wonder Eric had fucked her for as long as he had and that Chris said he loved her, but only Drew looked into her eyes the way she was staring into them now, as though he could clearly see the power behind her vulnerable mortal self. And all of a sudden, Maia realized no one could truly hurt her anymore than they could steal her shadow. For even though her body seemed to cast it, her shadow was actually part of the unfathomable darkness between the stars. She truly seemed to see herself for the first time staring into her dark eyes in the bathroom mirror.

* * *

Reluctantly, Maia returned to the party. The huge noisy gathering made her feel insignificant as a single blood cell slipped out of the Hall's main artery through a wound. She wondered what the consequences of her actions tonight would end up being. She had to find Drew again and ask him what was really going on. It was entirely possible she was only imagining that all the men she was involved with were Druids seeking to use her for their own mystifying purposes. Chris was right, desire was all she understood, because the truth was that she desired Drew as much or even more than any explanations he might be able to give her. Yet the man she wanted had let another man possess her, and part of her was tempted to resent him for this and to regret her erotic encounter with Eric like a tumor subject to the anti-bodies of shame and guilt. At the same time, another part of her dared admit she had thoroughly enjoyed herself and that the only problem now was how dangerously the experience had sharpened her erotic appetite. Every muscle in her body had been tenderized by how hard Eric fucked her as though she was being primed for something or for someone, and she found herself daring to hope it was for Drew's even more devastatingly pleasurable penetrations. She felt ready for a prolonged sensual feast in which her juices would flow until there was absolutely nothing left of her. She knew this was what she wanted deep down and that only Drew could give it to her. Whatever it took, she had to have him. She had to be taken by him. Whether or not she could hold onto him afterwards was a battle she would fight when she came to it, once he was deep in her sexual territory.

People were dancing together in what Maia assumed was the living room, where all the furniture had been pushed back against the walls. The instant she walked in, an attractive young man tried to pull her out onto the dance floor, but she wrested her hand out of his with a smile, shaking her head. After what she had just been through in the woods she did not need to feel another man's body pressed against hers in a subtle simulation of sex. She searched the room for Drew even though she didn't actually hope to find him there. She was stimulatingly aware of having lost her panties in a dark lake as her tender labial lips rubbed against each other… and grew slick and warm as she wondered whether she was destined to feel another cock thrusting between them tonight…

'Our host seems to have gone missing,' a woman's lilting voice said in her ear. 'Would you happen to know where he is now?'

Maia turned and saw a pretty blonde wearing a challenging smile on her heavily made up face. 'I have no idea,' she replied sincerely.

'Where was he when you last saw him? Come, do tell, love.'

Before Maia could reply the girl suddenly cast a familiar shadow.

'Would you care to dance?' Drew asked the blonde as he claimed one of her bare shoulders.

'I'd love to.' She promptly handed Maia her empty glass. 'Be a dear and ditch this for me.'

Drew led the girl out onto the dance floor holding Maia's eyes. She turned to discard the insulting glass on a table, but she could not escape the pain so easily, and she quickly realized her jealousy would only get worse if she didn't face it.

With the young woman's slender body clinging to his, Drew stared at Maia as he slowly wove the fingers of one hand through soft blonde hair as his other hand caressed a slim bare back.

Despite her indignation, Maia found herself breathlessly hooked on his smile as he deliberately held her eyes while fondling another woman's body. Her heart felt so painfully full she had to swallow a dry lump in her throat that felt as timelessly meaningful as the full moon outside. His partner almost looked unconscious she hung so limply in his embrace, her arms wrapped around his neck and crossed at the wrists evoking a white bow adorning his dark back as they turned around and around orbited by other slow-dancing couples. Maia experienced nothing but a cold rage during the few seconds Drew's gaze was directed away from her. His eyes had become the soul of her pulse and it seemed to flatline with fury until they looked at her again. In a form-fitting white evening dress, the slender young woman in his arms evoked a stream of smoke against his coal-black form, and Maia watched with pure murder in her mind as he whispered something in her ear and she kissed the side of his neck in response. She longed to turn away and run from the room, yet there was nowhere she wanted to be except with him, and the only thing that kept her from sinking into despair was the feeling that his true pleasure came from the fact that she was watching him. In her soul, Maia knew he was more aroused by the feel of her awareness embracing his actions than by the other woman's submissive body clinging to his. And somehow the way his naked stare spoke to her was more exciting than the casual way he whispered into the blonde's ear again and made her laugh.

Eventually, Maia did turn away. Enough was enough and she was too worn out by her encounter with Eric to endure the double-edged emotions Drew always seemed to bring with him like a sword. He was so kind and yet so cruel, so understanding and yet so perversely demanding, and suddenly she had lost the energy needed to deal with all these paradoxes.

'There's my little wandering pussy.' Chris grabbed her arm as she was about to leave the room. 'Enjoying yourself, my love?'

'Enormously!' She smiled up at him. 'And you?'

'Naturally I'm enjoying myself. Oh my, is that Drew dancing with someone else? Are you jealous?'

'I don't know, am I?'

'I believe you are.'

In an unconscious reflection of Drew's gesture with the girl, she ran her fingers through Chris' luminous hair. 'Why are you playing with me like this?' she sighed, feeling as numb as a mouse that has been under cats' paws for too long.

'Maia, take my advice and don't think about things so much.' He wrapped an arm around her shoulders and urged her towards the dance floor. 'Just go with the flow and relax and keep enjoying yourself. Everything will be all right no matter what happens.'

She rested her cheek on his shoulder as they began slow dancing, becoming one of the couples peacefully orbiting each other. She tried to forget that Drew was only a few bodies away. 'Chris, I don't believe you.' She sighed again.

'Maia, I love you.'

She closed her eyes. 'You do?' Then he couldn't possibly know about Eric yet...

'Yes, I do.'

She clung to him in desperation, her guilt and confusion suddenly so sharp it was almost a physical pain.

Drew's commanding voice slipped between her and Chris like a sharp blade, 'I'm cutting in now.'

'The hell you are,' Chris retorted mildly, holding her firmly against him.

'Let go of her,' Drew insisted. 'You had your chance.'

Maia kept her eyes closed. Her soul was already in Drew's hands and only a small frightened part of her continued trying to feel safe in Chris' potentially long-term embrace.

'Look, I don't know what you've been telling her behind my back,' Chris began, 'but you-'

'I said let go of her.' Drew's voice was harder than stone as his determination honed itself to a dangerous point, yet she was still surprised when Chris' arms slipped obediently from around her.

'Well?' Drew inquired, enveloping her in his arms with a tenderness that made them feel like the warm dark cloud of her own turbulent emotions.

'I did as you said,' she confessed.

'Very good, Maia, I'm pleased with you. Now tell me how you felt.'

'Very good,' she echoed mockingly, hurt by his casual response to the intense effort she had made for him, but then smiled apologetically up into his eyes.

'Was he rough with you?' he asked quietly.

'Yes, a little... I wanted him to be,' she confessed.

He granted her the ghost of a smile in return for this admission. 'Let's go upstairs.'

CHAPTER TWENTY-TWO

A cloaked figure formed by a cloud stained red by the dying sun was reflected in a full-length mirror abandoned by the side of a road, its wooden frame carved with diamonds and crosses, and the mirror was in its turn framed by a car window. A woman's hands rested on the black leather wheel in the foreground, the golden ring on her wedding finger shaped like a serpent swallowing its tail forming the center of the painting as the black asphalt of the highway stretched straight as a sword into a point on the burning horizon. The distant cloud-figure in the bloody sky reflected in the mirror abandoned on the side of the road was beckoning to her across a darkening field of grass.

Maia regarded her work with a mixture of pride and dissatisfaction because it was so important to her that Drew like it. Chris had constructed a frame that matched the one around the mirror in the painting, and the effect was haunting as the imagined led out to the real and then turned back on itself again endlessly. Eric had hung her work on the wall just outside his 'torture' room.

'I painted it, but I don't get it,' she admitted as Drew continued studying it.

'Then I'll explain it to you,' he offered.

'Please do.'

'Twilight is a traditional crossover time,' he began. 'Dusk is neither night nor day and, therefore, offers a doorway out of the structure of time and space.'

'I sort of knew that much…'

'The cloaked figure is part of the sunset, which makes him magical… he has the air of a priest mediating between this world and the next.'

'Like you.'

He squeezed her hand. 'The priest-like figure is formed by a cloud stained a deep red by the dying sun, by its metaphorical blood, which can be interpreted as a union of the spirit's pure lightness with matter's heavier flesh.'

'Go on, please.'

'The woman's hands in the foreground resting on the black leather wheel express the fact that the soul is outside of time and actually controls it, the clock being circular and the universe black and the leather once living skin. The golden snake ring on your wedding finger is our immortal energy flowing from form to form, from body to body, and using each one as a vehicle for experience and growth, herein represented by the car. The empty mirror frame is a gateway between this dimension and another one.'

'Between the shipper and the receiver of this magical parcel of blood-and-bones,' she concluded, remembering her thoughts in the luxurious bathroom.

'Exactly.' He squeezed her hand again approvingly.

'But Chris said there couldn't be anything exact between the worlds.'

'Never mind Chris. The mirror in its turn framed by the car

window reinforces the analogy of the body as the mysterious engine created and driven by our Spirit for the adventure of Self.'

'But what does the priest-like figure want? It's as though he made me paint him, and all these other images, without my even understanding them. Not even Chris was able to explain it all to me like this.'

'And he'll never be able to fuck you like I can either.'

'Is that all the cloud-being wants?' she demanded in order to cover up how her pulse took off in response to his sudden promise. 'Great sex?'

'I was coming to that.' He stepped closer to the painting. 'He's beckoning to you, Maia. He wants you to discover and fully explore your inner powers. He wants you to completely believe in them. He wants you to identify with the creative force of eternal blooming and not with the fragile petals it temporarily dresses itself in.'

'I wish it was so easy.'

'It is and it isn't, but then wherein would lie the pleasure if we climaxed in only a few seconds like animals? The sensual struggle is its own mysterious purpose and fulfillment.'

'Amen.'

'Let's have a look inside.' He opened the door to the room guarded by her painting.

In the center of the large space hung an enormous chandelier that came to splendid life when he flicked a switch. Apparently, the wall between two rooms had been knocked down to create one unusually large space, and the doors of what looked like two walk-in closets had been ripped off to form two cozy open alcoves, a black carpet soft and smooth as a layer of soot covering the entire floor. Directly beneath the chandelier, small wooden tables of varying styles clearly dating from different centuries were arranged in a circle, with a slightly larger space left between two of them to allow access to the pyramid of swords erected within them. The blades all pointed up at forty-five degree angles to each other, and it was impossible to tell that most of them were probably centuries old for they had been cleaned and polished until they shone as though freshly forged.

Maia watched as Drew was irresistibly drawn to the phallic blades. A ring of knives lying next to their scabbards decorated the little wooden tables, and nowhere else in the mansion was Eric's great wealth more apparent than in the ancient weapons he was able to afford. While Drew examined the swords, she found herself fascinated by the daggers, even though she had no idea what centuries they paradoxically represented. It was ironic how an instrument of death could so sumptuously evoke the life of its time. It was relatively easy for her to picture the men who had owned them because a few items of clothing, dull with age, were also laid out next to the virtually timeless metal blades. One black pair of gloves looked as though it had known at least a century of Time's merciless hand, ten decades for each finger, for only a thin shadow of cloth remained.

Drew held a sword admiringly out before him and she met his eyes over its fatal path for an instant before moving away from the gorgeous wheel of pain rimmed by the deadly clock of knives, exactly twelve of them. The room was laid out with an arcane significance that excited her in a way she was powerless to resist as she wandered through it, glancing back at the chandelier's luminous petticoats raised over so many phallic instruments of death. The edges of the room were in shadow as the objects of torture Eric had collected formed a loose cross-shape alongside one wall, in which an alcove black as a crypt contained a bed covered with white sheets. There was by far more empty black carpet than anything else in the room, a reflection of the universe itself that was not lost on her. She was pondering a scientific article she had read recently about dark-matter when she felt Drew walk up behind her.

'Are you ready to play now, Maia?'

'As ready as I'll ever be,' she replied in the same reverently hushed voice.

'The mistake everyone makes is not realizing that you have to know how to live in order to understand how to die,' he stated cryptically.

'They just expect death to happen,' she agreed, 'and that they won't have any control over it.'

'If that was how everyone felt about sex, we could never make love.'

She laughed out of nervous exultation as she turned to face him. It stunned her to discover that he had slipped on black leather gloves from one century and held a dagger with a jeweled hilt from another.

'I'm going to a lot of trouble for you, Maia.'

She somehow found her voice. 'I appreciate it, Drew.'

'You're beautiful soul is worth it.' He lightly traced one of her high cheekbones with the tip of the blade. 'You have such a stubborn skull,' he observed. 'How long is it going to take for you to fully realize and accept what's going on? Fear is the only thing that really hurts, Maia.'

'Yes, I know.'

'Then will you come with me?'

'Yes, I will, Drew.'

'Because you trust me?'

'No, because I have to.'

'That's not true, Maia, you have a choice.'

'No I don't... I love you.'

He glanced beyond her at one of the instruments of torture Eric had transformed to intensify pleasure. 'For years I sensed you were somewhere near,' he spoke as if to himself. 'I never dared dream you were Stella's own daughter.' He focused on her again. 'No other man would have been able to follow you into the fantastic illusion you conceived after that oak tree struck your womb, much less pull you out of it.'

She whispered, 'Because you love me, too?'

'As I love myself.' He smiled.

'Oh Drew...' She longed to throw her arms around him, but she was wary of the naked blade in his hand.

'However, I demand a lot from myself,' he warned, 'and I'm going to be just as hard on you, Maia.'

'But if you love me, how could you have told me to...? How could you have let Eric...? You're lying, you can't possibly really-'

'Stop giving into your fears so easily.' He clutched the front of her dress. 'You have to fight them. I'll help you.' He cut through the fine silk with one smooth motion to expose her breasts, and her pale skin was smoothly luminous in the shadows. 'No matter what happens, Maia, don't be afraid. This is your initiation into a new life. You know that nothing can happen to your divine shipper even if the body it sends itself is hurt, but it's a crime to return the gift unopened and unappreciated. Do you understand what I'm saying? Are you with me?'

Desire and doubt threatening to beat each other to the death in her pulse, she understood that only she could decide who the victor would be. 'Yes,' she said, 'I'm with you, Drew.'

* * *

Her dress hanging like bloodless black wings at her sides, Maia watched with growing excitement as Drew dramatically cut off his own shirt. She was surprised to see a silver cross hanging from a rough black cord against his chest as he tossed his ruined shirt away. She followed it with her eyes, not yet quite able to believe the sight of him half naked before her.

'Did you lock the door?' she asked anxiously.

Without answering, he pulled her against him.

She held her breath as she felt him rest the flat of the blade along her backbone.

'Relax,' he said firmly, and she knew he was slowly cutting her dress in the back, making her very much aware of the irreplaceable garment of her flesh the whole way down the seam of her spine. Her dress was now literally the rags she had felt it to be when she entered the festivities; there was no going back to the party for her now.'This is your rite of way, Maia.'

Lightning flashes of desire as he pressed her hard against the bulge in his crotch clouded her awareness; they made her pussy so warm and wet she felt her thoughts slipping away helplessly. 'I want you,' she whispered, burying her face in the tender harbor formed by his neck and shoulder.

'You're not afraid of me?'

'No, I'm not afraid of you.'

'Good.' He released her and stepped back.

She stared worshipfully up at his face waiting to see what he would do next. He was not as pretty as Chris or as sensually arresting as Eric, yet he was the most handsome man she had ever seen. It had to be the personality shaping his features that appealed to her so much, the ability of his mind to formulate profound concepts expressed in his fine bone structure.

He shifted the dagger in his hand so that he held it by the blade and abruptly offered it to her.

She took it from him without hesitation, and before she even knew what she was doing, she had cut the cross from around his neck, the sharp edge easily slicing through the black cord. She then grasped the silver icon of Christianity so fiercely in her left hand the sharp metal bit painfully into her flesh.

After a slight flicker of surprise, his eyes challenged her.

She stared back at him, basking in having his attention focused so intently on her as she held his weapon in one hand and his cross in the other. Symbolically, his body and his soul were now hers to command, both his sexuality and his spirituality resting in her hands.

'Do you know what your name means, Maia? It means Daughter of the Earth.'

She struggled with her ignorance, desperate not to disappoint him during this arousing ritual. She had no idea what she was supposed to do or what he wanted her to do, yet she couldn't tie up her intuition wondering why he had chosen to thrust her into a play where she knew none of the lines.

She slipped out of the shreds of black silk he had left her wearing, shrugging them off like shadows at the sensual moonrise of her luminously pale skin. She was aware of the party's raucous energy still going strong beneath them, and the contrast of their two bodies silently facing each other in the utterly still room made her feel curiously empowered, as though their attraction to each other was the eye of the night's sensual storm.

She had taken drama class in school. Perhaps being in a ritual was like improvising a scene for which no script was provided, only a general theme. The cross and the phallic instrument she was holding were obvious clues... Conflict was the issue here, conflict on every level, all the contradictions that shape life, reason and intuition, fear and faith, pain and pleasure, the list was endless. And together they were standing on the fine line between the sacred and the satanic as he dared her to walk this metaphysical tightrope with him. They were acrobats balancing on the 'sword-edge bridge' from which she could easily fall into a soul-shattering decadence… or she could use it to achieve a greater mastery and higher understanding of herself…

'Take what is yours,' she heard herself say, and raising the cross she parted her lips in order to rest the cold metal on her tongue's warm bed.

His expression was all she had hoped for as he obeyed her. Tilting her face up to his, he thrust his tongue into her mouth so the arching wave of his lust caught the cross and returned it to him.

She slipped the knife back into his hand and sank to her knees before him. She was confident that with her he could explore a whole new dimension where rites no longer had to be purely symbolic, as they had been with her mother. She unzipped his pants quick as a lightning flash, gently wrested the soft seed of his penis out into her hands, and planted it reverently in her mouth.

He caressed her face with the cool blade as she sucked him, her fulfillment as great as though it was truly his soul caught between her lips like the rosy horizons of the world in which he buried himself only to rise again stronger and greater with every plunge in the rhythm of death and resurrection… but she knew he would not let himself come yet so she was not surprised when he stepped back and slipped his erection out of her mouth. She had been sure his penis would not disappoint her, but she could never have hoped it would look and feel so perfect to her. She had seen no less than three fully aroused cocks today, and this fact both worried and thrilled her as she sank contemplatively back on her heels. All she was wearing now were her high-heeled sandals as she watched him return the cross to the black cord around his neck, his eyes burning in a way that turned her on even more than the sight of his hard-on.

'Stand up,' he commanded.

She obeyed him, struggling with a strange weakness. Deprived of his creamy nourishment she felt mysteriously drained. She had actually relished the flavor of his semen in a way she never had before. For some reason his pleasure tasted better than any other man's and she longed to continue absorbing his intensity as her soul curled dreamily up in the lap of his personality, which was at once infinitely stimulating and profoundly restful. He had obviously appreciated the passionate effort of her lips and tongue, and she admired his control as she focused on the silver cross gleaming amidst the sparse black forest of hair growing between his muscular pecs. He was whole again with the savior resting against his heart and a weapon gripped in his hand, and suddenly she became fully aware of the sinister sensual instruments surrounding them, rising out of the sooty black carpet like charred tree limbs.

'I should have died that night,' she heard herself speak again in a clear, self-assured voice she barely recognized as her own. 'Lightning struck the oak tree, but it really wanted me.'

'Why do you believe that?' he asked very quietly.

'I don't know…'

'Dreams and fantasies are not as interesting as life's journey, Maia.' His voice was so gentle she felt as though his lips were moving directly against her heart in a profoundly sweet kiss of understanding. 'It's all what you make of it.'

'Yes… Oh Drew…' She was dying to fall into his strong arms.

'What have you learned, Maia?'

She was suddenly so inexplicably tired she felt as though a python was tightening remorselessly around her bones. 'I've learned that I have to take command of my body,' she began earnestly. 'I cannot allow it to rule me, yet I cannot ignore it either. I've learned that my body is like the horse my soul is riding through life and I need to have a firm but loving relationship with it. Part of me has to understand just how much freedom to give it and how much control to exert, because that's what's best for it and therefore for myself.'

'And who are you?'

'I'm Maia, the earth, and your wisdom is heaven to me, Drew, I mean the way you seem to understand everything I'm feeling…'

'What about Chris and Eric, how do you feel about them?'

'Oh God, they don't even seem real when I'm with you.'

'But they are real, aren't they?'

'Not like you are… they obey you.'

'That's right, just as they'll obey you when you're my priestess.'

'They'll obey me?' She couldn't quite picture this, but it was an exciting concept.

'Yes, they'll obey you, but only if you don't run away from life, only if you're strong enough to make them face each other.'

'Face each other? What do you mean, Drew? How-?'

'They have to face each other over your body.' The door to the torture room suddenly opened behind him. 'You're both the wolf and its tamer, Maia, you can't let you're imagination run away from you and permit events to continue unfolding without your control. You have to take hold of matters.'

'What's happening?' she gasped, quickly rising so she could press herself against him and hide her naked body from whoever it was had entered the room. Then over his bare shoulder she glimpsed Chris' golden head along with Eric's unmistakable brown mane and she could scarcely catch her breath as the laws of gravity seemed to cave in on her with all her lovers suddenly in the same room. 'Why are you doing this, Drew?' she whispered desperately. 'What's going on?'

'Maia, I told you this is your rite of way. This is all happening on a metaphysical plain. Remember that and be yourself, your real self.'

She was saved from the distinct possibility of collapse when Chris very calmly took one of her hands and Eric gently grasped the other. Their faces were devoid of expression as they led her away from Drew, and for some reason she didn't even think of asking where they were taking her. The truth was she had no desire to question whatever it was Drew had planned for her, and heavenly clouds could not have felt much softer than the mattress she willingly lay back across in one of the dark alcoves. Eric and Chris stood on either side of the bed and each took hold of one of her ankles to help her spread her legs for Drew as he knelt between them. The high priest had removed his pants and all he was wearing now was the silver cross.

Maia was barely aware of Chris and Eric stepping back into the shadows she was so enthralled by the sight of Drew's beautifully rigid cock about to slide into her pussy, which had been nicely primed for him by two other men. Her sex was deep and slick and just tight enough to passionately embrace his hard-on all the way down to its deliciously thick base as he slowly entered her, making her gasp with pleasure as he relished filling her with him. It was inconceivable anything could feel so good. It was almost unbearable how ideally the dimensions of his erection fitted those of her fervently yielding depths, and the experience of his penetration was made doubly intense by the way he stared down into her eyes. She slipped her hands beneath her knees, forcing her legs wide open and shifting her hips so he could sink into her completely, but then he held himself motionless as she moaned in an agony of anticipation for him to begin thrusting. His presence inside her stimulated her to no end and made his patience almost impossible to bear.

'Please,' she begged. Her voice was hoarse from the night's endless friction of emotional torment and physical ecstasy, guilt and delight, dread and exultation, fear and desire. It felt like undeniable proof of life's divine nature in the microcosmic world of all her blood cells when his hips finally began moving.

'Come, Maia, expand your horizons for me... that's it... see how good it feels?'

'Yes, oh yes!' The seed of her clitoris bloomed beneath his deep, hard, spade-like thrusts as she started coming almost at once, her enchanted nature fully unfolding around him and devastating her...

CHAPTER TWENTY-THREE

The sun passionately being born between the leaves in a quivering net of light tugged at her awareness with its beauty, the pricking shafts of illumination threading themselves through her veins until she became fully aware of her body and the chill morning air... yet it was also very pleasant the way the breeze sighed over her where she lay cradled in Drew's hard, warm arms. She couldn't remember falling asleep after they made love, yet she must have drifted off because the last thing she recalls is the nearly unbearable joy of ascending into his eyes as she climaxed. Then suddenly she was looking at blue fragments of sky between the branches of trees as he carried her across the forest floor.

It startled and worried her just a touch when he gradually genuflected and spread her body at the foot of a tree – an ancient oak very much like the one whose branch had rammed into her womb. He stepped away from her and she had every intention of getting up to follow him, but the hard ground felt so inexplicably comfortable she couldn't bring herself to move. For a brief instant she thought with distaste of all the insects crawling around in the dirt beneath her naked flesh, but this tense concern dissolved almost at once as she seemed unable to hold on to any negative thoughts. And as she gazed at the oak tree rising endlessly above her, she sensed that Chris and Eric were also somewhere nearby… she was surrounded by her own personal pyramid of men… but she was mixing religions and this was a Druid rite…

She arched her back so she could look up even farther in admiration of the ancient oak's phallic might. Then she rolled languidly over onto her stomach and grasped two of its broad roots thinking to brace herself on them as she stood up, because she couldn't just lie there forever… yet her physical strength had no more substance than mist and her body felt impossibly heavy as she struggled to her feet, supporting herself with helpful knots in the gnarled old trunk. It was an endless process pulling herself to her feet, but she made herself do it and then rested her cheek against the rough, unfeeling bark. That was when she saw the altar. Small shining crystals hung from the lower branches of the trees surrounding it, and as they swayed in the breeze, catching the intensifying light of the rising sun, they flashed lovely prisms across the dark-gray slab of rock. Drew had vanished. She seemed to be completely alone, yet her intuition told her she wasn't. She could sense her three men standing behind the black trunks of the crystal-jeweled trees and somehow she knew what they wanted her to do next. She had to lie down again, but not on the ground.

Unable to walk, Maia sank down onto her hands and knees and crawled towards the altar's stone bed. It was such an effort to move at all she felt almost as though she was underwater, the rustling of the trees at once deafeningly loud and so strangely far away the sound didn't even seem connected to the dreamily silent swaying of the branches in the wind's invisible currents. Birds had begun to sing and the chirping music was so beautiful it hurt like needles pricking the pores of her skin. She paused to catch her breath and to try and dim the acute receptivity of her senses to a more tolerable level, and noticed that the grass had left deep imprints on her palms, darkly tangled paths superimposed over the more subtle map of her lifelines. She could even smell the morning dew, which wasn't so much a scent as a pure sense of well-being. Her razor-sharp sensory perceptions seemed to be cutting straight through into another dimension in which the gravity of fear and worry played absolutely no part at all...

When at last she reached the altar, Maia rallied one final surge of strength from the utterly relaxed army of her muscles to hoist herself up onto it. Then it wasn't at all difficult to relax against the unyielding stone and to wait... wait for her dream of Fate. She had no desire to run from Drew. Life would feel meaningless to her if he was not the man she believed him to be. His sensual intensity didn't frighten her. On the contrary, it was the reason for his power over her that he could prove the truth of their shared beliefs through the force of their lovemaking. Her heaven was the love she felt for him, her hell was this constant burning desire for him, and there was no separating the two. The only way she could feel whole was to give herself to him completely, to not hold any part of herself back from him, ever.

She closed her eyes, her body languorous as a cloud held together by bird-song, and it was more of a relief than a surprise when she opened her eyes and saw Eric standing at her feet, his face once again absolutely expressionless. And even though she could not see him, she sensed Chris standing behind the altar just beyond her forehead. She licked her lips as she let her head fall to one side, and Drew was there standing parallel to her heart, a different dagger in his hand now. This particular knife boasted a

Pleasures Unknown

golden hilt and a long, sinister blade. Looking at him she was half hypnotized by the rainbows of light appearing and disappearing and reappearing again in the shining black vest he was wearing, tiny prisms as evanescent and beautiful as life itself with all its emotional hues. He had stepped into the role of a pure power as high priest, and she fully acknowledged to herself now that this was what she had wanted from him all along.

He bent over to lightly kiss her mouth. 'Are you ready?' he whispered, his breath warm against her lips.

'You're never going to answer all my questions, are you?' she asked him, mildly surprised by her ability to speak.

'Don't you agree that our attempt to merge spirit and flesh is more interesting than anything else, more interesting especially than cut-and-dry answers you can never truly be sure of?'

'Yes, but you said they would obey me once I was your priestess,' she reminded him, referring to the other two men present. It worried her a little how unnaturally still and silent Chris and Eric were being.

Drew straightened up. 'They have come together and conceived your life, Maia.' He raised the dagger over his head so his muscular arms formed a pyramid framing his concentrated expression. 'Do you still feel torn between them?'

'No, I don't,' she replied serenely, 'because I know now that they're one inside me.'

'Amen, my priestess.' He shifted the dagger in his hands to get a firmer grip on the hilt. 'And this is your path into a realm where together we can command them at will.'

'Drew, what are you doing?'

'You want to live, don't you, Maia?'

'Yes, of course I want to live.'

'Then take the force of my spirit into your body, Maia,

Daughter of the Earth, receive me willingly, in absolute trust and without fear, for as much as you can give me is as much as I am able to love you. Life is a single blade with two sides. Are you ready to accept this painful duality and to grasp your immortal nature's golden hilt in an effort to fight for what you believe and increase the creative power of your love?'

'Yes,' she breathed, closing her eyes, but not before she saw the flash of the blade descending over her heart...

* * *

She didn't want to open her eyes because the last thing she remembered was the first thing she became aware of – an almost unbearable pleasure. She moaned and bit her lip praying it would never go away even though she wasn't sure she could stand the divine sensation another second...

'Look at me, Maia.' A man's voice whispered and the warm breath against her mouth shocked her into forgetting the blinding ecstasy for a second, long enough for her to open her eyes. 'It's all right,' he said gently, 'everything's all right now, Maia.'

As she gazed up into the stranger's steady blue eyes, the physical joy playing so loudly in her nervous system began turning itself down into an acute but somehow tolerable delight in which she could begin to hear herself think... The man she had seen smoking in the restaurant the other night was in her room, in her bed! She remembered seeing him that evening and not wanting him to leave, and now he was here beneath her feather comforter with her as if she had dreamed him there... that was it, she was only dreaming, and in this dream her bed-side lamp was still on and the sky had fallen impossibly close to her in his eyes, which narrowed as they stared down at her, making her heart contract in the most strangely wonderful way...

'It's all right,' he repeated quietly but firmly, 'you're awake now and everything is real, Maia. Do you hear me? Everything is real now.'

His statement contradicted what she had just concluded, but there was no mistaking the one very real fact of his cock was buried inside her, of his erection thrust as deep into her body as a dream that was intensely real.

'Don't you know me, Maia?'

She was struggling to catch her breath beneath the flood of feelings and sensations he was arousing in her on every level. 'I saw you the other night at the restaurant!' she gasped, the silver cross hanging from his neck striking her as reassuringly familiar.

'Say my name,' he commanded.

She reached up to brace herself on the back of his neck as his body continued moving slowly but devastatingly against hers. 'Drew,' she sighed. 'Your name is Drew...'

'How much do you remember?' he asked, smiling, and suddenly he began fucking her in earnest, driving his cock in and out of her fast and hard, forcing her to experience his full rending length as his head kissed a blissfully sensitive spot deep inside her over and over again, until she thought she would die the pleasure was so overwhelming. She didn't answer him because she couldn't hear her thoughts over how much it turned her own to watch her pert breasts bobbing wildly up and down beneath his onslaught.

'Don't you remember anything, Maia?'

'Yes... yes, I do!' She suddenly suffered a landslide in her mind as the images of a fantastic erotic dream tumbled back into her memory and for a few wonderful moments buried her dull life beneath a gloriously seductive landscape.

'You remember?' he insisted a bit breathlessly.

'Yes, I think so... yes, yes, I do...' She glanced down the tunnel of their converging bodies at the dark point where his erection was digging into her as passionately as if her body held all the secrets of the universe. 'Am I still dreaming?' she asked anxiously, desperately wanting what was happening to be real.

'No, you're not dreaming, Maia.' Leaning on one arm he slipped a thumb between her lips, gently gagging her with it to muffle her cries as he drove into her. 'I'm your dream come true.'

EPILOGUE

Maia woke to the sun's rays flooding her bed. Her first thought was that she had left the window open and somehow managed to sleep through the storm that had devastated her bedroom. An amazingly powerful and disturbingly conscious wind had moved almost everything around, even going so far as to raise the lid of her old toy box (which hadn't been opened in years) and spirit her once favorite doll out of it. The poor thing was lying naked in the middle of the hardwood floor now, her long black hair an incongruously sinister halo around her happy smile.

She sat up in bed and rubbed her eyes with both hands feeling utterly disoriented. Her window, she carefully noted when she looked around her again, was closed. There was no way the wind could have gotten into her room and wreaked such havoc on her possessions. Then her hands flew to her mouth in astonishment when she realized that whatever force had rearranged her bedroom had also succeeded in stripping off her nightgown. Yet no matter how powerful it was, a storm did not have hands, only a person could have... only a man...

'It wasn't a dream,' she whispered. 'He was real and I knew him, I really knew him...' She looked around her room again in disbelief even as part of her began to understand the mysterious order behind the apparent chaos.

The clay ashtray she had made for her father such a long time ago was on her nightstand and it was full of cigarette butts. She knew right away they did not belong to her father since Peter hadn't smoked for years. The nicotine-stained paper had touched another man's lips, and suddenly she recalled the slightly bitter taste in his mouth when he kissed her...

Flinging the sheet off her to kneel on the mattress, Maia reached for the ashtray, but then she didn't dare touch it. An unpleasant odor like an evil aura surrounded this undeniable evidence that something very strange had happened in this room...

Very tentatively, she left the illusory safety of the bed she had slept in alone until last night.

She searched the floor for her nightgown. She couldn't find it anywhere, but in the process she discovered many other strange and interesting things. Black and violet candles were set in a bronze candelabrum on her window seat, from which the pillows had been removed and laid side-by-side at the dark entrance to her walk-in closet. An empty wine glass was reflected in her vanity mirror, and the protective glass pane over the woven wicker frame was covered with recent photographs of herself that had all been tampered with in some way. Her most recent portrait had been burned around the edges into an egg-shape and two small magazine images, one of a white bird in flight and the other of a black panther, had been glued to its sides like wings. Her dresser had been moved so the reflection of her bed stretched out behind her in the mirror, and a glimmer of gold emerging from beneath one of her pillows caught her eye.

She whirled around and confirmed the sight had not been a trick of the light; the smooth round end of an object was indeed protruding from beneath her pillow, and she knew what it was at the same moment that she fully understood what had happened to her. The man she remembered seeing in the restaurant had entered the intensely erotic dream she had been living, and he had even helped create it with her. Her room was cluttered with the toys he had used to evoke its images, which meant he had been telling her the truth when he helped her imagine they were sitting by a lake – that her accident and her coma had not happened years ago, that they were happening now and she was only dreaming they were distant memories. He deliberately had not picked up the mess he had made playing with her subconscious in order to leave her proof of their haunting game, and the glint of gold in her bed was the spark that brought it all back to her in one burning rush of amazement. Somehow, he had managed to pull her out of her incredibly vivid imagination and back into her real, living body, and marvelously wicked images began licking through her memory that caused her to sink weakly into the wicker chair in front of her vanity.

The door to her bedroom opened cautiously.

It was too late to run and put on some clothes, so fortunately it was only Stella, who froze on the threshold as her hand flew to her throat.

'How long ago did Drew leave?' Maia asked her mother. 'I want to be a Druid, too. And by the way, I forbid you and daddy to drive anywhere on May Day!'

'Oh Maia…' Stella rushed over to hug her, and her mother's arms felt strangely soft and vulnerable to Maia after Drew's strong embrace.

'Mummy, lock the door please.'

'It's all right, dear, your father went over to Carol's house for a moment to check on her and see if she needed anything. The poor thing isn't used to walking around with a cane yet. How do you feel, sweetheart? Should you be out of bed?'

'There's a knife under my pillow.'

'A knife?!' Stella glanced at her daughter's bed as if it had suddenly caught fire.

'It's the kind of dagger the Druids used for their sacrifices. He left it for me.' Maia stood up and approached her bed. 'He used it in the dream.'

'He what?!'

Maia slipped her hand beneath the pillow, grasped the golden hilt and held the long blade up to admire it. 'He penetrated another dimension to come after me and to bring me back with him. He saved me.' She smiled. 'I woke up in his arms after he sacrificed me in my imagination just like in an ancient Druid rite.'

Stella stared at her with a dazed respect. 'You know everything now, don't you?'

'Yes. Is Carol all right?'

'She's fine. She was released from the hospital two weeks ago, but form now on she'll always need a cane to walk.'

'I know, she'll always have a bad limp, the poor dear.'

'Maia, how can you know that? I mean, you've been-'

'I've been in a coma for over a month, I know. Why hadn't you and dad ever told me you were Druids?'

'Because Peter has never been very comfortable with our involvement or really trusted Drew.'

'Well he'll have to start trusting him now.' Maia walked over to the window and looked down at the quiet street. The freshly laid black asphalt looked impenetrably dark even in the bright early morning sunshine. Then her heart literally seemed to stop for an instant when she saw Drew leaning against a small red sports car, his arms crossed over his chest as he stood looking directly up at her bedroom. He smiled when he saw her naked figure appear in the window, and the blade he had left her rang against the pane as she began lifting it out of her way. She ceased her effort, however, when he shook his head and formed a silent message with his lips her heart understood perfectly. She would see him again later. This was only the beginning for them, and it was not a dream, it was real. She smiled back at him, and then watched happily as he slipped into the shining modern armor of his car and drove away straight into her heart forever.

Other Magic Carpet Books

Maria Isabel Pita

Marilyn Jaye Lewis

Alison Tyler

Shauna Silverto

Lucy Niles

Laura Weston